Those golden-hazel eyes had once been her undoing.

In those eyes, she saw an echo of someone else entirely.

Bella.

Her throat tightened painfully at the thought of her daughter—their daughter—and instinctively, she took a small step back, both wanting to close the distance and desperate to create space, as if distance could somehow shield her from the turmoil of this moment.

"Patrick," she said at last, though her voice came out weaker than she intended.

His jaw tightened almost imperceptibly, his expression unreadable except for a flicker of something raw and unresolved beneath his composed exterior. When he spoke, his voice was deep and steady but carried an edge sharp enough to cut through steel.

"You have a daughter. No... *We* have a daughter..."

The words weren't a question—they were a statement, heavy with accusation and disbelief. And just like that, London felt everything inside her unraveling.

Dear Reader,

Love, much like honey, takes patience, care and courage. It can be messy, even painful, but when it's real, it's worth every risk.

In *A Family Worth Fighting For*, London Worthington has poured her heart into LW's Honey Farm, building a life with her daughter. She's convinced herself that romance is behind her, that some loves simply aren't meant to last.

Then Patrick Brown—the man who once held her heart—returns. Years apart have changed them both, but the spark between them is impossible to ignore. Patrick is determined to prove that this time he's here for good, and London must decide if she's willing to risk her heart once more.

Their journey won't be easy. Old wounds, lingering doubts and outside pressures threaten to pull them apart again. But London and Patrick discover that some love stories are too powerful to let go—and are worth fighting for, no matter the cost.

So, drizzle a little honey into your tea, curl up in your favorite spot and lose yourself in a romance about second chances, resilience and a love as sweet and enduring as honey itself.

Thank you for letting me share their story with you.

Jacquelin

A FAMILY
WORTH FIGHTING FOR

JACQUELIN THOMAS

Harlequin

HEARTWARMING

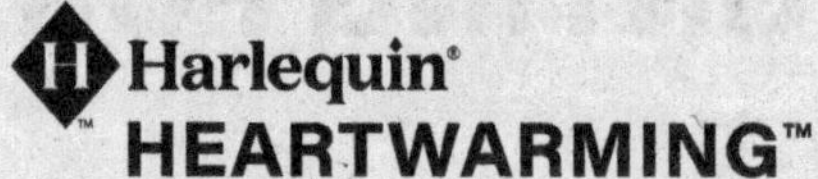

Harlequin® HEARTWARMING™

ISBN-13: 978-1-335-46051-6

A Family Worth Fighting For

Recycling programs for this product may not exist in your area.

Harlequin Enterprises ULC
22 Adelaide St. West, 41st Floor
Toronto, Ontario M5H 4E3, Canada
www.Harlequin.com

HarperCollins Publishers
Macken House, 39/40 Mayor Street Upper,
Dublin 1, D01 C9W8, Ireland
www.HarperCollins.com

Printed in U.S.A.

1 2 3 4 5 6 7 8 9 10 HDC 28 27 26 25

Jacquelin Thomas is a bestselling, award-winning author of 104 books in romance, romantic suspense, women's fiction, young adult and inspirational fiction. She has captivated readers with emotionally rich, relatable stories. With a background in psychology and clinical mental health counseling, Jacquelin brings depth and authenticity to her exploration of love, resilience and human relationships.

Books by Jacquelin Thomas

Harlequin Heartwarming

Polk Island

A Family for the Firefighter
Her Hometown Hero
Her Marine Hero
His Partnership Proposal
Twins for the Holidays
His Carolina Redemption
Fiancé Under the Mistletoe

Love Inspired Suspense

Sorority Cold Case

Love Inspired Cold Case

Evidence Uncovered
Cold Case Deceit

Love Inspired The Protectors

Vigilante Justice

Visit the Author Profile page
at Harlequin.com for more titles.

CHAPTER ONE

Polk Island awoke slowly, draped in soft hues of gold and rose on the morning after Memorial Day. At LW's Honey Farm, dew clung to the tall grasses like scattered jewels, the air thick with the salty Atlantic breeze and the sweet tang of wildflowers. The steady hum of bees wrapped around London Worthington as she worked the hives, her worn beekeeping suit clinging to her in the warming air.

Her hands moved with practiced ease, but her thoughts buzzed as relentlessly as the bees. Lifting a frame heavy with honeycomb, she traced the edges of the wooden box, lingering longer than necessary. Each cell held the fruit of relentless labor—theirs and hers. But this season felt different. The bees' dance offered no easy answers. Was the honey enough to keep the farm thriving? Was this place, her home, safe enough for Bella to grow up free from the shadows London fought to keep at bay?

The first golden streams flowed from the spout into a fine-mesh strainer, catching bits of wax and debris and leaving only pure honey behind. London watched the thick liquid catch the sunlight, thinking of how something so sweet had come from so much effort—just like the life she was building here, far from the past she'd left behind.

Around her, the bees moved with a purposeful rhythm, their tiny wings vibrating softly in the morning air. They never questioned their role in the hive's survival. London wished she could say the same for herself.

She exhaled slowly, brushing away a few bees and sliding the frame into a collection box, sealing it with deliberate care. Her eyes flickered toward the horizon where the sun climbed higher, painting the sky with hopeful pastels. But hope was fragile here, especially when so much remained unspoken.

Beyond the rows of apiaries stood her farmhouse—a warm, familiar sight with its wraparound porch bursting with fiery reds, sunny yellows, and deep purples. The towering oaks and palmettos bordering the property swayed gently in the breeze, welcoming another day.

Polk Island was her sanctuary, yet it was also a place that stirred a storm within her. London harbored a truth she couldn't speak aloud: There were fragments of her past and threads of Bella's future interwoven with shadows she feared to invite here. Four and a half years ago, she had faced an impossible decision—a choice she would defend even now, though it left her heart torn. Patrick Brown, the only man she had truly loved, had vanished from her life with a suddenness that cut like a blade.

His mother, Myra, had seen to that. Cold and calculating, wrapped in the armor of wealth, Myra had turned Patrick against her, convincing him that

London was undeserving of his future, his name, his love. London never fully grasped the depths of Myra's animosity—only that she couldn't let it touch her daughter. Bella deserved more than to be a pawn in a bitter game.

And so, London kept her secret, but the weight of it was a constant presence. She wanted Bella to explore the world, to uncover her roots, to eventually meet her father—but on her terms, not Myra's. She depicted Patrick as a distant star, close enough to inspire dreams yet always out of reach. Still, that narrative held its own quiet ache, a burden London had learned to bear, even as it gnawed at her resolve.

A soft giggle pulled London from her thoughts. "Mommy, look…the bees are dancing."

London turned to see Bella near the wildflower beds, bouncing on her toes in a pink sundress and yellow rain boots, dark curls springing with delight.

"They sure are, baby," London said, a soft smile warming her voice as she set down her tools. "They do a little wiggle to tell the others where the best flowers are."

"Can I dance with them?" Bella asked, eyes wide with wonder.

London crouched to meet her gaze, hiding the tightness in her chest. "How about we let the bees do their dance and you and I do our own?"

Taking Bella's hand, she watched her daughter twirl, laughter bright as the morning sun.

London held her close, pressing a kiss to her

cheek, quietly promising herself she'd protect this world, this fragile joy, no matter what.

Because here, on the island, London was determined to build a life where Bella could grow up free and full of hope—where the pain of the past wouldn't define their future.

PATRICK BROWN SHIFTED in his seat, the worn fabric creaking softly beneath him as he adjusted the angle of his iPad. The faint hum of the airplane engines filled the cabin, blending with the murmurs of passengers and the occasional clink of glassware from the flight attendants' cart. Outside, the night sky stretched endlessly, a velvet canvas speckled with distant stars.

It was morning in Charleston, South Carolina— a new day already unfolding on the other side of the world. But here, at thirty-five thousand feet somewhere over the Atlantic, Patrick remained suspended in the night. Not long ago, his journey had begun over the Indian Ocean, leaving behind the vast savannas and sunrises of Kenya. For months, he'd chased the light across that land, immersed in the rhythms of tribal communities whose way of life had captivated his lens. The Maasai, with their striking red shúkàs and rhythmic chants, had welcomed him into their world, allowing him to capture their stories—elders recounting history, young warriors practicing the Adumu dance, women threading intricate beadwork under the golden African sun.

Now, after almost five years away, he was finally heading back to the United States—not just to rest, but to find that special story…something close to his roots that his agent insisted would help him recalibrate. As a photojournalist, Patrick was drawn to stories that revealed the heartbeat of a community—the invisible threads that tied people to their land and legacy.

But this wasn't just about the honey farm.

It was about London Worthington—the only woman he had ever truly loved. He had spent years chasing the version of the story his mother handed him, trying to convince himself it was enough. But distance did nothing to dull the questions that lingered, nor did success fill the hollow space where London once stood.

The honey farm—*her* honey farm—surfaced in his research by accident, yet it gripped Patrick with a force he couldn't ignore. Beneath the professional curiosity pulsed an undeniable pull—writing about the farm had become more than an assignment—it was a bridge to London.

He didn't want to intrude or force his way back into her life. Instead, he planned to approach carefully—with respect and humility—knowing that London's trust would have to be earned, not demanded. He'd bring his camera, but more importantly, he'd bring an open heart, ready to listen and to see her for who she was now.

He wanted the story to be honest and authentic—no gloss, no clichés. He'd focus on the farm's heartbeat: the sweat, the resilience, the quiet moments that made it more than just a business. And beneath it all, he hoped to capture London's strength—the woman who had built a life of her own without him, who had built something remarkable despite the odds.

But the truth was he didn't know if she'd let him in. And even if she did, he wondered if he could face the ghosts of their past without breaking all over again.

He tapped the screen of his iPad, scrolling through old articles about the farm—features in local papers, lifestyle magazines, online blogs praising the honey's rich flavor, the farm's sustainable practices, and London's leadership in the community. Each story painted a picture of resilience and hard work, a legacy that went beyond honeycombs and beekeeping suits.

He wanted his story about the honey farm to be different from the usual feel-good features. No glossy, surface-level snapshot. He planned to dig deeper, to reveal the true heartbeat of LW's Honey Farm…the unspoken struggles, the sacrifices, the quiet strength of a woman who had built something remarkable on her own terms. Most of all, Patrick wanted to capture London herself—not just as the farm's successful owner, but as a fighter…a woman who was able to move on.

He eyed the photographs of London. Time hadn't erased her beauty; if anything, it had only deepened it. Her golden-brown skin glowed warmly under soft sunlight as she stood beaming in front of rows upon rows of beehives painted in cheerful pastel colors. Her waist-length locs cascaded down her back, catching the light with every subtle twist and coil. A navy-blue apron hugged her figure—a simple garment that somehow made her look even more radiant—and her smile… That smile….

Patrick's throat tightened painfully at the sight of it. That smile used to be his north star—the kind of expression that could light up even his darkest days. It was wide, real…joyful in a way that made it clear she had found peace somewhere he hadn't dared to look for himself.

For several seconds, he couldn't breathe—couldn't think—until finally, he forced himself to read past her photograph.

Nestled on the picturesque Polk Island… The words blurred slightly as his mind raced ahead of them. … *LW's Honey Farm has become a must-visit destination for tourists and locals alike…*

He skimmed faster now—faster than he could process—but then one line stopped him cold:

…beyond the honey, the bees, and the farm's success… London's greatest joy is raising her four-year-old daughter, Arabella.

His heart stuttered violently in his chest.

Four-year-old daughter.

The phrase looped through his mind like a broken record until everything else faded into background noise.

Four years?

No…it couldn't be possible—it couldn't be real. But even as denial clawed at him desperately like a drowning man grasping for air…something deep within him whispered otherwise.

His hands trembled as he scrolled further down until another photo appeared: small but striking enough to steal what little breath remained in his lungs.

Arabella.

She was perched on top of a hay bale beside London—the two of them laughing together under the golden haze of sunset—but it wasn't just any child's face staring back at him.

It was his face, too.

The wild curls framing her cherubic cheeks were hers…but those eyes? Those golden-brown pools filled with warmth and mischief. They were unmistakably his.

"No," Patrick whispered hoarsely under his breath before clenching his jaw tightly shut against the rising panic threatening to spill over inside him.

He wasn't just coming for an assignment anymore.

He was coming home for a daughter he never knew existed.

Patrick's thoughts churned as the plane began its descent. How would he approach London after all this time? After the years of silence and the gulf that had grown between them.

He knew he should probably reach out first—send a careful, tentative message, acknowledge her strength and the life she'd built. He wanted to be respectful, to give her time—but beneath that resolve burned the ache of all the lost years.

But the truth was he planned to show up unannounced.

He didn't want to give London a chance to put up walls or rehearse what to say. He didn't want her to have the opportunity to decide whether to shut him out before he even arrived.

Some part of him believed that honesty—raw and immediate—was the only way to break through the silence that had stretched between them for so long.

He wanted to believe he could come without demands, calm and open, but the thought of all the years he'd lost with his daughter tore through him. How did you make up for a childhood you'd never seen? But when the moment was right, he planned to tell her how much it hurt—how deep the pain ran to find out about his daughter this way, through an article and a photograph rather than from her.

He would demand answers, too. Why had she never told him about Arabella? Why had she kept that part of their lives hidden, deciding he wasn't worthy or trustworthy enough to know?

If she was willing to let him in despite everything, he'd tell her about his hopes for a connection, even if it was just from the sidelines.

If she wasn't ready—or didn't want him there— he'd have to accept that. Or at least try. But the truth was knowing he had a daughter had unsettled everything he thought he understood about his life.

He knew one thing for certain: He wanted to be in Arabella's life. To be there for his daughter, no matter what that looked like. That alone was worth risking everything.

THAT AFTERNOON, LONDON STOOD in the open-air barn, her sharp gaze sweeping over the rows of neatly arranged wooden crates filled with honey jars. Each jar seemed to capture the sunlight, the golden liquid inside glowing as if it held a piece of sunlight itself. The scent of beeswax mingled with the faint sweetness of wildflowers, a fragrance so familiar it felt like a second skin. She let the moment steady her, drawing in a deep breath to anchor herself before turning to face her staff. They stood in a loose semicircle, their faces attentive yet relaxed, the quiet hum of activity already beginning around them.

"We've got a big shipment going out tomorrow morning," she said, her voice calm but firm, the tone of someone who had spent years perfecting this balance of authority and approachability. "Triple-check every label. I don't want any repeats of last month's mix-up." Her eyes scanned each of them meaningfully, ensuring the gravity of her words landed. "And don't forget the sample baskets for the hotel—they need to be arranged and ready to go by two o'clock. Cia's taking them with her," she stated, referring to her sister. "The guests love those little honeycomb pieces," she added, her tone softening slightly at this last part. She wanted them to feel not just the weight of responsibility but also the pride in their work.

There was a murmur of agreement, heads nodding as her employees dispersed to their tasks. The rhythmic clinking of glass jars being carefully handled and the gentle rustle of packing paper filled the air almost immediately.

London watched them for a moment, allowing herself a flicker of satisfaction. Every detail mattered because this was more than a business—it was the life she had built brick by brick, hive by hive.

But just as quickly as that thought settled in her mind, she saw Kyla approaching from across the barn. Her assistant moved quickly but hesitantly, her hands fidgeting with the hem of her shirt—a telltale sign that something was wrong. London's brows knit together in concern even before Kyla reached her.

"London," she began, her voice lowered as though she didn't want anyone else to overhear. "There's…someone here to see you."

She tilted her head slightly, confusion flickering in her eyes. "A customer?" she asked, though there was something about Kyla's demeanor that suggested otherwise.

Kyla hesitated for a fraction too long before shaking her head. "No," she said softly, her gaze darting toward the barn's entrance as if the person might materialize there at any moment. "It's—"

Before she could finish, London felt it—a subtle

shift in the air, like the universe itself was both holding its breath and exhaling in relief. A ripple started in her chest, spreading outward until even the bees seemed uncertain whether to buzz or remain silent. Her breath hitched as she turned slowly toward the barn doors, caught between anticipation and dread, and that was when she saw him.

Her heart skipped a beat and then stumbled.

Patrick Brown.

The world seemed to tilt on its axis, and she felt both pulled toward and pushed away from this moment. Time folded in on itself, collapsing five long years into a single heartbeat that she both cherished and feared. For an instant, all she could do was stare.

He stood there, framed by the morning light spilling through the barn doors, his silhouette achingly familiar yet somehow different. Taller than she remembered—or maybe it was just his presence that seemed larger now. His dark brown hair was cut close to his scalp—the same way he'd always worn it—and his neatly trimmed mustache gave him that air of quiet confidence she used to tease him about. The beard was new... Broad shoulders, long limbs, and a stillness in his stance that both unsettled and captivated her.

But it wasn't his features that left her breathless.

It was his eyes. Those golden-hazel eyes had once been her undoing.

They were warm and rich like amber trapped in sunlight, yet now they held something else—

something that she reached for understanding while trying to turn from it. In those eyes, she saw an echo of someone else entirely.

Bella.

Her throat tightened painfully at the thought of her daughter—their daughter—and instinctively, she took a small step back, both wanting to close the distance and desperate to create space, as if distance could somehow shield her from the turmoil of this moment.

"Patrick," she managed to say at last, though her voice came out weaker than she intended—a whisper that barely carried across the space between them.

His jaw tightened almost imperceptibly, his expression unreadable except for a flicker of something raw and unresolved beneath his composed exterior. When he spoke, his voice was deep and steady but carried an edge sharp enough to cut through steel.

"You have a daughter. No—*we* have a daughter…"

The words weren't a question—they were a statement, heavy with accusation and disbelief. And just like that, London felt everything inside her unraveling. The careful walls she had built over the years—the ones meant to keep this exact moment at bay—crumbled in an instant.

She closed her eyes briefly against the weight pressing down on her chest, willing herself to stay calm even as panic clawed at the edges of her composure. She had known this day would come, just not that it would hit like this—as if the air itself had been pulled from her lungs and replaced with memories too painful to face, even in the wide openness of the barn.

"Let's talk inside my house," she said finally, forcing herself to sound steadier than she felt. Without waiting for his response, she turned on her heel and began walking toward the farmhouse at a brisk pace. Her hands clenched into fists at her sides to keep them from trembling. She didn't need to look back to know Patrick was following; his presence loomed behind her like a shadow that refused to be shaken off.

The farmhouse smelled comforting—like honey and vanilla—but today even those familiar scents couldn't soothe her frayed nerves. She led Patrick into the living room, without ceremony, gesturing for him to sit if he wanted to but not waiting to see if he did. Instead, she stood near one corner of the room where sunlight filtered through cream-colored curtains onto hardwood floors polished to a soft sheen.

Patrick didn't sit. He remained near the doorway with his arms crossed over his broad chest—a stance both defensive and commanding. His gaze locked on hers with unyielding intensity.

"Why didn't you tell me?" he asked finally, each word deliberate and weighted with emotion—hurt mingling with anger and disbelief in equal measure.

London exhaled slowly through her nose before answering. "Because you love your job," she began quietly but firmly, meeting his gaze head-on despite how much it hurt to do so. "Because you love traveling…you love your stories…taking pictures more than anything else." Her voice wavered slightly but steadied again as she continued, "And because…after everything that happened between us… I needed time."

Patrick's brow furrowed deeply at this explanation—or perhaps justification—and frustration rippled across his features like storm clouds gathering on an otherwise clear horizon.

"Four and a half years," he said bitterly after a beat of silence. "Nearly five years—and not once did you think I deserved to know about my own child?"

His words pierced straight through whatever armor London had left intact. Her chest tightened painfully as tears stung at the corners of her eyes—not from weakness but from sheer exhaustion at carrying this secret alone for so long.

"I thought I was doing what was best," she said softly but resolutely, despite how much it hurt to say it aloud now under his scrutiny. "For Bella—and for myself."

Patrick's expression darkened further; his voice dropped lower but no less intense when he responded: "You don't get to decide what's best for me—or for *her*—without me."

She flinched at that but stood firm even as guilt

gnawed away inside her like termites hollowing out wood from within.

"You walked away," London shot back quietly yet sharply enough to slice through tension now hanging heavy between them both. "You gave up on us."

Patrick's jaw clenched as he took a step closer, his eyes flashing with a mix of hurt and indignation.

London felt the weight of his gaze like a physical touch, prickling against her skin and settling like a leaden shroud around her shoulders. The memories of their past unraveling beneath the weight of their unspoken words, tugging at the frayed edges of her composure.

"You think walking away was easy for me?" he retorted, his voice tinged with the raw edge of emotion laid bare. "You think I didn't carry the weight of that decision every single day?"

London's chest constricted at his words, the ache of their shared pain reverberating between them like an invisible thread binding them together despite the chasm that had grown over the years. She wanted to reach out, to bridge that gap between them, but years of hurt and silence held her back like an invisible barrier. "Sometimes it's easier to walk away than to face what's really going on."

A charged silence stretched between them, thick with all the words left unspoken over the years. London could hear the uneven rhythm of her own breathing, feel the rapid pulse at her throat as Patrick stared at her, his gaze a storm of emotions she couldn't fully decipher.

Then, Patrick exhaled sharply, raking a hand through his hair before pinning her with an unwavering look. "Well, I'm here now," he said, voice rough with a promise that sent a shiver down her spine. "And I'm not walking away this time."

Her heart lurched, torn between relief and fear—because if Patrick was back for good, it meant every carefully built wall around her and Bella's world was about to come crashing down.

And London wasn't sure she could survive the fallout.

CHAPTER TWO

"I WANT TO meet my daughter," Patrick said, his voice low and urgent, as if every second without her was an eternity. "*Now.*"

London's eyes softened with a mixture of sympathy and resolve. "I never had intentions of keeping her from you," she replied, her tone steady despite the tremor in her hands. "But I need you to understand why I did what I did before you see Bella."

Patrick tightened his jaw, the muscles ticking along his temple. His chest tightened, a knot of frustration and longing twisting inside him. Four and a half years. That was how long he'd been away, chasing stories and capturing truths through his lens in far-off places. Four and a half years of silence, distance, and missed moments.

"She's four," he said, quieter now but no less intense. "Four birthdays without me. Four years of first words, first steps... Did she say *Mama* or *Dada* first?"

London flinched.

He caught it—the flicker of pain in her eyes—and a part of him wanted to reach out, to ask gently why she'd made this choice. But the rest of him was still raw, desperate for answers.

"Patrick, I didn't want to derail your life," London said, her voice low but steady. "You were about to leave on another assignment—a dangerous one—and every time we talked about the future, it always came back to your career. It mattered more to you than anything else. I knew where I fit on your list of priorities. And then your mother…" Her throat seemed to tighten as she forced the words out. "She made sure I knew I'd never belong in your world. She told me that, flat out. And as much as I wanted to fight for us, I realized I was the only one fighting."

She looked at him then. "Your mother didn't have to tear us apart, Patrick. You made that choice yourself. She just gave you the push. You chose your career. You chose to walk away from me." Her voice cracked, but she didn't back down. "I chose to protect our daughter from becoming a weapon in a war I couldn't win. I wasn't going to let Bella be caught in your mother's games or feel like she had to compete with your ambitions. She deserved better."

"That's not fair," he shot back. "You knew what I was trying to build—for us."

"No," she replied, her voice slightly elevated. "You were focusing on creating something for yourself, and I was no longer included. Your mother persuaded you to prioritize your career, especially as your reputation and success as a photojournalist soared. She insisted that this was your destiny— that you had to pick it above all else."

The words landed like a blow, and his heart clenched tight. He rubbed his face as if to shake off the weight of them. "So, you kept my daughter from me as punishment?"

Tears shimmered in her eyes, but she blinked them back. "I kept her a secret because I loved you enough to let you go, and I loved our daughter enough to keep her safe—from all of it."

Patrick's jaw tightened.

"Do you blame me for protecting Bella?" London asked, crossing her arms as if to brace herself. "Especially after your mother made it her mission to break us. She humiliated me, spread lies, planted doubt where there should've been trust. And you—" her voice cracked "—you let her."

"I didn't know the full extent," he murmured. "Not until it was too late."

"Exactly," she said bitterly. "By then, I was already pregnant. Alone, Patrick. I couldn't fight your mother *and* fight to keep you. I had to focus on the child I was carrying."

He didn't argue, because he knew she was right. Myra's poison had seeped in, and he'd been powerless or unwilling to stop it.

"But you should've told me about the baby," he said, voice rough with emotion.

"You were determined to leave," she whispered. "I didn't think you'd come back. Not for me. Not for a baby."

Silence stretched between them, thick and fragile.

Patrick took a step closer, eyes burning with longing and determination. "I'm here now. And

I've been kept away from her long enough. London… I'm not asking anymore. I *need* to meet my daughter. I need to see her. I need to start making up for lost time. Today. Now."

London blinked back tears, her mouth trembling. She studied him, then nodded slowly. "Okay. But we must take this slow."

Patrick swallowed hard, voice steady though his heart threatened to break. "I can do slow. But I *will* be in her life. You won't have to do this alone anymore."

His fingers flexed at his sides, restless and unsure.

When London called out, her voice tight with strain, Patrick swallowed hard. His heart stumbled when he heard the light patter of small feet rushing across the floor.

Then she emerged.

Arabella—his daughter.

Her dark curls, like little spirals of midnight, bounced with every eager step, and her lavender sundress, dotted with tiny white daisies, caught the light as it clung delicately to her small legs. In her tiny hand, she gripped a crayon drawing so worn and creased by her grip it seemed like an extension of her spirit.

Patrick's eyes, though wide, barely registered the drawing; he was entirely consumed by the sight of her face—soft, round cheeks flushed with excitement, large warm eyes filled with innocent wonder, and a barely perceptible dimple that appeared when her slightly parted lips formed gentle words.

"Mommy... I was drawing," she offered, her voice a blend of sweetness and clarity that resonated in the silent space between them.

His chest constricted painfully, as if every beat was a reminder of the years lost.

Before he could step forward, London interjected, her tone threaded with hesitation and a measure of hope. "There's someone here who..." She paused a moment as if gathering her thoughts. "Who wants to meet you."

Patrick steadied himself as his entire world contracted to the two of them. Standing motionless, he took in the fragile figure before him—a little girl whose mere presence seemed capable of mending years of absence. His eyes locked onto her, and a tidal wave of longing crashed against him. This delicate child—his little girl—lifted her gaze, a questioning innocence shimmering in her eyes, and he swallowed hard.

"Hi," Bella whispered, holding her crayon drawing so close it was as if it were a precious talisman against the fear of abandonment.

With a trembling exhale, he managed, "Hi." His voice wavered as uncertainty and overwhelming joy mingled in his words, forcing him to sink to one knee to meet her at her level.

In that vulnerable moment, she seemed so small, and his own hands, grasping his legs, trembled as if to keep the unsteady surge of emotions from overwhelming him. "I'm…" he murmured, then faltered as if the words were stuck behind a dam of emotion. "I'm Patrick."

Her eyes flickered toward London, her brows knitting into a puzzled frown.

London swallowed hard, the sound echoing like a secret finally being revealed. "He's your dad. Remember, I told you about him. You have pictures of him in the photo album."

At those words, a sharp, bittersweet throb pulsed through Patrick's heart. He watched Bella's face intently, marveling as she tried to piece together the sudden puzzle of her identity. For a suspended moment, she regarded him with a measured tilt of her head, as if sorting through a series of mysterious clues.

"*You?*" Bella's voice was tiny but unyielding. "You're my daddy?"

Patrick nodded slowly, each movement laden with belief and remorse. "Yeah…yeah, I am."

"Mommy says you have a very important job. You take pictures all over the world."

Patrick remained crouched to her level, knees stiff but heart softer than it had been in years. The camera pressed against his ribs—familiar, grounding— yet for the first time, it felt like it didn't matter. Not here. Not with *her.*

Mommy says you have a very important job. You take pictures all over the world…

The words caught him off guard—not the innocence of them, but the *knowledge*. She knew. London had told her. He wasn't a ghost or a blank page in this little girl's story. He existed. And somehow, through the miles and mistakes, London had made sure their daughter knew his name, his purpose.

Emotion swelled behind his ribs, thick and sharp.

He cleared his throat, voice low. "Yeah. I'm a photojournalist. I take pictures in parts of the world most people don't get to see—sometimes places they'd rather not."

She tilted her head, curious. "Like what?"

He hesitated. *War. Hunger. Protests. Grief.* But those weren't words for a child. Not yet.

"Like…people who are brave. Or hurting. Or just trying to live their lives," he said finally. "I take pictures, so the world doesn't forget them."

Her eyes lit up. "Like a superhero?"

Patrick let out a soft laugh, broken and awed all at once. "Not quite. But sometimes, yeah…it feels like I get to show the world something important."

He didn't say what really shook him—that her mother had made room for him in their daughter's world. That he wasn't starting at zero. That maybe he had a chance to *become* something to this little girl who already saw him as someone worth knowing.

The silence stretched briefly as Bella's expression morphed from confusion to astonishment, and then—like the sudden burst of the sun on a rainy day—her face bloomed into a radiant, gap-toothed grin. "Do you know how to draw puppies?"

A startled laugh, raw and joyful, escaped Patrick as if his heart had finally found its rhythm. "Yeah," he responded, his voice rough with emotion. "Yeah, I can draw puppies."

"Wanna see mine?" Bella said, thrusting her crayon drawing toward him as she inched closer with an earnest sparkle in her eyes. "I made one at camp. He has blue ears, a green belly, and a tail that sparkles."

With utmost care, he took the creased paper as though it were spun glass, his fingers trembling around its delicate edges. "Wow," he murmured, voice laden with wonder and a thick throat of gratitude. "That's amazing."

As Bella giggled a pure, unrestrained laugh, she leaned in to point at each vibrant scribble, explaining her masterpiece with the unfiltered enthusiasm only a child can muster.

Patrick followed her every gesture, nodding, questioning, and absorbing every detail that made her beam with pride.

In the background, he sensed London's steady presence—watchful and tense—reminding him that the path ahead was still fraught with uncertainty. Yet as Bella's animated chatter filled the space between them, centered on her colorful concept of rainbow puppies, a fragile hope stirred within him. It was small and uncertain but real—an ember of possibility lighting up what had once seemed irreparably dark.

LONDON STOOD IN the doorway, leaning against the frame, unnoticed. She hadn't meant to linger, but the sound of their voices had rooted her in place. Bella's animated storytelling. Patrick's low, attentive murmurs. It all felt…intimate. Familiar in a way that made her chest ache.

"He lives in a sky house," Bella was saying now, her voice dreamy. "With clouds and jellybean bushes. And his name is Pickle. But only on Tuesdays."

Patrick let out a soft laugh. "Why only Tuesdays?"

"Because on Wednesdays he's a cat."

That earned a real laugh from him, quiet but warm. He glanced over at Bella, who was giggling at her own joke, and the pencil paused in his hand. "You've got quite the imagination."

Bella nodded solemnly, then leaned closer to inspect his work. "You forgot the sparkles."

Patrick held up the pencil. "I don't have sparkle color."

Bella grinned. "You have to pretend the sparkles. That's what Mommy says when we run out of glitter glue."

London's throat tightened. The mention of her didn't pull Bella's attention toward the doorway, but it pulled Patrick's. His head turned slightly, as if sensing her before seeing her.

Their eyes met.

She didn't move, not right away. There was something about watching them like this—something whole and heartbreaking. Bella with her wild stories. Patrick with his quiet focus and gentle presence. And between them, the sketch of a rainbow puppy coming to life in lines and color.

London finally stepped into the room, her shoes quiet on the hardwood floor.

"You're forgetting the jellybean bushes," she said softly.

Patrick blinked, surprised by her voice, but his expression softened. "Guess I'm out of practice."

Bella beamed. "Mommy, he's really good. Like, better than Miss Pam at camp."

London smiled, eyes on the half-finished drawing. "He used to draw all the time. Once he turned a napkin into a whole story."

Patrick looked up at her. "Still have a few napkins in me."

The silence that followed wasn't awkward—it was weighty. Fragile. A moment suspended in something neither of them could name yet.

Bella reached for another pencil. "Can you draw me next?" she asked. "But like a princess who flies dragons."

Patrick raised a brow. "That's a tall order."

She grinned. "You can pretend the dragon sparkles, too."

London's laughter was quiet, but it felt like something cracked open inside her—just enough to let the light in.

She settled on the edge of the couch, watching

them, the ache in her chest still there—but now threaded with something else.

Not peace.

But maybe the start of it.

For months, London had rehearsed this moment in her head, every version ending in more pain than comfort. She never let herself imagine what it might feel like to watch Bella with her father. Her heart hadn't dared to hope it would look like this: joyful, unguarded, easy. She had feared so many things: resentment, awkwardness, rejection. But none of those fears fit the picture unfolding before her.

What she hadn't accounted for was the tenderness. Or the way it would gut her.

Bella had always asked about her daddy with a mixture of curiosity and acceptance. She never cried about not having him here, not really. She filled in the blanks with stories and colors and wild what-ifs. When London had finally told her Patrick's name, there had been no tears—just a spark of fascination, a quiet gasp. *My daddy draws stories with a camera.* That had been the anchor.

And now here he was.

Drawing her stories. Listening to every silly detail as if they were sacred. Making Bella laugh with a laugh that used to belong to London alone.

The weight of it settled over her shoulders, not heavy but undeniable. A cloak of memory and consequence.

London looked at him again, really looked.

Patrick—older, yes. More tired around the eyes. But there, beneath all of it, was the man she had loved and mourned.

And God help her; she still felt that pull. That ache. That part of her that remembered him with all the gentleness in the world.

But that was before. Before the nights she cried herself to sleep. Before the labor pains alone. Before the colic and the daycare juggle and the moments she felt like she was drowning while the world carried on.

She'd built a life without Patrick. She'd become someone new—a mother, a provider, a woman who survived.

And yet the sight of him beside Bella threatened to unravel it all. Because maybe it had never been about survival alone. Maybe it had always been about protecting this very moment.

"Look, Mommy…" Bella waved the sketchpad at her. The rainbow puppy now had wings and a shimmering tail. "He can fly to the moon now. Daddy said so…"

London forced her smile to stretch wider. "He's beautiful, baby. You and Daddy make a good team."

Patrick looked up, eyes searching hers. That word hung in the air between them. *Daddy.*

He didn't flinch. Instead, he nodded slowly, something unreadable flickering in his gaze.

"You okay?" he asked quietly.

London blinked, startled by the directness.

She nodded too fast. "Yeah. Just…watching."

Watching a piece of her heart exist outside her body, wrapped in giggles and colored pencils and the long-lost touch of a man she wasn't sure she could forgive.

Patrick set the pad aside and stretched his legs, careful not to jostle Bella, who had now taken to pretending her dragon princess needed a castle drawn, too.

"Thank you," he said, voice barely above a whisper.

London frowned. "For what?"

"For this. For letting me be here."

She looked at him, and for a beat, the years of silence and grief and confusion bubbled to the surface.

"I didn't do it for you."

He nodded. "I know."

"She's not a door you get to walk through when it suits you, Patrick. She's a whole world."

His jaw tightened, but he didn't argue. "And I want to learn how to live in that world."

London swallowed against the lump in her throat.

Bella was humming now, lost in her own universe. Her curls bounced with each exaggerated movement of the pencil. Unbothered. Unaware of the emotional minefield just inches away.

London rubbed her palm along her thigh, grounding herself. "She's a lot. Her mind never stops. Some nights, she dreams up whole musicals in her sleep. I don't always get it right."

Patrick shook his head slowly. "She's amazing. And you... You got everything right that mattered."

She closed her eyes for a second. She didn't want his praise. She didn't need it. But it felt good to hear.

"This doesn't fix anything," she said, voice barely audible.

"I'm here to stay. If you let me."

Her heart twisted. Because she wanted to believe him. For Bella's sake. For her own. But belief was a risk she hadn't taken in a long time.

Still, she looked at Bella—the way she leaned against Patrick like she'd always known him. As if some invisible cord had tied them together from the start.

And maybe it had.

Perhaps this was how healing began.

London leaned back against the couch cushion, not ready to say yes. But not willing to say no.

She whispered, "I think you should draw a castle, Patrick. Every princess needs a castle."

And he picked up the pencil.

Because some things didn't need words.

Some things needed time.

And the space to pretend the sparkles.

"SAMPLE BASKETS ARE READY," Kyla announced, brushing a stray curl out of her eyes as she stepped inside.

"Thanks, Kyla. How do they look?" London asked, her voice smooth out of habit.

Grinning, she responded, "Gorgeous. I tucked the mini honey jars in with the balm samples and added the new info cards. If this doesn't impress the Polk Island Hotel guests, nothing will."

London smiled back, but it didn't quite reach her eyes. The motion felt automatic, like she was mimicking an old version of herself—one who wasn't constantly balancing hope and dread. "I appreciate you. Headed back to the barn?"

Kyla nodded. "Need to prep for the harvest demo next week." She glanced down at her clipboard, already lost in the next ten things on her list. "I'll check in after lunch."

As the door clicked shut behind her, silence wrapped around the house like a thick shawl.

London exhaled, the breath catching slightly in her chest. She turned toward the living room.

There they were. Patrick was still perched on the floor beside Bella, their heads nearly touching as they giggled over a new drawing. Crayons were scattered across the rug, the half-finished sketch between them showing a little girl in a tiara riding a smiling dragon. Bella's laughter, bright and unguarded, filled the space.

London's hand curled around the back of the chair beside her, steadying herself.

She should be happy. And a part of her was— deeply, achingly happy. Watching Bella's face light up, hearing that soft rumble of amusement in Patrick's voice as he praised her drawing…it tugged at something raw and hopeful inside her. They were finally meeting, finally connecting in a way she'd prayed for during countless sleepless nights.

But beneath that joy lay something darker. A tight knot of worry twisted in her gut. Because while this moment was beautiful, it wasn't the whole picture. Patrick's parents didn't know. And they wouldn't be gentle. Their judgment could cut deep—through him, through her, through Bella. And London wasn't sure how much more slicing her heart could take.

She pressed her lips together, watching them. Love and fear warred in her chest, neither quite winning. She didn't want to interrupt. Didn't want to risk breaking whatever fragile bridge was forming between father and daughter. But in the back of her mind, the clock was ticking.

Soon, the rest of the world would catch up.

And she wasn't sure if it would welcome them with open arms—or tear them apart.

She hesitated, then cleared her throat. "I'm about to make some lunch. Want to join us?"

Patrick looked up, a little surprised, but nodded. "Yeah. I'd like that."

As if summoned by the invitation, Cia emerged from the guest room, yawning and barefoot, her natural hair in two-strand twists.

She stopped short when she saw Patrick. "Hey, stranger…"

He broke into a smile. "I know it's been a while."

"Too long, in my opinion…" Cia turned to London and whispered, "Can I talk to you?"

London's heart ticked up a notch, but she nodded and followed her sister to the kitchen. Cia leaned against the counter, arms crossed. "I heard his voice and stayed in the guest room as long as I could. Is everything good with you two?" she asked softly, her voice low and even. "*You* good?"

London nodded. "I'm okay."

Cia studied her a moment longer, then nodded back. "All right. Just checking."

Together, they pulled out fresh sourdough, tomatoes, avocado, turkey, and greens. The easy rhythm of working with her sister grounded London for a moment. It was something solid in a day that had started feeling increasingly abstract.

"Bella's eating at the table?" Cia asked, slicing tomatoes into neat, even rounds.

London's gaze drifted toward the porch. That was where her daughter usually insisted on eating—curled up on the swing, her plate balanced on her lap, humming to herself while watching birds flutter around the feeder. Lunch outside was one of the few routines Bella clung to like clockwork.

"I have a feeling that she'll want to be wherever Patrick is," London said, the words tumbling out before she could pull them back.

Cia didn't say anything, but the glance she shot in London's direction said enough.

Curious. Measuring. Careful.

London shifted her weight, suddenly too aware of the unspoken questions hanging between them.

She forced a smile, trying to push past the tangle of nerves and emotion.

"I mean, if she wants to eat outside, we can set everything up on the porch," Cia offered easily, her tone light. "Wouldn't be the first time we followed her lead."

London blinked, caught off guard by the simple generosity in her sister's voice. Then she nodded. "No, we'll eat in the dining room."

As Cia squeezed lemons into a pitcher, Patrick's voice called out from the other room. "Mind if I ask something?"

London turned as he stepped into the kitchen, hands in his pockets. "What's up?"

He leaned against the doorframe like he belonged there—too casual, too familiar—and said, "I'd like to do a feature on LW's Honey Farm. A deep dive—story and photos for *American Journey*."

Cia's knife stilled mid-slice, a tomato half slipping off the cutting board. "That's a big deal."

"It is," Patrick replied, though his eyes were locked on London, not Cia. "They've picked up pieces of mine before. I think this would be a great fit."

London didn't answer. She reached for the pitcher instead, tossing in sprigs of mint with more force than necessary. The honey slid thick and slow off the spoon, but her mind spun fast. His words stirred something in her chest that felt too much like hope—and that scared her more than suspicion.

"London?" Cia's voice broke the silence, gentle but firm.

She kept her gaze on the pitcher. "It's a flattering idea," she said finally, the words measured. Neutral. Safe. "But… I'm not sure."

She heard the shift in Patrick's posture before she looked up—feet uncrossing, shoulders tensing.

"Why not?"

London turned, slowly. Met his eyes. Her voice didn't rise, but it didn't need to.

"Because it feels convenient," she said, each word smooth as glass and just as cold. "You show up out of nowhere, say all the right things, sit on the floor drawing dragons with my daughter…and now you want to spotlight my business?"

The question didn't need answering. It hovered between them like bees disturbed from the hive—silent, swarming, and far too close.

Patrick took a breath. "I get it. But this isn't some angle. I pitched the idea because I'm proud of what you've built. I've seen the photos online, the product reviews, the buzz. But being here—it's more than that. There's heart in what you're doing. I think people should see that."

"And then what? You write the article and disappear again?"

Patrick's voice dropped. "I'm not disappearing. Yes, writing is still part of who I am. I can do both. I can be a father to Bella."

Cia stirred the lemonade and gave Patrick a look.

"You sure you're not trying to make up for time by fast-tracking everything?"

"No," he said. "I'm trying to do right by both. I'm not pretending I didn't miss years. But I want to earn my way in. And this? This article? It's one small way I can start showing up."

London looked at him—really looked—and saw the weight behind his words. Still, the ache in her chest didn't ease. Because if he left again, if this was all temporary, it wouldn't just break her heart.

It would break Bella's.

And that was a risk she wasn't sure she could afford.

"We'll talk about it later," she said quietly, setting the lemonade on the table. "Let's get through lunch first."

Patrick nodded, stepping forward to help carry the plates.

And though her hands were steady, London's heart beat a quiet rhythm of warning—hope, guarded. Trust, not yet.

The smell of warm cookies mingled with the citrus tang of fresh lemonade as Patrick sat down at the worn oak table, the wood scarred with years of life. He took it all in with quiet reverence: the delicate clink of glasses being set down, the shuffle of plates, the hum of Cia and London moving in tandem like they'd done this a hundred times before.

Bella had already claimed her spot beside him,

swinging her little legs under the table as she reached for a sandwich with both hands.

Across from Patrick, London poured lemonade into mason jars, her movements precise but somehow distant.

Cia chatted cheerfully, tossing out compliments on the pickles and how the honey-roasted turkey paired perfectly with the sourdough bread from the Polk Island Bakery and Café.

Everything felt domestic, easy. Like he'd stumbled into a picture he hadn't known he'd been missing. Patrick reached for a sandwich, his hands steady even though his insides were anything but.

He could still hear Bella's laughter from earlier, see the way her eyes sparkled when she told him about her rainbow puppy and the jellybean bushes. But it was the way her eyes had crinkled at the corners, the tilt of her head when she was thinking hard—those were echoes of himself. Reflections that brought with them a sharp, unexpected ache.

He took a bite of the sandwich. Turkey, sharp cheddar, a hint of honey mustard. Good. Familiar in a way that tugged at his chest.

Cia passed him a cookie with a wink. "London's still got the touch. Best peanut-butter cookies in three counties."

He accepted it with a small smile, but his attention drifted back to London, who finally slid into the seat across from him.

Her fingers brushed against the rim of her glass, eyes lowered.

He wanted to ask her then. Why had she let him walk through the world while his daughter grew up learning to pretend sparkles and invent jellybean bushes without him?

But now wasn't the time. Bella was watching him with open curiosity, her mouth full of sandwich. So, he smiled at her instead, even though his insides were a knot of grief and disbelief.

He hadn't come to Polk Island to find this. He'd come to breathe, to slow down. But discovering the truth in that magazine article... He was walking into a storm he hadn't even known was brewing.

"These pickles are amazing," he said aloud, his voice even.

Cia grinned. "My mom brined 'em herself. With a dash of LW's honey, of course."

London nodded, still not quite meeting his eyes. "Even my brother has created a couple of dishes for the hotel featuring my honey."

He set his glass down. "That's great. This is why the farm should be featured in *American Journey*. They said if I can get the feature turned around in six weeks, they'll run it in their fall issue. Full spread. Print and digital."

Cia let out a small gasp, nearly dropping her cookie. "London, that could change everything. You said you wanted the brand to grow globally. A feature like that can help."

London's gaze shifted from her sister to Patrick. Her mouth opened, then closed again.

"The editor asked for stories that featured innovative small businesses with community impact. Yours…it fits."

Cia reached over to squeeze London's hand. "That's incredible."

Bella, oblivious to the adult tension, hummed a tune and reached for another cookie.

London glanced at her daughter, then back to him. "I don't know if I'm comfortable with you doing a piece on me."

His stomach sank. "Why not?"

"You tell stories for a living. Beautiful, powerful stories. How will the magazine feel about you featuring this story…and your connection to it? It just may be a feature for you…but I have to protect this one."

He looked at Bella, her curls bouncing as she whispered something to Cia about dragons and cookie crumbs. His chest ached.

"I didn't know at the time, London," he said. "If I had…"

She nodded. "I know you didn't, but that doesn't make this any easier."

Patrick sat back, the weight of it all pressing in. He'd covered war zones, famines, civil unrest. He'd photographed faces full of grief and triumph, despair and resilience. But nothing had prepared him for this.

"You asked why I pitched it," he said after a moment. "It wasn't just because the editor needed content. It was because I saw something in the farm—in your work. Something steady. Alive. Worth honoring."

She looked at him then, really looked. And he continued.

"I've spent years chasing other people's stories. For the first time, I want to tell one that matters to me. One that might help me reconnect with what I lost—with what I didn't even know I had."

Cia had gone still, her eyes wet. She placed a hand on her sister's back but didn't speak.

London stared at her lemonade, lips pressed into a line.

"I don't know if I can trust that yet," she whispered. "You being here…it feels good. But if it's temporary—if this is just until your deadline—it'll hurt Bella, and I won't let that happen."

Patrick nodded, understanding cutting deep. "Then let me prove it's not."

The silence returned, thick but not empty. Full of things unsaid.

Bella reached over and handed him a cookie, crumbs on her fingertips. "You didn't eat yours yet. It's the best part."

Patrick took it, heart aching. "Thanks, sweetheart."

She beamed, and he saw it again—the unmistakable echo of himself in her.

He bit into the cookie, the sweet-salty taste grounding him.

He didn't know what would happen next. But in that moment, surrounded by turkey sandwiches, lemonade and pickles and peanut-butter cookies, he knew one thing with absolute clarity.

He wanted to stay.

Not just for the story.

For them.

London stood in the quiet of Bella's room, the soft hum of the old ceiling fan a steady background to the rustle of pajamas and the faint scent of strawberry-bubblegum soap. Outside, the last streaks of sunset melted into the deep blue of night, but her mind was still replaying the moment Patrick had driven away from the farm an hour ago—his smile, the uncertainty in his eyes, the way Bella had clung to his leg before finally letting go.

Bella sat cross-legged on the bed, a tangle of damp curls around her face as she hugged her favorite worn-out bunny. London tugged the sleeves of Bella's pink nightgown down over her little wrists, then sat beside her, smoothing the coverlet over her lap.

"How are you feeling, sweetie?" she asked softly, brushing a curl from her daughter's forehead. "After meeting your daddy today?"

Bella's eyes lit up instantly, and she bounced a little in place. "Happy," she said without hesitation, her smile wide and genuine. "He's nice. He smells like the woods. And he knows how to draw puppies and lots of stuff."

London's throat tightened. "I'm glad you're

happy," she said, managing a smile. "You waited a long time to meet him."

Bella nodded, gaze drifting toward the window where the fireflies were beginning their nightly dance. "Do you think he'll come again tomorrow?" she asked, hope threaded through her small voice.

She hesitated. Patrick had said he wanted to see Bella again soon, but his life had always been unpredictable, dictated by far-flung assignments and stories that had pulled him thousands of miles away. "We'll see," she said gently. "I know he wants to spend time with you."

Bella hugged her bunny tighter. "Will he leave again to tell more stories with his camera?"

The question hit London like a stone to the chest. She could still picture Patrick with that camera slung around his neck, chasing light and shadows in faraway places. She had loved him for that passion once, before it had taken him so far from her—and now from Bella, too.

London swallowed and reached for Bella's small hand. "I don't know exactly what will happen," she admitted, her voice steady but quiet. "But I do know he wants to stay in your life. That's important to him."

Bella seemed to consider that, her brow furrowing as she toyed with the bunny's floppy ear. "So… even if he has to go, he'll come back?"

"Yes, sweetheart." London squeezed her hand. "He'll come back. He wants to be part of your world. And I'll make sure you two get to see each other."

A small, relieved smile returned to Bella's face. "Okay. I like him. He's funny. He made my apple slices into a butterfly."

London chuckled, remembering the scene in the kitchen right before he left—Patrick arranging the fruit just to hear Bella giggle. That sound had filled the house with a warmth she hadn't realized she'd been missing.

"Come on, sweetie," she said, shifting to tuck Bella in properly. She pulled the coverlet up to Bella's chin and kissed her forehead. "Close those eyes and get some sleep. You've had a big day."

Bella yawned, curling onto her side. "'Night, Mommy. 'Night, Bunny. 'Night, Daddy—wherever he is."

The words caught London off guard, but she kept her smile, smoothing Bella's hair until her breathing evened out.

When she finally stood and crossed the room to switch off the lamp, London glanced back at her sleeping daughter. Patrick had left, yes—but he had also left a new spark in Bella, a joy she couldn't ignore.

And as much as London's heart wanted to protect her daughter from disappointment, she knew she couldn't stand in the way of that connection. Not anymore.

CHAPTER THREE

THE SCENT OF lavender and warm earth drifted in through the kitchen window as London tightened the lid on the jar of honey she'd just finished sealing. The air was thick with the sweetness of summer and the low hum of bees somewhere in the clover. She was rinsing her hands at the sink when she heard the creak of the front screen door, followed by a familiar voice.

"Where's my girls?"

London turned just in time to see her mother, Madelyn, step into the kitchen, a wide-brimmed straw hat pushed back on her salt-and-pepper curls and a mason jar nearly the size of a beehive cradled in her hands.

"Mama…" London said, smiling despite the thrum of nerves that had been riding her all morning. "You didn't have to bring that huge jar of pickles."

Madelyn kissed her on the cheek, then made a beeline for the fridge. "Of course I did. You know Bella loves my pickles just as much as you did at her age. Don't pretend like you didn't eat a whole jar one summer afternoon and then deny it."

London laughed, but her heart fluttered. "I had help with those greedy brothers of mine."

Madelyn raised a brow. "Uh-huh… So, where is she?"

"I'm surprised you didn't see them when you drove up to the house. She's out in the garden with Kyla and her daughter, Leah. Last time I checked on her, the girls were pretending to be bees."

Madelyn nodded approvingly and set the jar down with a gentle clink. Her sharp eyes scanned the kitchen, taking in the open cookbook, the cooling tray of oatmeal scones, and the still-steaming kettle. Then, her gaze landed back on London, softening just slightly.

"Cia called me last night," she said, voice low but direct. "She told me that Patrick is back."

The scones suddenly looked a lot less appetizing. London turned to busy herself at the counter, wiping crumbs that didn't need wiping. "She shouldn't have bothered you with this…"

"Well, she did. And I'm glad she did. Don't be mad at your sister for caring."

London sighed. She could feel her mother's eyes on her like the sun through a magnifying glass. "I'm not mad. Just…tired. Confused."

Madelyn pulled out a chair at the small breakfast table and sat down, setting her purse on top with a familiar *thump*. "*So…?* Where do things stand between you two?"

"There's not really a *two* to stand anywhere," she replied. "Patrick's here, and he's spending time with Bella. Getting to know his daughter."

"And?"

London shook her head, forcing a smile. "He wants to do a piece on the farm for *American Journey* magazine. Said it was time the world saw what we built here."

Madelyn tilted her head. "Sounds like admiration to me."

"It sounds like a temporary assignment." Her voice was sharper than she intended. London lowered it. "What happens when it's over, Mama? When the last picture's taken and the last word is written? Patrick is an award-winning photojournalist. He's spent his career chasing stories around the world. That doesn't just…change."

Madelyn folded her hands on the table. "But sometimes priorities do."

London leaned against the counter, arms crossed. "He missed the first four years of Bella's life. How do I let her fall in love with someone who might be gone again in a few weeks?"

"You protect her," Madelyn said gently. "But you don't close her off from something—or someone— that might be good. You're scared, baby. And I get it. Lord knows I get it. But you don't have to have all the answers right now. Take it one day at a time."

London's throat tightened. She blinked rapidly, trying not to let the tears rise. "It's not just about Bella. What about his mother?"

Madelyn blinked. "What about Myra?"

"You know she's never liked me. She's going to find out she has a granddaughter and hate me even more for keeping it from her."

With a small shrug, Madelyn responded, "Maybe she will. Maybe she won't. But that's not your burden, London. Patrick's a grown man. If he wants a relationship between his daughter and his mother, he needs to be the one to build that bridge. Not you."

London felt the ache of truth in her mother's words. She glanced toward the window, where she could just make out Bella running through the yard, a daisy crown askew on her head, Leah chasing her with mock bee wings made from old tulle.

"She deserves the world," she whispered.

"Then give Bella the chance to see if her father can be part of it. *One day at a time*."

London crossed the room and sat down beside her mother, her fingers curling around Madelyn's. "Okay," she said softly. "One day at a time."

Her mother gently squeezed her hand. "That's all any of us ever get."

They sat there in silence, the summer breeze stirring the curtains, the clink of laughter echoing from the garden. And for just a moment, London let herself breathe. Let herself hope.

Just for today.

Just for now.

Just one day at a time.

THE EARLY FRIDAY-AFTERNOON sunlight filtered through the gauzy curtains of Patrick's short-term rental, softening the edges of the modest living room. He had chosen a place tucked away on the quieter side of Polk Island, away from the bustle and memory-soaked corners he wasn't ready to face yet. It was temporary. Everything in his life felt that way right now. Except for one thing.

Bella.

The weight of her name pressed softly but steadily on his chest. He had spent the morning pacing, straightening throw pillows, making coffee and forgetting it on the counter. His parents were due any minute, driving in from Savannah after he'd called them two days ago.

He had debated waiting longer, telling them after he'd had more time with Bella, after he and London had established some kind of rhythm. But there was never going to be a perfect moment. And this truth couldn't stay buried any longer.

At precisely 1:03 p.m., their car pulled into the gravel driveway. He saw the familiar silhouette of his father, Robert, behind the wheel, and his mother, Myra, already craning her neck to peer out of the passenger window.

Patrick opened the door just as they stepped out of the vehicle.

His mother pulled him into a tight hug, the scent of her signature jasmine lotion instantly transporting him back to childhood. "You look too skinny," she said, patting his cheeks. "What are you eating?"

"Food, Ma," Patrick responded. "I'm fine."

His father gave him a firm handshake that quickly turned into a hug.

"It's good to see you, son," Robert said. "You look well."

They settled into the living room, Myra pulling her coat off and immediately rearranging the pillows on the sofa. Robert wandered toward the small bookshelf, eyeing Patrick's travel-worn copies of photojournalism anthologies.

"Son..." Myra uttered, settling on the edge of the couch with practiced poise, her eyes sharp with expectation. "It's so good to have you stateside finally. I feel like you've been traveling forever. What brought you back to this island? I ask because I just naturally assumed you would've come straight home to Savannah."

Patrick braced himself. This was the moment. The words were heavy in his chest, like they'd been waiting for years, and maybe they had. He curled his hands into fists, then relaxed them. One breath. Just one truth.

"I had a reason for coming here," he began, voice low, steady. "There's something I need to tell you—"

"Please don't tell us that you're trying to get back with London," Myra cut in, her tone brittle with warning. "Son, you know this isn't going to work out between you and that girl. She's not leaving this island, and your work calls you all over the place. Be practical."

The words hit him like a door slammed in his face.

His mouth closed, jaw tightening. That wasn't

what he'd been about to say—not exactly—but now the weight in his chest turned into something sharper.

He glanced at his father, who stayed quiet, studying the worn grain of the coffee table like it held answers.

"I'm not here for a second chance with London," Patrick said finally, though it tasted like a lie. Or maybe just a half-truth. "This isn't about us."

But the real words—the ones he *needed* to say—stayed lodged in his throat. He tried to picture how to begin. *I have a daughter. Her name is Arabella. She's yours, too, in a way you never expected.*

But with Myra watching him like a strategist sniffing out weakness, her disapproval already crackling in the air, he faltered.

"It's more complicated than that," he said instead.

Myra waved a dismissive hand. "Everything's always complicated with *that one*. You need someone who fits your world. Not someone who wants to tether you to a place like this."

Patrick nodded, almost imperceptibly, retreating behind the familiar armor of silence.

His parents turned in unison, the energy in the room shifting instantly.

"Okaay…" Myra said, suspicious and curious all at once.

Patrick swallowed hard, then uttered, "I have a daughter."

Silence.

Not a stunned silence. A loaded, bracing-for-impact kind of stillness.

"A daughter," Robert echoed slowly.

Myra blinked, then smiled broadly. "A *daughter*? You have a baby girl? Patrick, that's—that's incredible…oh my goodness! Why didn't you call us sooner? How old is she? Where is she? What's her name?"

Patrick lifted his hand. "Her name is Arabella, but everyone calls her Bella. She's four."

The joy in Myra's eyes faltered.

"Four?" she said sharply.

Patrick nodded. "Yeah. *Four.*"

Myra stood up. "And we're just now hearing about her? Who's her mother?"

He met his mother's gaze. "London."

Myra blinked.

"London?" she said slowly, as if she couldn't quite parse the syllables. "London *Worthington*?"

"Yes."

Myra recoiled as if slapped. "That—that *woman* kept your child from you?"

Robert had gone still, his jaw tight. "You mean that she didn't tell you? Not a word?"

Patrick shook his head. "I found out a few days ago. But yeah…she never told me before."

Myra's face turned red with indignation. "Unbelievable. I *knew* she was trouble the minute I laid eyes on her. All that sweetness hiding a conniving little agenda."

"Ma…"

"No. No, I won't be calm. She took *four years* from us, Patrick. From *you*. From your dad and *me*. That's our *granddaughter*, and she didn't even have the decency to give us a chance to know her. How dare she?"

"Ma—"

"Where is she?" Myra interjected. "Where's Bella? I want to see her. *Today*."

Patrick held up both hands. "Stop. Just…stop. You're not going over there. Not like this. How can you be so surprised? After the way you've always treated her."

Myra placed both hands on her hips. "You're defending London?"

"No. I'm saying this is *not* the way to handle it. Bella doesn't even know about you yet. I've only just met her. Right now, I'm trying to earn my daughter's trust. I need you to respect that."

His mother paced the small space like a caged cat.

Robert finally spoke. "I can't believe London would do that to you. To *us*."

Tension simmered in Patrick's gut. "It isn't that black and white," he responded. "I'm not saying it was right—it wasn't. But you need to understand something, Ma. London didn't trust you."

Myra froze. "*Excuse me?*"

"She didn't trust you. Or us, really. But especially you," Patrick said, his voice low and tight, simmering with years of pain. "You have always made it clear that you didn't think she was good enough for me. And you did everything you could to make sure we didn't stay together."

Myra's eyes flashed. "I was only trying to protect you. She was—"

"Pregnant," Patrick cut in, his tone flat. "And she didn't know how to tell me. You think your pressure made that easier? You iced her out. You accused her of being a distraction. You told me she wouldn't last."

Myra turned toward Robert as if for backup. "I never said that."

"You did, Ma. Repeatedly. You were never welcoming to her. You were determined to break us up. London felt it. And she remembers every second of it." His voice broke on the last word, and he looked at his mother, pain flickering beneath his steady gaze.

"You pulled strings to get me that assignment in Syria, didn't you?"

Myra stiffened, saying nothing. The silence said everything.

"I knew it," Patrick whispered. "You went behind my back, used your contacts at the Horizon Press Agency, sold me as the perfect candidate. And then you stood there and pretended it was a blessing. Like it just happened out of the blue."

"Eleanor Vance is a dear friend of mine, and she was immediately interested in you. You had just won the World Press Photo of the Year, Patrick," she snapped, her voice rising with indignation. "Do you even understand what that meant? You were finally being seen. You had real momentum. And I don't regret it. Your work covering those refugee camps on the Syrian-Turkish border earned you a National Photojournalism Award for Excellence. I didn't want you to throw all that away."

"No, Ma," he said, his voice rising with fury. "You didn't want me to throw *you* away. You were scared I'd choose her over you and everything you'd planned for me. And you were right—I might've."

"London was emotional. She clung to you. She made things complicated."

"Her father was terminally ill, and she was *pregnant*, Ma." Patrick's voice cracked. "When Angus Jr. died, I couldn't be there for London because you made sure I was chasing a dream that *you* thought mattered more than the life I was building with her."

Myra's face hardened. "I did what any mother would've done to protect her son."

"No," he said bitterly. "You did what *you* always do. You pulled the strings. You shaped the story. You decided what my life should look like—and anyone who didn't fit, you erased."

He took a shaky breath. "Well, I'm done letting you do that."

"Patrick—"

"I have a daughter I didn't even know existed because of the decisions you made behind my back. I'll never be able to redeem those years, Ma. But I can make sure I'm here from now on."

Myra folded her arms. "So now what? You want

me to just sit back and wait for her to *maybe* let me be a part of my granddaughter's life?"

"Yes," Patrick said. "That's exactly what I want. Because Bella is what matters. Not your pride."

The room was quiet again, but now the air felt heavier, charged with the pain of old wounds.

Myra lowered herself back onto the couch, deflated.

Patrick exhaled slowly. "We both walked away. I chose my career. London chose to survive the best way she could. And she raised a beautiful little girl who loves glitter, believes in rainbow puppies, and makes everyone around her laugh."

He looked at his mother, softening. "If you want to know Bella, you have to earn London's trust first. And I don't know if she'll ever give it. But I'm asking you to try. Without forcing it. Without resentment."

Myra wiped the corner of her eye. "I want to meet my granddaughter."

"I know. Just let me talk to London. Let me try to get us all there the right way."

Robert nodded solemnly. "We'll follow your lead, son."

Patrick sat down beside his mother. "Bella is incredible. You'll love her. But don't come in expecting anything. Come in giving. That's the only way this works."

Myra took a long breath, then nodded.

"All right. Just take it one day at a time." Patrick looked at his hands, burdened by the four and half years that had slipped away and the delicate hope of what the future might hold.

One day at a time, he reminded himself silently. Each day brought him a step closer to being the father his daughter deserved.

LONDON SAT AT a corner table at the Polk Island Café, the coastal light pouring through wide windows, dappling the worn wood floors and casting soft glows across the glass mugs lining the back shelf. Outside, the breeze off the water fluttered the café's awning and sent the scent of rosemary and brine drifting in every time the door opened. The low murmur of conversation filled the room—locals lingering over crab melts, summer tourists hunched over cell phones and iced lattes.

It should've been comforting. Familiar.

But nothing about this moment felt easy.

She crossed her arms as she waited, the blue-checked tablecloth beneath her fingertips rumpled and fading in places. Her tea had gone cold. She resisted the urge to check the door again, even though the tiny bell above it had been drawing her attention like a moth to flame every few minutes.

Patrick had asked to meet here, of all places. Not her place. Not the beach. Here—the café where once they'd shared slices of peach pie and whispered promises, where they used to dream aloud over sweet tea and hush puppies. Here, where the ghosts of what could have been still clung to the woodwork.

The bell above the door finally jingled, and there he was—looking somehow the same and yet completely different. His sleeves were rolled up just the way she remembered, forearms browned by sun, camera strap marks faint against his tan. But there was a tension around his eyes now. Not weariness. Something heavier. Regret, maybe.

He spotted her and made his way through the tables.

"Hey," he said, voice low and careful.

"Hey," London echoed, gesturing to the seat across from her.

Patrick settled into the corner booth—their booth, though neither of them acknowledged it. His eyes lingered on her a beat longer than necessary.

London shifted, clearing her throat and pushing the teacup away.

"Thanks for meeting me," he began. "I figured this place might be…neutral ground."

"That depends on what you plan to say."

He gave a faint chuckle. "Still sharp as ever."

"Just direct. Let's not waste time rehashing what went wrong," she said, her voice steady. "I want to talk about what happens now. With Bella."

Patrick leaned in, forearms braced on the table. "Okay. Good. I want that, too."

London studied him quietly. The sharp line of his jaw. The furrow between his brows. He looked older. More worn. And yet beneath the scruff and sun, the boy who once snuck handwritten poems into her recipe cards was still in there somewhere.

That realization unsettled her more than she wanted to admit.

"I told my parents about Bella," Patrick announced.

Her breath caught. "And?"

"They were shocked as you can imagine," he said. "My mom…she was thrilled. Then I told her you were Bella's mother."

London stared at him. "Let me guess. That joy didn't last long."

"No," he admitted, wincing. "Not exactly."

"Not surprising since your mother never liked me."

"She doesn't understand you."

"She didn't try," London said, heat in her voice. "She looked at me like I was some…tarnished thing you picked up on a dare."

"She was wrong," Patrick said softly. "She's still wrong."

London's gaze flicked toward the café window. Outside, the marina shimmered in the afternoon light. Kids tossed breadcrumbs to gulls. The tide rolled in slow and patient.

"My parents really want to meet Bella," Patrick said. "Before they leave the island on Sunday. I'm hoping you'll agree to maybe having dinner later."

London blinked. "Dinner? *With your mother?*"

"She'll be on her best behavior. I promise."

London gave a brittle laugh. "Patrick, your mother's best behavior is still emotional warfare. She doesn't raise her voice—she just cuts you with a look. And I won't let her turn that blade on Bella."

"She missed four years of her granddaughter's life," he said. "That's not something my mom can ignore."

"And whose fault is that?" London asked, even though the answer was obvious.

He didn't flinch this time. "Mine. And yours."

She looked at him for a long moment. The hurt. The history. All of it hung in the air between them like steam off the cappuccino machine behind the counter.

"I'm not ready," she said quietly. "Honestly, I don't know if Bella is either."

"I'm just asking you to consider it," he said. "We don't have to go far. What about here? Familiar ground. Safe."

London hesitated.

The café. Her sanctuary. Their battleground. The memory of him across this very table with salt in his hair and laughter in his voice twisted something inside her. How many times had they eaten here, dreaming about careers and a little cottage just off Harbor Drive?

And now here they were. A daughter in the balance. A past they could never fully unpack.

The door to the café opened again, and Misty Rothchild swept in from the kitchen, her polka-dot apron flapping like a flag. She spotted them instantly.

"Well, look who's making my café prettier just by sitting here," Misty teased, beaming at London before raising an eyebrow at Patrick. "And the one who got away. Back in town, are you?"

London mustered a small smile. "Hi, Misty."

She leaned on the edge of the booth, eyeing them both with a playful grin. "How's your mom doing? I've been craving those pickles of hers. I even offered to stock them here at the café, but Madelyn shut me down before I could finish the sentence."

London chuckled, shaking her head. "She only makes them when the mood strikes. I told her she's sitting on a gold mine, but you know how she is. She always says that if her spirit isn't settled, the batch won't turn out right. And if the jar doesn't seal with that perfect pop, she'll toss the whole thing. Mama swears she can taste stress in the brine."

"She's probably not wrong," Misty said, laughing. "Her pickles could bring about world peace, one jar at a time."

London agreed.

Misty turned to Patrick. "Are you sticking around this time?"

He hesitated. "I'm stateside for a while. Still figuring out the rest."

Misty gave a knowing nod. "Well, don't figure too long. Some roots don't take if you wait too late to plant 'em."

She gave Patrick's shoulder a pat and disappeared behind the counter again, the scent of baking bread trailing behind her.

London stared after her, Misty's words echoing louder than they should've. *Roots don't take if you wait too late.*

She looked at Patrick, whose expression had turned unreadable.

"All right," she said slowly. "Dinner. But if your mother so much as breathes the wrong way near Bella, we're leaving."

"No arguments," he said. "I swear."

London pushed away from the table and stood. "We'll meet you here. Five thirty."

Patrick stood, too. For a second, it looked like he might reach for her, might take her hand or brush her arm like he used to. But he didn't. He just nodded.

As he left, London lingered by the booth. Her gaze settled on the chair he had just vacated, the ghost of their past etched into the grain of the wood.

This wasn't the conversation she'd imagined when she first saw him again. But maybe it was the one they needed.

Still, as she stepped outside and let the breeze wrap around her, the same question gnawed at her insides:

How do you protect your child from someone who claims to love them—when once, they shattered you without warning?

Dinner would come soon enough. And with it, the storm.

But London knew her anchor now. Her daughter. Her voice. Her boundaries.

And this time, no one—not even Patrick's mother—would shake her from that truth.

CHAPTER FOUR

Patrick led the way into the Northwinds dining room at the Polk Island Hotel, the warm scent of fresh herbs and sea air wrapping around them like a welcoming shawl. The soft clink of silverware and low murmur of conversation filled the space with a quiet elegance that soothed and unsettled him all at once.

This wasn't the original plan.

They were supposed to meet at the Polk Island Café—familiar, cozy, a place that felt safe. But two hours before dinner, Patrick changed his mind. Something about the weight of the moment, the significance of what they were walking into made the café feel too small. Too casual. Too close to the past they were still trying to make sense of.

So, he'd picked up the phone and made a quiet call, asking for a last-minute table at Northwinds. It wasn't just a nicer restaurant—it was intentional. Northwinds sat inside the hotel London's family owned, a place that had always carried her family's fingerprints and pride. Choosing it was more than about ambiance.

It was about respect.

He wanted London to feel steady in her space. This wasn't just dinner. This was a new beginning, if they could survive the tension long enough to reach it. If things went well tonight, maybe the scattered pieces of his life—past, present, and future—could start finding their way back into alignment.

He glanced to his right, where London walked with one hand resting on Bella's back. She looked calm, but he could see the effort in her posture, in the controlled curve of her mouth. Bella, blissfully unaware of the undercurrents swirling around the adults, grinned up at the glowing lanterns and whispered a running commentary as they walked.

Patrick slowed his steps, giving them room to come beside him.

He wasn't just bringing his daughter to dinner with his parents. He was walking into the beginning of everything he'd missed—and praying it wasn't already too late.

The hostess led them to a table on the veranda Patrick had requested this exact spot—far enough from the bustle inside, close enough to hear the rhythmic hush of the tide.

As they settled in, Patrick positioned himself between Bella and London, as if his presence could shield them from what might come.

Myra and Robert Brown arrived not long after, his father greeting him with a warm hug, his mother offering a kiss on the cheek and a searching look that landed squarely on Bella.

"Oooh," she murmured, her tone high and polite, "she's...darling." However, her smile didn't quite reach her eyes when her gaze landed on London.

Patrick introduced Bella formally, then gestured for everyone to sit.

Unspoken tension surrounded them. The conversation started slowly. Menus were opened, water was poured, and an unspoken tension lingered between them.

Bella giggled when the server asked if she wanted a "big girl drink" and opted for sparkling water.

Patrick smiled but kept a close eye on London, who was doing her best to remain neutral. Her posture was poised, her words minimal.

Then Myra, with the unmistakable sweetness that often carried a bitter aftertaste, remarked, "Such a lovely place. I imagine London picked it. Her family does own the hotel, after all."

Patrick didn't hesitate. "Actually, it was *my* choice. I wanted something quiet. Familiar."

He didn't miss the flicker in London's eyes, the way she seemed to shrink back slightly.

"Oh," Myra said, adjusting the silverware near her plate. "Well. Very thoughtful."

It shouldn't have mattered, but it did. That assumption—that London would steer the ship, manipulate the setting, set the tone—had taken root.

He watched his mother carefully, feeling like a referee in a match where no one acknowledged the competition.

His father, to his credit, remained quiet but present, giving small nods of encouragement when Bella spoke or reached for more bread.

Patrick tried to guide the conversation, keeping it light. Bella talked animatedly about her current obsession—drawing dragons and living on clouds. She described how her dragon, Muffin, only ate blueberry pancakes and lived in a floating palace above Polk Island.

Myra, surprisingly, leaned in with a small smile. "That's lovely, sweetheart. I'd love to see one of your drawings someday."

It was the first moment of connection all evening, and Patrick clung to it like a lifeline. The tension at the table had been tightly wound from the moment they sat down, and now—finally—it was beginning to loosen. Even Robert chuckled, playing along by asking if Muffin had his own cloud-sized toothbrush.

Bella giggled and nodded. "And bubblegum toothpaste."

Still, Patrick's attention kept drifting to London. Her plate sat nearly full, the lemon garnish on her grilled sea bass untouched, her fork moving more out of habit than hunger. She smiled when she should, nodded when expected, but he could see the distance in her eyes. She was retreating inside herself, behind the wall she'd spent years building up to keep his family from hurting her. And she had every reason.

He leaned in. "You okay?" he asked, his voice just above a whisper.

"I'm fine," London replied, offering a tight smile. "Just…observing."

But Patrick knew better. Her silence wasn't apathy. It was armor.

Myra shifted the conversation, her tone brightening as she turned to London. "So," she began, her voice laced with something that wasn't quite curiosity. "I've been hearing great things about your honey farm. Someone mentioned it at the garden club I belong to in Savannah. It appears you've made quite a name for yourself."

Patrick caught the way London blinked in surprise, as if unsure how to process the unexpected compliment.

"Yes," she said carefully. "We've been fortunate. The harvest was strong this year, and we picked up a few more retailers on the mainland."

"Sixteen hives now, I heard, or maybe I read it somewhere…" Myra said, lifting her wineglass and swirling it delicately. "That's a lot of bees."

"It is," London said with a slight smile. "We started with two hives in the back field. Now we have several across the orchard."

Myra hummed, the sound both appreciative and…uncertain. "And you're really out there working the hives yourself?"

"Every week," London said. "It's hands-on work. And we've learned a lot. The bees teach you if you're willing to listen."

"That's very…poetic," Myra replied. Then her smile faded just a touch, and she tilted her head toward Bella. "I imagine that's a little dangerous, though. All those bees. Does Bella go out there with you?"

London's expression didn't change, but Patrick saw it—the flicker of irritation beneath her calm. "She doesn't go near the hives," she said, even and firm. "She knows the rules. We talk a lot about safety. But she loves helping bottle and label the jars."

"I see." Myra nodded slowly, her eyes flicking toward Patrick as if silently asking, *And you're okay with that?*

Patrick's jaw tightened. "Bella's not in any danger," he said, careful but direct. "London runs a tight operation. Safer than half the kitchens I've walked into."

Robert chuckled, trying to cut the tension. "I got stung just mowing the lawn last week. Bees don't discriminate."

London gave him a polite smile. "Exactly. It's about respect. And staying calm. They only sting when they feel threatened."

Myra offered a tight nod.

And there it was again. That subtle tug-of-war beneath the surface of every word exchanged.

Patrick reached for his water glass, his fingers curling tightly around the base. He hated how every interaction felt like a test. Like London had to prove herself. Like Bella's life was being measured against some silent ledger of what was safe in Myra Brown's eyes.

"This hotel is really nice. Robert and I stayed here once. It was many years ago…" Myra stated then, shifting her gaze toward the softly lit dining patio, likely hoping to redirect the conversation.

Patrick stuck a forkful of chicken into his mouth, chewing slowly.

"Yeah," Robert interjected. "We came here on vacation, and we had a great time on the island. Didn't we, sweetheart?"

"Well," Myra said, "it was lovely. Just…very local."

"It's home," London said simply.

They fell into a strained silence, broken only by the clinking of silverware and Bella humming a tune under her breath.

Later, when dessert came—vanilla custard and fresh berries—Bella asked if she could walk to the koi pond. London agreed, rising from her seat, and Patrick joined her without hesitation.

"We'll stay here," Myra said, patting her lips with a napkin. "Let you get some air."

As they stepped into the dusky evening, warm with the scent of roses and salt air, Patrick exhaled for what felt like the first time all evening.

"She meant it as a compliment. Her words about the honey farm…" he said after a moment.

"Sure," London murmured. "Wrapped in worry. Laced with judgment."

Patrick sighed. "She doesn't understand it. Yet. But I think she wants to."

"Wanting and doing are two different things."

"I'll talk to her."

London didn't respond right away.

Bella giggled in the distance, tossing bread-crumbs toward the koi as they swam in lazy circles.

Her arms were crossed loosely over her chest, her eyes on their daughter. "She asked if Bella goes near the hives," London said, quiet but steady. "Like I'd just let her wander into danger."

"She doesn't know you."

"That's because she never once tried to get to know me. She'd already made up her mind the first time we were introduced."

Patrick stepped closer. "Maybe this is her try-ing now."

London's silence was heavy.

"I know it's not perfect," he said. "But it's a start. And she saw you tonight, London. Not just the woman from the past, but the one you are now."

"I don't need her approval."

"I know," he said. "But Bella deserves a family that's not always one conversation away from rip-ping Band-Aids off old wounds."

That got her attention.

London turned, really looking at him. "So, what are we, Patrick? Old wounds?"

"No," he said. "We're the part that's healing."

Her expression softened, just a little.

"I want this to work," he said. "All of it. You. Me. Bella. My family. Yours. I want us to find a way forward."

London didn't say yes, but she didn't pull away

either. She looked back toward Bella, who was now crouched at the edge of the pond, whispering something to the fish.

"You picked this place," she said quietly. "Thank you."

"For what?"

"For understanding that I needed a space where I would feel safe. The café holds a special place in my heart, but the hotel…" She trailed off, her gaze drifting to the polished wooden beams overhead, the familiar hum of quiet conversation surrounding them like a soft blanket.

"I didn't want you walking into a space that might feel…complicated," he said. "I wanted you to have the room to just…be."

He reached out and touched her hand. Brief but warm. Solid.

For the first time that night, she didn't flinch. But she didn't quite reach back either.

Her hand stayed where it was, still and uncertain beneath his.

She let the contact linger. Just long enough to let him know she noticed. Just long enough to let him stay.

It wasn't trust. Not yet.

But maybe it was the start of something that could hold.

If he was patient enough to earn it.

LONDON WAS SEATED behind the large oak desk in her farmhouse office, with the early-afternoon sun streaming through the tall windows. She absent-mindedly rotated a jar of honey in her hands, observing how the golden liquid shimmered in the light.

A gentle yet assured knock came from the front door.

She stood up and headed toward the entrance. London recognized who it was without having to inquire.

Opening the door, she found Patrick standing there, wearing a blue T-shirt and jeans with a camera bag over one shoulder. His expression was cautious, yet his eyes held the familiar warmth—the same eyes that once regarded her as if she had hung the stars.

"Hey," he greeted.

"Come in," London replied, stepping aside to let him in.

The farmhouse was quiet today. Bella was with Madelyn, spending the day making pickles and playing in the backyard. London had needed the break—space to think, to breathe, to come down from last night's dinner.

They walked through the rustic living room to her office, the walls lined with books, photos, and framed newspaper clippings of her honey farm's rise in popularity. Patrick's gaze lingered on a black-and-white photo of her and Bella holding hands in front of the apiary, their faces partially hidden by veils and sun.

"You've built something incredible here," he said.

London gestured to the chair across from her. "Have a seat."

He did, carefully placing his camera bag beside him. For a moment, neither of them spoke.

"So," she began, resting the jar back on her desk. "Are you here to talk about last night? Or are we pretending that didn't happen?"

Patrick gave a short breath, somewhere between a laugh and a sigh. "I'm here for both. And I brought my camera because I still want to do the article. If you'll let me."

London leaned back, watching him carefully. "I'll agree to the article. But I want you to keep Bella out of it. No pictures of her. No mentions of her. This is about the farm. One article slipped a photo of her in its magazine… I didn't find out until after it was published. She deserves her privacy and a normal childhood away from the spotlight."

He nodded slowly. "That's fair. I respect that."

"Good."

A beat passed before Patrick leaned forward, elbows on his knees. "London…last night didn't go quite how I wanted it to. I hoped it would feel like a fresh start for everyone involved. Like we could… move forward."

She met his gaze. "You mean you hoped your mother wouldn't say something terrible. You were trying to manage everyone's feelings."

"I was trying to protect Bella. And you."

London stood and crossed to the window, arms folded as she looked out over the hives. "I still can't believe she asked if Bella was safe around the bees. As if I'd put our daughter in danger. And that was after she admitted she's been reading about my business. She knows exactly what I do here."

"I'm telling you that she doesn't understand. Not really," Patrick said. "She's not used to being out of control."

London turned back to him, fire in her eyes. "Then maybe she shouldn't have tried to control everything to begin with. She didn't just disapprove of me—she made me feel small. Like nothing I could do would ever be good enough for you or for her."

Patrick's jaw tightened. "I know. And I didn't stop her. That's on me."

The silence that followed was thick—but not hopeless.

Finally, London returned to her seat, her arms folded, her walls firmly back in place.

"You want to write about this place? Fine. Take pictures. Interview the staff. Highlight the community events." She paused, her voice tightening. "But don't spin it into some redemption arc."

Patrick opened his mouth, but she cut him off. "People love those stories, you know?" London shook her head, firm but calm. "That's not my story." She leaned forward, making sure he understood. "I didn't stumble on a yummy jar of honey and decide to turn it into a business. I didn't get struck by inspiration and magically find my purpose. I didn't fall into this. I chased it. I studied bees—read every book I could get my hands on, took classes, watched hives for hours, asked a thousand questions. I didn't just wake up one morning and know how to build this. I *learned* it. I *earned* it."

"I remember how excited you were," Patrick responded. "I once complained that I thought you loved the bees more than you loved me."

She chuckled at the memory. "Do you remember how I started in my kitchen, using what little savings I had, packing jars by hand and selling them out of my trunk at farmers markets? I spent nights figuring out spreadsheets I didn't understand and mornings forcing myself out of bed when quitting would've been easier. I nearly lost everything trying to scale up. I've had to fight for every inch of this land, every brick, every contract. People think you find places like this. You don't. You *build* them."

Patrick sat quietly, the weight of her words settling between them.

"This story…if you're going to tell it—tell that part right."

"That's exactly what I want to write."

She studied Patrick for a long moment, then nodded. "Then let's get to work."

Outside, the bees kept humming. Inside, the air shifted just slightly—less tension, more resolve. They weren't healed. They weren't whole. But they were talking.

Patrick stood awkwardly at the edge of the room

while London handed him the white beekeeping suit, folded neatly over her arm. Sunlight streamed through the window of her home office, touching the pale wooden floors and glinting off the glass jars of honey lining one wall. There was a weight between them—yesterday's dinner, Myra's barbed concern, Bella's bright innocence. London hadn't spoken much after Patrick left last night, just let the silence wrap around her like a shawl. But now she was focused, resolute, and somehow that steadied him.

"You'll need to tuck your pants into your socks. Bees find their way into the smallest places," she said, offering the mesh-veiled helmet next. "I assume you're not allergic."

Patrick smirked as he held up the helmet. "Nope. Stung once as a kid. Cried…but I survived."

"Well, I haven't lost a visitor yet," she replied, pulling on her own gloves. Her voice was dry, but there was a note of amusement buried in it. Not quite a smile—not yet.

Once he was suited up, she led him outside. The mid-morning air was warm, thick with the scent of sunbaked earth and rosemary from her herb garden. A gravel path wound between the outbuildings until they reached the first row of hives. Painted in soft pastels, each wooden box bore a small plaque with a name etched on it: *Magnolia, Ivy, Rose.*

"You name your hives?" Patrick asked, lowering his camera bag to the ground.

"Only the strong ones," she said. "And the troublemakers."

Patrick chuckled and adjusted the strap across his chest. He was already reaching for his camera. "Got it. Which one bites?"

"Daisy," London said without hesitation, stepping closer to one of the hives. She moved with easy confidence, lifting the smoker from a small cart nearby and puffing a gentle cloud toward the entrance. The bees buzzed louder, a low hum like a living engine. "This hive is the most temperamental of the bunch."

He snapped a few shots, watching her through the viewfinder. Her movements were methodical, practiced. She lifted the lid from the hive with care, revealing frame after frame thick with bees. The sun caught on the golden glisten of the honeycomb, and Patrick's breath caught behind the mesh of his helmet.

"This is incredible," he murmured.

London didn't look at him. She was studying the bees, checking each frame with a careful eye. "Most people don't see the beauty. They see a stinger and run."

"I see the beauty," he said quietly, aiming his camera again.

For a long moment, the only sounds were the click of the shutter and the low, contented hum of the bees. Patrick moved in a slow arc around her, capturing the way the light filtered through her veil, the curve of her hand as she held a frame up to inspect it.

"My mother read the article from last year," he said after a while. "The one in the local journal."

London arched a brow, gently returning a frame to the hive. "I'd guess she was surprised I was capable of running a successful business."

Patrick winced. "She doesn't know how to say things without poking a little. But she was impressed. Truly."

London replaced the lid and stepped back. "That doesn't change the fact that she thinks raising Bella around bees is dangerous."

"She was nervous, yes. But wrong. I see it now. You're careful. You know what you're doing."

London exhaled, her breath fogging the mesh for a second. "I don't need validation. Not from your mother, and not from *you*."

Patrick lowered the camera. "I know. But I want to understand. Really understand what you built here. That's why I asked about the article. Not just to showcase the farm—but to do it right. With respect."

Her eyes softened, just a touch, then turned toward the next hive. "Come on, then. You haven't met the bees in Violet yet."

They moved down the row, and Patrick followed her lead, more comfortable now in the suit, more in tune with the rhythm of the morning. With every click of the shutter, he caught a different angle: honey gleaming in the cells, bees clustered like dancers on a stage, the steady strength in London's posture.

When she paused to sip from a water bottle, pulling the veil back, he asked, "Did you ever think this is where you'd end up?"

London wiped her brow. "Not even close. I wanted to travel, to write, to disappear into something bigger."

"And now you're rooted."

She glanced at the hives, then back to him. "Now I protect something smaller. But no less important."

Patrick met her gaze. "You're good at it."

London gave a short laugh. "There was a time I thought I had to prove that to you. I don't anymore."

"I know."

They stood in silence again, the moment stretching. The bees carried on around them, unbothered by human tension.

"Let's finish up. The sun will be overhead soon, and they'll get agitated."

He fell into step beside her, camera at the ready, grateful for the chance to follow her lead—not just today, but in some small way, going forward, too.

"Is there a reason you chose a circular design for the hives?" Patrick asked.

London nodded. "I didn't want the rigid lines and military order some beekeepers seem to prefer. I wanted something that reminded me of family—of the kitchen table where my father used to sit, the same table where he'd first tasted my wildflower honey and called it gold. I chose it for practical reasons as well."

She smiled faintly. "When hives are in straight lines, bees tend to drift. They come back from foraging and end up in the wrong hive—especially the ones on the ends. It disrupts the colonies, throws them off balance. The circle helps them orient themselves. Less confusion. Less competition. Less stress."

Patrick let the silence settle between them, respectful and unhurried. "You didn't just build a honey farm," he said after a moment. "You built a sanctuary."

Her throat tightened, but she didn't look away. "That's what I wanted. For the bees. For Bella. For me."

THE LATE-AFTERNOON sun dipped low behind the coastal pines, painting the sky in streaks of pink and gold as Patrick peeled off his beekeeping hood. The suit was warm, awkward, and cumbersome—but entirely worth the discomfort. He'd spent the day shadowing London through the fields, his camera never far from his hands as he snapped photos of hives, honeycomb, and London herself—poised, focused, utterly in her element.

He'd known London was capable. She always had been. But what he witnessed today was something else. Commanding her bees with calm assurance, explaining their habits, their roles, and the intricate life of a hive with passion and precision... London had built a life here, a purpose rooted in resilience and care. The woman he had once loved had blossomed into someone even more remarkable.

And she had done it all without him.

The thought sat heavy in his chest as he drove back from the farm to his rental cottage. The old gravel roads gave way to paved lanes lined with swaying marsh grass. The silence in the car stretched, a contrast to the day's buzz and rhythm.

Patrick didn't mind. It gave him time to think.

Bella had been with Madelyn for the day— London's mother doted on her granddaughter with boundless energy, and Bella thrived under her warmth. Patrick had initially hoped to bring her with him, to spend the afternoon taking pictures and showing her more of his world, but London had asked for the time alone.

"Just us," she had said that morning, her voice gentle but firm. "I want you to see what I've built. What I've protected."

And he had.

He'd seen the hand-painted signs marking wildflower paths, the careful circular arrangement of the hives in the sunniest fields, the workshop where she and her employees jarred honey and prepared gift boxes with seasonal herbs and beeswax candles. He saw the photos on the office wall—local awards, smiling customers, a feature in a regional lifestyle magazine. She had made something real, something lasting.

And through it all, she had done it with Bella in tow.

When he stepped onto the porch of the cottage, the scent of steamed vegetables and roasted chicken wafted from inside. He reached for the door handle, but the door yanked open before he touched it.

Myra stood there, arms crossed, lips pinched, her polished brows arched in immediate disapproval.

"You're late."

Patrick sighed. "I wasn't aware I was on a schedule."

"Dinner was an hour ago. And where is Bella?"

He stepped past her, setting his camera bag on the foyer bench. "With Madelyn."

Myra followed him into the kitchen, heels clicking against the hardwood. "Of course she is. Isn't that just convenient? For London."

Patrick turned, tired from the heat and the weight of the day. "Don't start."

"Start what? I'm your mother, Patrick. I've waited years to meet my granddaughter. I'm only on this island for one more day, and it seems I'm the last person on the list when it comes to spending time with her."

"It's not about you being last. It's about easing Bella into all of this."

Myra's eyes flashed. "She's a child. Children adapt."

Patrick poured himself a glass of water, buying time. He took a long sip before replying. "Bella is not just any child. She's thoughtful. Sensitive.

She's been through a lot of change in the last few days. I'm not going to throw her into a situation she's not ready for."

"You mean a situation *you're* not ready for."

He set the glass down harder than he intended. "That's not fair."

"And what's fair? That her other grandmother gets to monopolize her time because London's family lives on this island and I don't?" Myra's voice rose, brittle with frustration. "You talk about what Bella needs, but what about what I need? I'm her grandmother, too."

Patrick inhaled deeply. "Yes. You are. And maybe if you had started this conversation with empathy instead of accusation, we'd be having a very different discussion."

Her lips tightened. "Don't you dare turn this around on me."

"Why not? You spent dinner last night scrutinizing every choice London's made. Where she lives. What she does for work. You act like she's an obstacle instead of the reason Bella exists in the first place."

Myra blinked, stunned into silence. Patrick rarely raised his voice. He had inherited his father's even keel—until now.

"Do you know what I saw today, Ma?" he continued, quieter now but just as firm. "I saw London in the middle of her life's work. I saw a woman who built something out of nothing. Who wakes up every day to take care of living things. Who made a home for our daughter when I didn't even know she existed."

Myra folded her arms again, but this time the movement was slower, her posture less rigid.

"She could have told you," she said, softer.

"She didn't owe me that. Not after how we left things. And maybe it would've gone differently if she had, but that's not the point. The point is she's done everything on her own, and she's done it well. She deserves more than your side-eyes and not-so-polite judgment."

A long pause passed between them.

"I'm trying," Myra said finally, her voice more tentative. "Dinner…it didn't go the way I imagined."

He picked up his camera bag again, heading for the stairs.

"Where are you going?"

"To upload the photos," he said. "London agreed to the article."

Myra arched a brow. "She did?"

"With one condition. Bella stays out of it."

"Why? She's a beautiful child."

"Because London wants to protect her. From attention. From scrutiny. From, well, from everything you've shown you're capable of. She was not happy when the last article included a photo of Bella."

He didn't say it to be cruel. Just true.

Myra sat heavily at the kitchen table, her hand drifting to her necklace. "I didn't know I was coming off that way. I simply thought I was being honest."

"You were," Patrick said, pausing on the steps. "But not kind. There's a difference."

Upstairs, he closed himself in the guest room and opened his laptop.

As the photos of London filled his screen—her gloved hands checking a frame of honeycomb, the sunlight catching in her hair, the bees swarming around her like a living halo—he exhaled.

This was the story he wanted to tell. Not just about bees and honey. But about perseverance. About a woman who had loved, lost, and rebuilt. About the life he could have missed entirely if fate hadn't brought him back here.

And maybe, just maybe, about a second chance.

But that would come later. For now, he clicked open a blank document and typed *The Beekeeper of Polk Island: A Story of Honey, Heart, and Home.*

He paused, then added *By Patrick Brown.*

CHAPTER FIVE

THE HOUSE WAS quiet now. The comforting hum of the dishwasher in the background barely registered as London moved through the living room, turning off stray lights.

Bella was tucked into bed upstairs, her bedtime story finished, her little body curled beneath a quilt patterned with daisies and honeybees. The monitor on the coffee table crackled softly, a gentle reassurance that her daughter was safe and sleeping.

London paused at the kitchen counter to pour herself a glass of lemon-balm tea, the steam curling around her face like a whispered lullaby.

Outside the window, the darkness settled over the honey farm like a well-worn blanket, the stars distant and cold. The day had stretched long—too long—and though her body ached from the physical labor of tending the hives and managing orders, it was the emotional strain that had left her raw.

Patrick.

He'd been with her most of the day. Snapping photos, watching her work, asking questions she hadn't expected him to ask. Thoughtful questions. Respectful. And if he didn't look ridiculous in that bee suit, the mesh veil slipping sideways more than once. She'd wanted to laugh—had laughed—but the ache beneath it remained. Because she'd seen the way his eyes followed her. The way he listened. The way he looked at the farm as though he finally understood what it took to build something from nothing.

But understanding didn't erase the years.

He'd left to build his own successful career. And she'd raised their daughter alone.

London carried her tea to the living room and settled on the couch, tucking her legs beneath her. She grabbed the remote and flipped through the streaming menu without really seeing it. She needed something light. A comedy. A baking show. Anything but the heavy silence of her thoughts. She finally landed on a gardening competition and let the cheerful theme song fill the room.

She sipped her tea, letting the warmth anchor her.

Patrick being back on Polk Island had disrupted everything. For years, she'd focused on Bella. On the bees. On building a life that was safe, self-sustaining, and stable. She'd worked long hours, leaned on her mother and siblings when she needed to, and cried into her pillow when it all felt like too much.

But even in the quiet, even in the grind, the ache of losing her father never fully left her. It sat in her chest, a weight she'd learned to carry but never put down. He had been her compass, her calm, the first person to taste her wildflower honey when she was just experimenting in her kitchen. He'd smiled— soft, proud—and told her it was the best thing he'd ever tasted. This was her legacy. A deliberate empire rooted in her own hands—and in the memory of the man who believed in her first.

And now Patrick was here, wanting to be a father.

London's chest tightened as she thought of Bella's face when he had spoken to her like he truly wanted to know her. The way her daughter lit up at his attention. It was too soon. Too precarious. And she couldn't afford for Bella's heart to be broken the way hers had been. She didn't doubt Patrick's sincerity.

Not entirely. But sincerity didn't build trust. Consistency did.

He had to prove he meant to stay. Not just for a weekend. Not for a summer. But for the long, hard seasons that followed.

Her phone buzzed on the side table, breaking into her thoughts. A message from Patrick.

Thank you for today. I learned more in a few hours than I have reading a dozen books. You're amazing, London. Truly.

She stared at the message for a long time, thumb hovering over the screen. She didn't respond. She couldn't. Not yet.

Because words like *amazing* and *truly* didn't erase the ache of years she'd spent staring at her daughter's face and wondering why he hadn't called. Why he hadn't written. Why he hadn't come back.

He was a beautiful memory wrapped in too many jagged edges.

London leaned her head against the back of the couch and closed her eyes. Her tea had gone lukewarm, but she didn't move. On the television, contestants debated the best soil for dahlias, their voices lilting and British and utterly foreign to her life.

She thought of Patrick's mother and the conversation that still prickled beneath her skin. Myra had smiled, had asked about the farm, even praised its success—but beneath it all had been skepticism. A worry about Bella's safety. A subtle judgment that no number of polite words could mask.

London had fielded worse. But it didn't make it easier.

She opened her eyes and stared at the ceiling. Could she forgive Patrick?

That was the question she didn't want to answer. Because if she forgave him, then she had to open the door. And if she opened the door, he might leave again. And she wasn't sure she could survive that.

London finished her tea and stood, switching off the television.

Upstairs, Bella murmured something in her sleep, and she smiled despite the weight in her chest.

She climbed the stairs and peeked in, brushing a curl from Bella's forehead before heading to her own room.

London stood at the window for a long time, looking out over the moonlit fields where the hives sat arranged in a perfect circle—her choice, deliberate and symbolic. Circles had no edges, no harsh corners where things could get trapped or pushed away. They were whole. Continuous. Safe.

She had built this. With her hands. With her heart. And no matter what happened next, she would protect it.

She would protect Bella.

Even from Patrick, if she had to.

THE FARMHOUSE WAS Sunday-afternoon quiet except for the soft clink of mason jars at the sink. A gentle breeze drifted through the open screen door, carrying the faint, calming scent of lavender from the garden. From a distance, near the orchard, the steady drone of bees hummed faintly—a soothing backdrop to the familiar sweetness of honey that filled the air, a constant presence in the space London had carefully shaped.

Her hands moved on autopilot, rinsing jars while her thoughts circled—unfinished orders, upcoming shipments, and the memory of Bella's bright laughter from that morning.

London's eyes settled on the small vase of freshly cut lavender sitting on the windowsill, its purple sprigs bending gently in the breeze. She inhaled deeply, the orchard's hum blending with the lavender's soothing fragrance.

An unobtrusive idea took root—soft at first, then growing more certain.

Lavender honey.

Not just for its market appeal or to fit the brand. But because it captured this moment—the distant buzz of bees, the lingering sweetness in the air, Bella's laughter, the calm she'd fought to build.

A soft smile curved her lips as she tipped the water from the jars.

Yes. Lavender honey.

The idea settled warmly in her chest, but the peace unraveled in the next breath. The low crunch of tires on gravel pricked her attention, pulling her out of the quiet.

Her body stiffened just before the knock sounded at the door.

She dried her hands quickly and headed to the door, her instincts already on alert.

When London opened it, she was not surprised to find Myra Brown standing on her porch, crisp and poised, as if the visit had been an appointment penciled in on a carefully curated schedule.

"Good afternoon," Myra said, her voice clipped but polite, the kind of civility that often preceded one of her barbed observations.

London folded her arms. "Afternoon."

As Myra's sharp gaze swept over the porch, then toward the open stretch of the property, London felt the familiar prickle under her skin. Myra had a knack for slipping little digs into conversation— remarks about London's choices, her work—they never sounded outright rude but always left their sting. London couldn't remember a single time Myra had spoken to her without some hint of judgment tucked neatly between the words. "May I come in?"

She hesitated only a moment before stepping aside. "Sure."

The older woman entered with a measured grace, taking in the interior with cool eyes.

London watched her every move, aware of every silent judgment hidden behind those composed expressions.

They settled into the living room, the distance between them as firm as a boundary line. Myra sat on the edge of the couch, not relaxing into it, while London took her armchair, angled for both defense and command.

"I came to talk," Myra began. "Woman to woman."

London arched a brow. "Is that right?"

"Yes. I think we both know this…situation with Patrick and Bella is complicated."

She held her stare. "It didn't have to be. But it got complicated the moment you decided I wasn't worthy of your son's love."

Myra's lips thinned. "I never said you weren't worthy."

"You didn't have to," London replied. "You said it in every cold look. Every time you referred to me as *that girl*. Every time you insisted Patrick could do better."

Myra looked away, her composure flickering.

"You were very young. He had just started his career."

"And I was building a business," she countered. "Your disapproval wasn't about my age. It was about control. You didn't like that Patrick was in love with someone you couldn't control."

Myra bristled. "I was protecting my son's future."

London let out a quiet laugh, the sound more bitter than amused. "Well, *congratulations*. You got what you wanted. You broke us up."

The words sat between them like a cracked plate, sharp and undeniable.

Myra's face tightened. "I didn't know you were pregnant. If I had—"

"If you had," London interrupted, her voice rising, "you still would've pushed him to walk away. And maybe you would've insisted I was trapping him. Or worse."

Silence.

She leaned back. "You don't get to rewrite history, Mrs. Brown. You planted doubt. You made Patrick feel like his life would be ruined if he stayed. And I wasn't going to beg him to choose me."

Myra swallowed, visibly shaken for the first time. "You can't keep Bella from us."

London narrowed her eyes. "I'm not keeping her from anyone. *I'm protecting her.* That's my job as her mother."

"She deserves to know her family."

"She does. But she also deserves to be safe. To be surrounded by people who love her without trying to manipulate her parents."

Myra sat straighter, her jaw set. "You don't trust me."

Her eyes flashed. "You're right… I don't."

"We're heading home to Savannah this evening. I would like to spend the day with my granddaughter. However, Patrick says it's too soon."

"It is," London responded flatly. "Bella is not a pawn in a redemption story. She's a little girl who needs stability and time. And Patrick and I are working through how to do this right."

Myra studied her, then stood. "You're determined to keep me at arm's length."

"Until you prove you can respect the life we've built? Absolutely."

Myra smoothed her jacket. "I'm not the enemy, London."

She rose up and strolled into the foyer. "Then stop acting like one."

As London opened the front door, a breeze slipped in to cool the heated words.

Myra lingered on the threshold long enough to say, "Patrick loves his daughter, you know. We all do. She's a cherished member of our family."

The door closed with a soft click behind her.

London stood in the silence of her living room. She exhaled slowly, her shoulders heavy but her spine straight.

She walked to the window, watched Myra's car trail dust down the drive, and felt no regret.

She would fight for her daughter's peace. And for her own.

Whatever happened next, it would be on her terms.

THE POLK ISLAND HOTEL stood like a quiet sentinel on the edge of the shore, its whitewashed walls softened by years of salt and sea air. Beyond the sweeping back terrace, the ocean stretched wide and endless, its steady rhythm brushing against the sand. Ancient oaks framed the property, their branches draped with veils of Spanish moss that swayed lazily in the coastal breeze.

Patrick crossed the terrace, his camera bag slung over his shoulder, taking in the slow, breathing beauty of it all—the soft rustle of the moss, the muted crash of distant waves, the way the hotel seemed to belong to both land and sea. He wasn't here for an assignment today—not officially, at least. After emotionally complex conversations with London and his mother, his mind needed space.

He figured a walk might help clear his thoughts. The scent of jasmine drifted in from the edge of the garden. He paused briefly to snap a photo of the light playing against the tall glass windows of the dining room.

"Never could resist chasing the light, huh?" a voice called from behind him.

Patrick turned, squinting slightly into the sun. Kenyon Worthington stood just beyond the patio doors, dressed in his kitchen whites, his apron folded over his arm. Tall, broad, with the calm, grounded demeanor that came from years in high-pressure kitchens, he had always exuded the kind of quiet strength Patrick had admired from afar during his early days with London.

"Kenyon," Patrick greeted, forcing a smile. "Didn't expect to see you out here. I figured you'd be buried in prep for dinner service."

He shrugged. "Took a break. It's a good day for air. Thought I saw you out here squinting at the sun with a camera and figured I'd say hey."

Patrick nodded. "I needed a little room to think. It's been…a week."

Kenyon gestured to the shaded table near the railing. "You got time for a sit?"

Patrick hesitated, then nodded. "Yeah. I do."

They sat, the hum of the island surrounding them—palm fronds whispering in the breeze, the rhythmic hush of waves meeting the shore, the distant call of seagulls riding the wind. From the restaurant beyond came the faint clatter of dishes and the low murmur of voices, soft and familiar like the island itself.

Kenyon leaned back, crossing one ankle over his knee. "You know, I've been thinking about whether I'd ever get the chance to talk to you. Man to man."

Patrick met his gaze, prepared for whatever was coming. He knew it was only a matter of time before one or all of London's brothers cornered him for a heart-to-heart. Kenyon had always been the quietest, but that didn't make him any less protective.

"I figured this conversation was coming," Patrick said honestly.

Kenyon tilted his head. "Did you? That means you know why."

He exhaled slowly. "Because I hurt your sister. Because I left. Because I missed everything about my daughter's life up until a few days ago."

Kenyon didn't respond right away. Instead, he studied Patrick as if weighing whether the man sitting across from him was worth his sister's time or her trust.

"London didn't talk much after you left," Kenyon finally said. "She buried herself in work, in building something from scratch, in raising that little girl with more grace than most people could ever hope for. We didn't know all the details of what happened between you two—she kept that part of her life locked tight. But I've seen heartbreak before. I've cooked for it. Sat next to it. Held it. Even lived it once. And I saw it in her."

Patrick swallowed against the tightness rising in his throat. "I don't have an excuse that will make what I did okay. I made choices back then that were about survival. Fear. Pride. Immaturity. I thought walking away was best for her, for me. I didn't even know about Bella."

Kenyon nodded. "And now?"

He leaned forward, elbows on the table. "Now I know better. I know I can't undo the time I missed, but I can show up now. I can fight to be in my daughter's life. And I can try to rebuild trust with London. On her terms."

Kenyon watched him for another long beat. "You say you want to be in your daughter's life. And I respect that. But let me be clear, Patrick. If you so much as waver, if you break London's heart again or cause chaos in my niece's life, you'll answer to *all* of us."

Patrick nodded solemnly. "I wouldn't expect anything less. Honestly, I wouldn't trust me either if I were in your shoes. But I'm not running from this. I missed everything...*everything*. Bella's first steps. Her first words. London had every reason to shut the door in my face. But she's let me in—just a crack. And I'm trying to earn the rest. For Bella. For her, too, if she ever wants that."

Kenyon rubbed a hand over his jaw. "London doesn't let people in easily. Never has. You knew that, even back then. And now, with Bella...you're not just asking her to trust you. You're asking her to risk her daughter's heart, too."

"I know." Patrick met his gaze evenly. "I think about that every minute."

Kenyon let the silence settle before finally nodding. "Well. You being here is a start. But it doesn't make up for years. Don't expect this to be easy. We Worthingtons protect our own, Patrick. Bella may be your daughter, but she's ours, too."

He smiled faintly, not offended but oddly comforted. "I wouldn't want it any other way."

Kenyon stood and adjusted his apron. "I'd better get back before my sous chef turns the seafood special into rubber." He paused. "You know where to find me if you need help navigating this. I'm not your enemy. But I am London's brother. Don't make me regret this conversation."

He stood as well. "I won't. And thank you. For saying what you needed to say."

Kenyon gave him a short nod before heading back toward the kitchen, disappearing into the soft murmur of evening prep.

Patrick stood there for a long while after, the weight of the conversation grounding him more than it unsettled. He had no illusions about the uphill path ahead of him, but as he turned back toward the quiet road that led away from the hotel, he felt something he hadn't in a long time—resolve. Maybe even the beginning of redemption.

LONDON BALANCED THE peach cobbler in one hand and steadied Bella with the other as they approached Patrick's cottage. She truly hadn't planned on making this visit. She'd convinced herself it would be easier to keep her distance, to leave things as they were, but Bella changed her mind for her.

Can we see them again, Mommy? she'd asked over lunch, her eyes wide, her sandwich paused halfway to her mouth. *My Nana and Pop. I liked them.*

London had hesitated, her chest tightening as

the protective walls she'd built threatened to rise. But Bella's simple, earnest request softened her resolve. This wasn't about convenience or boundaries anymore. It was about family—the kind Bella deserved to know.

So here they were, walking the narrow path that led to the small white cottage, the salty breeze from the ocean tugging at Bella's curls. In her free hand, Bella carried a modest bouquet of wildflowers they'd gathered from the edge of the orchard.

As they neared the cottage, London's steps slowed. She wasn't entirely sure what she was walking into, but she was certain of why she was doing it.

Bella wanted this.

Patrick answered the door, his surprise flickering quickly into something warmer.

"Hey," he said, stepping back to let them in.

His gaze dipped to the cobbler and the flowers, and for a moment, London saw the emotion shimmering in his eyes.

"We brought dessert," London said, feeling suddenly self-conscious but pressing forward. "And flowers. Bella wanted to see your parents again before they left."

Patrick's throat worked around the words he didn't say, but his smile said plenty. "They'll love that. Come on in."

The cottage smelled faintly of coffee and the lemony cleaner someone had recently used. Myra and Robert were seated in the cozy living area, their travel bags tucked near the door.

His mother's face lit up when she saw Bella, and her expression softened even more when she noticed the flowers in the child's small hand.

"You came!" Myra rose, her arms outstretched. "And you brought us something beautiful."

Bella beamed as she crossed the room to hand over the bouquet. "We picked these. Mommy said they're wildflowers. Do you like them?"

"They're perfect," Myra said, her voice thick with appreciation as she knelt to Bella's level. "Thank you, sweetheart."

London set the cobbler on the kitchen counter, watching the easy way Bella slipped into the space, how she settled on the rug near Myra as though this visit was the most natural thing in the world.

Patrick appeared beside her, his shoulder brushing lightly against hers. "Thank you," he murmured, his voice low and sincere. "It means a lot. To them. To me."

London glanced up at him, noting the slight tension around his mouth, the way he seemed to be holding back something deeper. "Bella wanted to see them," she said quietly. "She's the one who asked."

"Still," Patrick said, his gaze steady on her. "You could've said no."

She could have. Part of her still felt the weight of all the boundaries she'd drawn, all the rules she thought she needed to keep herself and Bella safe. But maybe some walls weren't worth keeping.

"It seemed like the right thing to do," she admitted.

Myra called out from the living room. "Is that peach cobbler?"

London smiled, stepping toward the counter. "It is. Still warm."

"Then you've officially made my day," Myra said, her voice rich with gratitude. "And we have ice cream in the freezer."

They settled around the small dining table, plates filled with sweet, cinnamon-laced cobbler, laughter filling the air as Bella recounted her version of picking the flowers, complete with wildly exaggerated bee encounters that had Patrick and his father chuckling.

London relaxed into the rhythm of the conversation, surprised by how comfortable it all felt. Myra's warmth was genuine, and Robert's quiet humor balanced it well. They didn't pry, didn't push, just shared stories and listened, weaving Bella into their lives with gentle threads.

Later, as they stood near the door saying their goodbyes, Myra pulled London into a brief, heartfelt hug.

"Thank you for today," she whispered. "You didn't have to come, but I'm so glad you did."

London's throat tightened, emotion catching her off guard. "Bella wanted to see her grandparents. I did this for *her.*"

"I hope we can do this again."

London offered a small nod. "I'd like that. I want my daughter to know her family."

Patrick's eyes met hers as they stepped outside, the late-afternoon breeze stirring around them. "You sure?"

"Yeah," she said, watching as Bella skipped ahead toward the hotel's path. "I'm sure."

He smiled, something soft and grateful passing between them. For the first time, London let herself believe that maybe she could share this part of Bella's life with them—without fear, without regret.

Maybe family didn't have to come with conditions.

And maybe, sometimes, the right thing was simply the kind thing.

As they walked away, Bella's hand slipped into hers, small and certain.

"Mommy?"

"Yeah, baby?"

"I love my daddy, Nana, and Pop. They feel like home."

London squeezed her hand gently, her chest full of something she didn't quite have words for yet.

"Yeah," she whispered. "They do."

CHAPTER SIX

THE FOLLOWING DAY, London heard the crunch of gravel just past six. She wiped her hands on a towel and glanced at the window over the sink.

Patrick was early.

She wasn't sure if that meant he was eager or anxious. Maybe both.

London opened the door before he could knock.

He smiled, hands tucked awkwardly into his pockets. "Hey. I know I'm an hour early, but…"

"It's fine," she said, stepping aside. "Come in. Bella's been waiting for you."

As soon as he stepped into the foyer, the little girl came running, arms wide and face glowing. Patrick bent low, scooping her into a hug with ease.

"Hey, bug," he said, his voice catching.

London watched them, heart tugging in two directions. She wanted Bella to have this—this joy, this connection. But she also remembered what it had cost her the first time.

"We were just about to start dinner," she said after a moment. "You can join us, if you want."

Patrick looked surprised, then pleased. "I'd like that. Thank you."

The meal was simple—grilled chicken, roasted vegetables, and cornbread that Bella had insisted on helping with. They laughed when Patrick took a bite and declared it the best cornbread he'd ever had.

"Really?" Bella's eyes were wide.

"Absolutely," he said solemnly. "Better than any five-star place I've been."

London raised an eyebrow. "Now I know you're exaggerating."

"Only a little," he said with a wink.

After dinner, Bella curled up on the couch beside Patrick with her favorite picture books.

London cleaned up slowly, listening to them read together, the sound of Patrick's voice somehow both familiar and foreign in her home.

After about twenty minutes, she broke in to announce, "I have to go over the inventory for Saturday's summer festival and handle the new orders before the team heads out. It should only take a couple of hours."

"We'll be fine," Patrick responded. "Take your time."

"Are you sure?" she asked.

He gave a quick nod.

"Have fun, Mommy."

London broke into a grin. "Bella is allowed *two* cookies and a glass of milk. Nothing more."

He chuckled at the expression on his daughter's face.

As she walked across the yard toward the barn, London felt the quiet tangle of emotions weaving through her. Work usually centered her, especially on busy Mondays, when the team prepped shipments and logged product counts for the week ahead.

Inside the barn, the rich scent of beeswax, wildflowers, and lavender filled the air as her employees moved through their tasks with practiced efficiency. London joined Kyla in the office, double-checking the week's inventory sheets and reviewing the new online orders. Her hands were busy, jotting numbers and labeling boxes, but her thoughts drifted.

Patrick was showing up. Not just as a visitor passing through Bella's life, but as a father—present and attentive in ways she hadn't expected. She'd braced herself for distance, for him to hold Bella at arm's length out of guilt or uncertainty. But instead, he was leaning in, learning her rhythms, making room for her curiosity.

Was she jealous? The question settled over her like a fog, unexpected and uncomfortable.

Bella's easy affection for Patrick should have stung, shouldn't it? But what she felt instead was something warmer, something that surprised her. Relief. Gratitude. Even joy.

She wanted Bella to know she was wanted.

She wanted her daughter to feel chosen.

And it felt good to know that she wasn't doing this alone anymore. That maybe they could find a way to build something whole out of all the broken pieces.

When London returned to the house, she peeked into the living room.

Bella was drifting off, head on Patrick's shoulder.

"Would you like to put her to bed?" she asked softly.

He looked unsure for a moment, then nodded.

Patrick carried Bella to her room like he'd done it a hundred times. When he came back out, his expression was unreadable.

London poured two cups of tea and handed him one. "Want to sit outside?"

The porch was quiet; the sky streaked with the last light of day.

They sat side by side, a careful distance between them.

"Thank you for tonight," he said after a while. "For letting me be here."

London nodded. "She needs you."

He exhaled. "I want to be here. Not just tonight. I want to be part of her life. *Your life*."

"That wasn't always the case," she said, not unkindly.

He turned to her, his eyes shadowed. "London, I didn't leave because I stopped loving you."

She didn't look at him. "Then why did you let your mother gain a stronghold into our relationship?"

There was a long silence before he spoke. "I've asked myself that same question many times. I was twenty-four. I was scared. My job was chaotic—I was traveling constantly. I didn't know how to build something stable. And my parents convinced me that leaving was…protecting you."

"You broke my heart and called it protection," she said softly.

He winced. "I believed them. That you deserved better. That I would only drag you down."

"You let me think I wasn't enough. That I wasn't worth fighting for."

"You were always worth fighting for," he said, voice thick. "But I didn't know how. I regret it every day."

London stared out into the darkness. "I survived without you. I built something here. I raised our daughter. Alone."

He nodded. "And you did an amazing job. I see that now. I see you. And I want to earn my place—with her, and maybe, one day, with you."

London took a long sip of her tea. "It won't be easy. I don't trust easy anymore."

"I'll be here," he said. "As long as it takes."

She didn't offer forgiveness. Not yet. But she didn't send him away either.

BACK AT THE COTTAGE, Patrick set his camera bag down on the wooden kitchen table and rubbed the back of his neck. The stillness wrapped around him like a heavy cloak.

He wandered over to the window and looked out. The marshland stretched in lazy swaths toward the horizon. The tide was low, and the sweet smell of salt and earth drifted in. This place, so quiet and distant from the rush of his old city life, should have felt like a refuge. But inside, Patrick's mind was racing—tormented by memories and tangled feelings.

London.

He tried to hold on to the image of her face from earlier. The way she had watched him as he read Bella a story. The softness in her eyes when Bella smiled. But there was also the steel beneath—the boundaries she set without apology. The way she reminded him gently but firmly that she was no longer the girl he'd once loved but a woman who had built a life without him.

He took a deep breath and sank down into the threadbare armchair by the fireplace. His hands, calloused from years of wielding a camera, rested on his knees, clenched tight. He thought about the admission he'd made to London—the truth about his parents' role in their breakup.

It had been easier in some ways to blame himself, to carry the guilt alone. But hearing it aloud, seeing it reflected in London's calm but wary expression, had cracked open a part of him he thought was long sealed.

They didn't just force me to leave. He remembered her words. *They manipulated you. Made you believe it was for the best.*

He closed his eyes, the memory of those conversations with his mother and father flooding back—the subtle digs, the relentless insistence that London wasn't the right fit, that his career demanded stability he couldn't give. They painted her as a complication, a distraction. They told him London deserved better, even if it meant walking away.

And blinded by self-doubt and the fear of failure, he'd believed it.

Now, sitting in this quiet cottage far from the city lights, Patrick felt the ache of all that lost time. Years spent apart, moments with Bella he hadn't shared, laughter and tears he'd only witnessed in photos and stories.

He glanced down at his hands. The hands that once framed images on the other side of the world, capturing war zones, distant cultures, fleeting moments of beauty and heartbreak. Hands that now trembled slightly with uncertainty.

What kind of father was he, arriving late to a life already so fully formed?

He took a sip from the glass of bourbon he'd poured earlier, the burn a sharp contrast to the softness of his thoughts. The sound of the tide outside mingled with the distant calls of birds settling in for the night.

He thought about Bella—how much she resembled London, with the same curiosity and stubborn streak. The way she had clung to his side during the story time, trusting him enough to fall asleep in his presence.

That small, fragile connection gave him hope but also fear. Could he make up for the years he'd missed? Could he be the man London and Bella needed him to be?

The room seemed to close in as Patrick's mind

drifted back to their early days—the laughter they shared in the Polk Island Bakery and Café, the lazy Sunday mornings when the world felt uncomplicated. London with her fierce intelligence, always challenging him, grounding him.

He remembered the promises whispered in the dark, the plans they made before everything unraveled. Back then, love felt simple. The future was a wide-open road, not the tangled mess it was now.

He clenched his fists.

Then came the slow, insidious pressure from his parents. The phone calls filled with disappointment veiled in concern. The dinners where London was subtly dismissed, where Patrick was urged to focus on his career and think about his future.

He had wanted to believe them, to believe that ending things was an act of protection for London. That leaving was the sacrifice a man had to make for love.

But now he knew the truth had been much darker.

He had been a pawn in their game—used to keep the family image intact. And in that, he had hurt the two people he cared about most.

Patrick shifted in the chair, a knot tightening in his chest. He wanted so badly to repair what was broken. To build a relationship with London, to be the father Bella deserved. But he also knew that trust wasn't given lightly—and that his family's shadow loomed large.

Would London ever truly forgive him? Could

she see past the years of absence to the man he was now trying to be?

He thought of the honey farm, London's sanctuary. How fiercely she guarded it, how proud she was of what she had created. Maybe that was the key—letting her lead, supporting her on her terms.

He reached for his notebook and began jotting ideas for the article—ways to tell London's story, to show the strength and resilience she embodied.

But beyond the article, beyond the words and pictures, he knew the real story was about healing—a slow, fragile process they had to navigate together.

Outside, the sky was a deep navy, stars blinking awake like distant promises. Patrick stood and moved back to the window, watching the tides of the marsh ebb and flow.

This was more than a story. It was a chance to rebuild a family fractured by time and circumstance. To be the man, the father, the partner London deserved.

He didn't know what tomorrow would bring. But as he blew out the lamp and settled into the darkness, a quiet determination settled over him.

He was done running.

Patrick sat back down, the chair creaking under him as his mind kept turning over everything London had said—and everything he hadn't yet said aloud.

He wrote in his notebook again, but the words felt inadequate. He wasn't writing a story here. He was trying to understand himself, to reckon with years of mistakes and missed chances.

He thought about the way London had looked at him when he admitted the truth about his parents. Not anger. Not accusation. Just a quiet, guarded understanding, as if she'd known all along but never wanted to confront it. She didn't seem surprised. Maybe that was the hardest part—realizing that the woman who had raised his daughter had carried the burden of his absence without bitterness, just quiet resolve.

Patrick ran his fingers through his hair, rubbing his temples. He remembered a time when he had believed he could balance everything. His camera in one hand, London's in the other, a little family carved out against all odds. But life, and his parents, had other plans.

Patrick stood and walked toward the small bookshelf where a few scattered volumes leaned precariously. One was a photojournalism anthology he'd been meaning to reread; another a gardening book London had lent him when he first arrived. He picked up a framed photo of Bella, her chubby cheeks pressed against London's cheek, both smiling in the golden sunlight of the honey farm.

He traced the outline of Bella's face, and a fierce determination flared inside him. He owed it to her to be better.

Not just the occasional visitor or a man with camera in hand, but a real father. One who showed up. One who stayed.

Patrick sank back into the chair, pulling his phone from his pocket. He scrolled through London's number, thumb hovering over the Call button. The words he wanted to say were tangled and heavy, but one phrase kept coming back.

I'm here now.

As he set the phone down, Patrick's mind drifted again to his mother. Myra had always been a force, commanding attention and loyalty in equal measure. But that strength had often twisted into control and judgment.

Patrick hated the way she had treated London— like an intruder, a threat to her perfect family narrative. And he hated how easy it had been for him to slide back into his parents' expectations without questioning them.

That conversation had been the first time he'd challenged her. The first time he'd tried to stand up for London instead of bending to Myra's will.

He wasn't sure if it was enough.

His heart clenched at the thought of how much time had slipped away, how many moments with Bella he'd lost to fear and family politics. The thought made him want to fight harder—not just for his daughter, but for London, too.

She didn't have to carry this alone anymore.

Patrick glanced once more at the framed photo on the shelf. Bella's smile was wide and innocent, unaware of the complexities swirling around her. But she was the reason he had to get it right. He was tired of running from his past. Tired of being a man haunted by what-ifs and could-have-beens.

On Saturday, he told himself. He'd talk to London after the summer festival. Really talk her—not just about the article or the farm, but about them. To figure out how to move forward together, in whatever way they could.

For the first time in a long time, he believed it might be possible.

He stood and stretched, the weight on his chest a little lighter than before. Outside, the tide whispered against the shore, promising renewal and change.

Patrick walked to the door, paused, then stepped outside into the cool night air. The stars were bright, the sky endless.

And for the first time in a long time, he felt like he belonged.

THE LATE-MORNING sun filtered warmly through the towering pines lining the festival grounds just a short walk from North Beach, casting dappled light over the bustling crowd. The air was alive with the mingled scents of fresh-cut grass, sizzling barbecue, and the faint sweetness of wildflowers tucked into the edges of the wooden booths. It was Saturday, the day of the Polk Island Summer Festival—a cherished tradition where locals and visitors alike gathered to celebrate community, music, food, and craft.

London's honey farm had its own little corner

near the main stage, proudly showcasing the fruits of her labor. She stood behind the booth, her hands busy arranging small jars of golden honey. The label was simple but elegant, emblazoned with the farm's logo—a delicate bee hovering over a blooming magnolia.

Her product line had expanded over the years, each variety a reflection of the land and the seasons. There was her signature natural raw honey, pure and unfiltered, with a clean, mellow sweetness. The wildflower honey captured the vibrant flavors of spring and summer blooms, its taste shifting subtly depending on the year's harvest. Her coastal blossom honey carried soft citrus undertones, a nod to the nearby groves. London also offered creamed honey, smooth and spreadable, perfect for morning toast.

She had also brought along several sample jars of her newest creation—lavender honey. Small tasting spoons rested nearby, inviting curious visitors to experience the delicate blend of natural sweetness and soothing floral notes. The lavender honey shimmered in the light, its subtle aroma drawing people in for a taste of something both familiar and entirely new.

But the jars that drew the most attention were the new honeycomb-infused products—amber-hued honey encasing delicate pieces of comb, like edible jewels suspended in gold. There were samplings of lavender honeycomb, lightly floral with hints of the herb's calming fragrance, and the Polk Island reserve honeycomb, rare and buttery, harvested in small, prized batches. Each variety was carefully labeled, their hexagonal jars catching the eye in the afternoon breeze.

She smiled as she watched Bella playing at the end of the booth with a plush unicorn, her soft giggles drifting back to London like a warm melody.

At her side, her assistant, Kyla, expertly manned the booth. Her slender frame leaned casually against the table, but her eyes scanned the crowd with practiced attention, greeting customers and sharing tidbits about the farm's latest harvest.

"It's a perfect day," she said, glancing at London. "The turnout's great. I think the summer's really drawing people out after last year's storms."

London nodded, keeping an eye on Bella. The festival was always a whirl of activity, but having Kyla here made things easier. It gave her the freedom to step away for a few moments, to breathe in the buzz of the crowd, and even, secretly, to watch for Patrick.

Because she knew he would show up.

And sure enough, moments later, she caught sight of him weaving through the crowd, camera slung casually around his neck. His eyes were already scanning, looking for scenes to capture—children laughing, couples dancing, vendors chatting—but when his gaze met hers, something softer flickered. Relief. Hope.

London felt a tight knot in her chest loosen just a little.

The festival's soundtrack drifted around them, a vibrant blend of styles that mirrored the island's eclectic charm. Near the main stage, a local band was picking up momentum—singing in bright harmony. The rhythm was lively and infectious, drawing a small crowd who tapped their feet and clapped along.

Down by the food court, a reggae group played steady, pulsing beats with a laid-back groove that made people sway in place or bob their heads while they ate. Over by the craft tents, a solo guitarist strummed folk tunes—soft, contemplative melodies that wove between the louder sounds like gentle whispers.

London loved how the music layered together, each sound a thread in the festival's colorful tapestry.

Just as Patrick approached the booth, Cia appeared, her wide smile lighting up her face.

"Hey, Bella..." her sister said, kneeling to the little girl's level. "Want to come check out the kids' area? There's face painting and a petting zoo—and I hear the cotton candy is the best."

The little girl's eyes lit up immediately, and before London could say more, Cia was scooping her up with practiced ease. Her giggles followed them as they disappeared toward the colorful tents and bouncing inflatables.

London turned back to Patrick, who was now setting his camera to a low angle, focusing on the jars of honey that caught the sunlight in golden glints.

"Looks like you've got the place buzzing," he said, nodding toward the booth with a small smile.

London shrugged. "Kyla is doing most of the work today. I'm just here for moral support."

Before Patrick could respond, movement near the booth caught London's eye. Her mother, Madelyn, approached with her usual confident stride. Trailing behind her was Ace, London's sister-in-law, whose round belly was unmistakable evidence of the baby growing inside her.

Ace greeted London with a warm smile. "Hello, London…the honey smells incredible, as usual." Her eyes lingered on the lavender honey. "I believe this will be my favorite. I won't open my sample— I want to enjoy it for as long as possible."

Madelyn glanced around, her sharp eyes scanning the crowd before settling on London.

"I'm so proud of you."

London gave a small laugh. "Thanks, Mama. As you can see, the farm's been busy this season."

Moments later, Shane, London's oldest brother and one of the farm's biggest supporters, joined them. Tall and broad-shouldered, Shane carried the easy confidence of someone comfortable in his own skin. His grin was quick and genuine when he spotted Patrick.

"Hey, Patrick," Shane said, extending a hand that Patrick took readily. "Good to see you here."

Patrick nodded, appreciating the gesture. "Thanks. It's good to be here."

London felt a brief swell of something hopeful as the group settled around the booth, the chatter and laughter floated on the breeze, mingling with the rhythmic thump of a live drum circle and the high-pitched squeals of delighted children. The scent of kettle corn and grilled seafood wafted through the air as families strolled between vendor tents.

She adjusted her sunglasses and tucked a wayward braid behind her ear, glancing up just as Bella darted back toward the booth.

"Mommy... Daddy..."

She launched herself at Patrick, arms flung wide.

He scooped her up effortlessly, spinning her in a quick circle that drew a delighted squeal.

London felt it like a ripple through her chest—the sound of her daughter laughing, wrapped in the arms of her father.

"Daddy, come see the petting zoo. There are baby goats and a bunny that sleeps like a baby. Please, please, can we go? Mommy, you come too?"

London hesitated, hand already moving toward the edge of the booth. "I need to help Kyla with the—"

"Go," her assistant responded, appearing beside her with a knowing smile. "I've got this. It's a festival, London. Try to enjoy it."

Cia gave a playful nudge from behind. "I'll stay with Kyla. Consider this a forced break."

Bella's hand was in hers now, tiny and insistent.

Patrick stood beside them, waiting. London glanced once more toward the booth, then let out a breath and gave in.

"All right," she said, her voice soft. "Let's go pet some goats."

The path to the children's area wound past a string of artisan stalls, the clatter of wind chimes mingling with the jangly tune of a bluegrass band playing nearby. London walked between Bella and Patrick, acutely aware of the way their shadows stretched across the ground.

It was a strange, quiet symmetry.

Bella skipped ahead, tugging her father forward with enthusiasm. The petting zoo was penned just beyond a line of cypress trees, filled with hay and the scent of animals.

London stayed back for a moment, watching.

Patrick knelt beside Bella as she reached a hand toward a sleeping rabbit. His voice was low, gentle. He guided her hand, and she beamed up at him, pride shining in her hazel eyes. Something tugged in London's chest, sharp and unexpected.

This moment was the kind of thing she had told herself she didn't need.

It had lived only in the soft, aching corners of her imagination—the quiet fantasy of the three of them together. Her daughter laughing with her father. Her hand in his. Peace.

But peace had a price. And London wasn't sure she could afford it.

She stepped closer, her sandals crunching over

straw, and knelt beside them as Bella turned to show her the bunny.

"He's so soft," Bella whispered, her voice reverent. "He likes me."

"How could he not?" Patrick said, smiling over her head.

London met his gaze for a heartbeat too long, then looked away.

They stayed for a while—longer than she planned. Watching Bella feed the goats, giggling as a kid nuzzled her shoulder. London found herself laughing more than she expected. It felt...easy. Familiar in a way that twisted her insides.

Patrick didn't try to dominate the moment. He was present. Focused. And every so often, London caught him watching Bella not with guilt or awe but something deeper. Love. The kind that made her throat go tight.

They walked slowly back toward the vendor booths, Bella perched on Patrick's shoulders, waving at familiar faces and pointing out cartoon mascots roaming the grounds. Her laughter floated above them, bright and content.

London tried not to imagine what it would feel like if this wasn't a one-off day. If this could be a pattern. A rhythm.

But that dream was dangerous.

Patrick had walked away once. No matter how many explanations he offered—his parents, his doubts, his misguided attempts to protect her—the truth was she'd been left behind. Pregnant. Alone.

And letting herself hope now meant tearing down the walls she'd carefully erected.

What would it cost to open her heart again?

Everything, a voice inside her answered.

If she let him in—truly in—and he left again, it wouldn't just be her heart shattered. Bella's laughter would go quiet. Her bright eyes would dim. The cost wasn't hers alone to bear anymore.

Patrick helped Bella down, and she immediately darted to London, slipping her small hand into hers.

"Mommy, can Daddy eat dinner with us tonight?" she asked, looking up with hope that felt like a dagger.

London hesitated. Patrick said nothing. He looked at London, not pleading, just…open.

She swallowed the knot in her throat. "We'll see, baby. Let's enjoy the festival for now."

As they neared the booth, London slowed. She felt like she was returning to reality, stepping back into the roles she knew—mother, businesswoman, protector. But something had shifted.

She glanced at Patrick, walking just behind them. He wasn't the man who left her. Not entirely.

There was something quieter in him now. Something grounded. But was it enough?

Did he want more than a relationship with Bella?

Did he want her?

The question hovered between them, unspoken but heavy.

London gripped Bella's hand a little tighter as

they approached the booth. She wasn't ready to answer it. Not yet.

But for this moment, she let herself pretend. She let herself enjoy the laughter, the sunlight, the way Patrick's hand almost brushed hers as they walked.

She let herself dream—just for a little while longer.

And tomorrow she would remember the cost of dreaming.

But for now, she held her daughter's hand and walked beside the man who once held her heart.

Today she didn't pull away.

Not yet.

CHAPTER SEVEN

PATRICK STOOD IN the kitchen, a glass of lemonade in his hands, untouched. Outside, the trees rustled in the summer breeze, their shadows dancing on the ground. But inside him, everything was still. Still and heavy.

He hadn't been able to get London out of his head. Not since the festival.

He'd gone to Polk Island Summer Festival expecting to snap a few photos, capture a slice-of-life piece for the magazine, and quietly observe the world Bella lived in. He didn't expect her to come running into his arms, cheeks flushed from the heat and excitement, eyes shining. He didn't expect her to beg him to come see the petting zoo, her small hand warm and eager in his. And he definitely hadn't expected London to follow, slightly wary, trying so hard to act unaffected.

But something had shifted between them in that moment. Walking together, side by side, with their daughter between them—he'd felt it. A thread pulling taut and familiar. Something fragile but unbroken.

He set the mug down on the counter with a soft clink and rubbed the back of his neck.

London was strong, self-contained, fiercely protective of Bella and the quiet life she'd built. He admired her. Respected her. Loved her?

That word, even in his own mind, made him pause.

He walked into the small living room and grabbed his camera bag. Sitting down on the edge of the couch, he opened it and ran his fingers over the familiar contours of the gear. His passport was tucked in the outer pouch. A reminder of the life he'd led for more than a decade: conflict zones, natural disasters, uprisings, revolutions, elections. He'd lived in six countries, spoken four languages fluently, and his photographs had graced the covers of magazines and newspapers around the world.

It was a life that had always felt worth the risk. Until now.

Now there was Bella. Now there was London, with honey on her hands and exhaustion in her eyes but still standing. Still brave. Still beautiful.

He'd missed four years of his daughter's life. He couldn't change that. Couldn't rewind time and be the man he should have been. Being here now meant change. Real change.

His next assignment had been waiting for weeks. A contact in South Sudan was trying to get him embedded with a relief convoy documenting the impacts of drought and displacement. It was work that mattered. Work that paid well and gave him a purpose.

But could he go? Could he pack up, hop on a plane, and leave Bella behind? London?

He leaned back against the couch, closed his eyes.

What would it cost him to give his heart to her again?

It wasn't just about showing up and being a father. It wasn't just about supporting her or helping with bedtime or trips to the grocery store. It was about trust. About commitment. And about confronting the very real possibility that she might not want him in that way anymore.

She had every right not to.

Patrick pushed himself off the couch and moved to the window. Outside, the long drive curled beneath the live oaks. No cars. No visitors. Just the quiet beat of a humid southern afternoon.

He pulled his phone from his pocket and opened his Notes app. Then, in a new entry, he started typing.

Pros of staying:

Bella gets to know her father

More time with London

Stability (finally)

New opportunities (freelance, local paper, maybe a book?)

Cons:

Giving up international work

Losing professional identity

Potential fallout with parents

Risking heartbreak if things fall apart

He stared at the list. Then added another line.

Unknown: Does London even want me here?

The truth was he didn't know. She'd invited him

to dinner. Trusted him with their daughter for brief stretches. Talked to him late into the night more than once.

But she hadn't opened the door to anything more. Not yet. Maybe not ever.

And yet…

There had been a moment at the festival. When Bella was busy feeding a goat and he and London had stood just outside the pen, shoulder to shoulder, not talking. The music from the main stage drifted toward them, and she'd closed her eyes. Only for a second. But he'd seen it.

Peace. Maybe even contentment.

He'd wanted to reach for her then. Touch her hand. Tell her he still remembered the night they danced barefoot in the rain behind his old apartment, soaked and laughing, her hair sticking to her cheeks.

But he hadn't. Because fear was a hard thing to shake.

And what did he really have to offer her?

A used-up dreamer with a bag full of cameras and an itch to keep running?

He sat back down and opened his laptop. He navigated to a job board he rarely checked and typed in *photo editor* and *documentary producer*.

Opportunities blinked back at him. Local television stations. Regional news outlets. A nonprofit based in Charleston looking for a visual storyteller to run campaigns on coastal conservation.

Nothing glamorous. Nothing headline-grabbing.

But they were real. And they were stable.

He closed the laptop.

Maybe it wasn't about what he had to give up. Maybe it was about what he had to gain.

He stood and grabbed his keys. The air outside was thick with the scent of salt and pine as he stepped off the porch and into the warmth. He had a few hours before sunset. Dinner wasn't until later, but maybe he could come early. Maybe Bella wanted to show him her new drawing, or what she'd planted in the garden.

Or maybe he just needed to see London.

THE EVENING SETTLED gently over Polk Island, the sky brushed in pale gold as London heard the crunch of tires on the gravel drive. Through the window, she saw Patrick climbing out of his truck, a small bouquet of daisies in one hand and a plate wrapped in foil in the other. Lemon brownies, she guessed—Bella's favorite. For a moment, she just watched him. There was a nervous energy in the way he adjusted his collar, as if he wasn't sure what to do with himself. And despite everything—despite the history, the questions still between them—her chest tightened.

When he reached the porch, she opened the door before he could knock. "Hey. You made it."

"Wouldn't miss it." He held up the brownies.

Bella's excited shriek pulled them both into the living room, where she'd already set up the movie, a well-worn animated favorite she insisted on re-watching.

The three of them settled on the couch—Bella nestled between them with a blanket tucked around her, her small hand occasionally reaching for Patrick's.

London watched them from the corner of her eye, her chest tightening with something she wasn't quite ready to name. Bella's giggles filled the room, and each time she leaned into Patrick's side, London's heart did a complicated twist. Not because Patrick was showing up now, but because Bella had never asked for anyone else to fill that space before.

When the credits rolled, Bella's eyelids drooped. London scooped her up, kissed her soft curls, and carried her to bed without protest. Patrick waited in the living room, his elbows resting on his knees, his hands laced tightly.

London returned and sat on the opposite end of the couch, her nerves humming low and steady like distant thunder.

"Thank you," he said quietly, breaking the stretch of silence between them.

"For what?"

"For everything."

She shrugged, trying to mask the storm beneath her ribs. "It was good for Bella. She loves spending time with you."

His gaze didn't waver. "And what about you?"

London's throat tightened. She toyed with a loose

thread on the couch cushion, searching for the right words. "I'm figuring it out."

Patrick exhaled, his fingers tightening briefly. "I need to be honest with you, London. I want to be a real father to Bella. Not just weekends or vacations. Full-time."

Her head snapped up, breath snagging in her chest.

"I mean it," he pressed, his voice firm but gentle. "I want to be in her life every day. I want to help with school pickups, bedtime stories, scraped knees—all of it. I don't want to be some man who drops in and out of her life. I want Bella to know she can count on me."

London's pulse roared in her ears, a kaleidoscope of memories flashing through her mind—the nights she'd cried quietly after Bella fell asleep, the weight of parenting decisions she'd made alone, the ache of not being able to offer her daughter both parents at the dinner table.

"Patrick, it's not that simple."

"I know it's not." He shifted forward, elbows on his knees again, his expression open and steady. "But it's worth figuring out. I've already started looking into what I need to do legally. I want my name on Bella's birth certificate. I want her to carry my last name."

London's mouth parted, but no words came.

"I've read up on South Carolina's process. I know it'll mean filing a petition to amend her birth certificate. I'll do whatever's required. I want to

make this right. I want to give her my name because she's mine."

The sincerity in his voice chipped at her walls,
leaving her raw and exposed, every word a reminder of the fault lines between them. Her stomach knotted, and she tightened her grip on the
edge of the counter, as if bracing herself against
the weight of the conversation. "You should've discussed this with me first, don't you think?"

"No," Patrick shot back, his tone sharp, wounded.
"I don't need your permission to give my daughter
my name. Honestly, I never thought you'd object."

London's pulse quickened. Beneath the edge in his
voice, she could hear the hurt—deep and personal—
as if her hesitation had cut him in a place still tender.
"I feel it warranted a conversation between us," she
said, forcing her voice to stay calm, even as tension
coiled tighter between them.

His eyes hardened. "So did you telling me I was
going to be a father."

The words landed like a blow, and for a moment,
London's breath caught. She could see it now—the
anger simmering beneath his controlled exterior,
the betrayal Patrick still carried from being kept
in the dark.

Meeting his gaze, she felt the space between
them shrink into something sharp and unyielding.
"I'm sorry, Patrick."

He nodded. "You need to understand that I am
going to be in my daughter's life front and center—

not on the sidelines. We will make important decisions when it comes to Bella...*together*."

She hadn't expected him to push back. "I've been the one—"

"And why is that?" Patrick interjected. "Look, I'm asking you to trust me. Trust me with our daughter. One more thing... I want Bella to spend the weekend with me. My parents will be in town."

"I think it's too soon for that," she responded.

"I don't agree. Bella's comfortable with me— she's comfortable around my parents. I can never get back the time I lost with her. I'm not willing to give up any more time—*I won't*." Patrick paused a moment before continuing. "This isn't just about Bella. I want you back in my life, too. I want us to be a family."

The words hung between them, thick and electric.

London's chest constricted, her mind spiraling through the weight of what he was asking. Letting him take Bella for the weekend wasn't a small thing—it wasn't just about time with her father, it was about opening the door to his parents, too, the same people who had once judged her and nearly pushed her out of his life. Opening the door to her heart...

"You're asking me to trust you with everything," she whispered, her voice nearly trembling.

"I am." His brown eyes held hers, steady and sure. "I'm asking you to let me earn that trust, every day if I have to."

She wanted to say yes. But fear coiled tight in her stomach—the fear of Bella getting hurt, of Myra and Charles's influence, of losing the fragile stability she had fought so hard to build. The idea of her daughter spending nights away, under their roof, churned uneasily inside her.

London looked down at her hands, at the faint callouses earned from years of working the honey farm, from raising a daughter on her own. "I need time, Patrick."

"I can give you that."

She met his gaze again, and something inside her softened, just enough to let the smallest thread of hope slip through. "I need to think about what this looks like. About how we move forward."

"That's fair. I don't want to disrupt her life. I want to be part of it. I want to be part of yours, too."

Silence stretched again, but it wasn't heavy this time. It was charged with something else…possibility.

"You've shown up for her," London finally said. "She lights up when you're around. I can't ignore that."

Patrick's shoulders eased, the smallest crack in his guarded expression appearing. "She's my daughter. I love her."

The words landed deep, reverberating in places London hadn't dared visit in years.

"Give me time," she whispered, but there was a faint tremble of a smile tugging at her lips. "Just… don't disappear."

"I'm not going anywhere."

He stood, crossing the room with a deliberate slowness that gave her time to pull away if she wanted. When he cupped her cheek, she didn't move. Her skin tingled beneath his palm, her heartbeat a wild, skittering thing.

"I meant it, London. I want this."

She closed her eyes, leaning the smallest fraction into his touch. "I know."

"Good night."

"Good night," she responded.

When he left, the house felt different—less like a fortress to keep the world out and more like a place where something new could begin.

She lingered in the quiet, her fingers brushing over the spot on her cheek where his warmth still lingered, and let herself imagine, just for a moment, what it might be like to say yes.

THE SCENT OF saltwater drifted through the open windows of the Polk Island Hotel restaurant, mingling with the faint aroma of fresh-baked bread. The polished wooden floors gleamed, and the sea-glass-colored upholstery added a calm, coastal charm to the space. London adjusted her sunglasses atop her head and slid into the booth near the window.

The view overlooked the water, where sailboats drifted lazily. It was the kind of view people paid extra for, but for London, it was simply home. She drummed her fingers against the cold glass of her iced tea, nerves dancing low in her stomach.

Cia arrived a moment later, cheeks flushed from the coastal breeze, her curly hair tucked into a loose bun. "Sorry, sorry," she said, dropping into the seat across from London. "There was a group of tourists asking about the bee tours. I had to redirect them to the website."

She smiled faintly. "You're becoming quite the honey-farm ambassador."

Cia grinned. "It's my sister's business. I've got to represent."

Their banter settled into a quiet lull as they perused the lunch menu. London kept her gaze on the door, watching for the rest of their siblings. Her stomach tightened.

"You're thinking about Patrick."

London sighed. "He wants to get Bella's birth certificate amended, which I really don't have a problem with…but I would've preferred he talk to me about it first."

"Why?" Cia asked. "You think he should've asked your permission?"

"Something like that."

As if summoned by her unease, Micah strolled in next, dressed casually in board shorts and a linen shirt, his ever-present sunglasses perched on his head. He slid into the booth beside Cia. "Hey, sis. Hey, London. What's up?"

"I didn't know you were off today," she said.

"Yeah, I took a couple days. I'm driving to Atlanta to hang out with some friends from college."

Kenyon walked up to the table, wiping his hands on a towel. Clearly, he'd come straight from the hotel kitchen. Shane wasn't far behind, laughing at something Ace must've said before she veered off toward the spa. The brothers took their seats with casual familiarity. Shane reached for the breadbasket without missing a beat.

"This is starting to feel like a family meeting," Kenyon joked. "Should I be worried?"

"No ambushes today," London replied, lips twitching at the corner. She cleared her throat and looked around the table. "But I do need your opinions."

Micah raised an eyebrow. "This sounds serious."

"It's about Patrick," London said, her fingers curling around the rim of her iced tea glass.

Cia reached over and squeezed her hand in support.

"He wants to amend Bella's birth certificate," London said. "He wants to be legally acknowledged as her father. He wants her to carry his last name."

The table fell quiet as the server returned to take their lunch order. Without hesitation, they each ordered the shrimp-and-lobster salad, a house specialty they all favored.

Shane leaned forward, his brow furrowed. "How do you feel about that?"

"Initially, I wished he'd asked me, but the more I consider it… I'm okay with it," she admitted, surprising even herself with how certain the words felt as they left her lips. "Bella deserves that. She deserves to know where she comes from. And honestly, I think she'd be proud to carry his name."

Kenyon gave a small nod, his expression softening. "That's big, London. That says a lot."

"But that's not all," London continued, her voice dipping as if the weight of what she was about to say could buckle her resolve. "Patrick doesn't just want his name on her certificate. He wants us to be a family. He asked me to give him another chance."

Micah's brows lifted, and Shane leaned back, crossing his arms. "Whoa. He wants you back. Like…as a couple?"

London gave a small, almost imperceptible nod. "Yes."

Cia studied her carefully. "Do you still love him?"

London stared into her iced tea, tracing the rim with her fingertip. The silence pressed in, thick with the weight of the truth she'd never said aloud. "My heart never got over him." The confession slid out, fragile and undeniable. "Even when I thought I had, even when I moved on with my life, there was always this part of me that held on to him."

"Then, what's holding you back?" Shane asked gently.

She exhaled, feeling the knot in her chest tighten. "The stakes are different now. Back then, it was just me. If I made a mistake, if I got my heart broken, I could live with that. But now? There's Bella. If I let him in and he walks away again, she's the one who'll pay the price."

Kenyon leaned forward, resting his arms on the table. "You really think he'd walk away this time?"

"I don't know." The words burned in her throat. "That's what terrifies me. I see him showing up. I see him trying. He wants to be her father. He wants to carry the weight of that. But people want a lot of things. That doesn't mean they can always handle it."

Micah rubbed his jaw thoughtfully. "But you're not the same girl who fell in love with him years ago. You're stronger now. Smarter. If he messes up, you'll see it coming."

"And Bella isn't alone," Cia added. "She has us. If he fumbles, we're here. She won't have to go through it by herself."

Shane studied her carefully. "What does your gut say, sis?"

"It says he means it. That this isn't some temporary wave of guilt. He wants to be here. He wants to be her father in every way."

"Then maybe you give him the space to prove it," Kenyon said. "Start with the birth certificate. Let him take those steps."

"It's a big step, but it doesn't mean you have to rush the rest," Shane added. "You don't have to answer right now about being a family again. Take your time. Let him show you what he's willing to fight for."

London looked at each of them, gratitude swelling in her chest. This—these people, this table, their steady, unwavering love—was her safety net.

"I'm going to talk to him," she said. "I want to make sure the process is done right. I want him to have that legal connection to Bella. And maybe… maybe I'll let myself believe in second chances."

Cia squeezed her hand again. "We'll be here, no matter what."

"Always," Shane echoed.

London smiled, but deep inside, her heart trembled with the weight of what she was about to risk—for herself and for Bella.

The server and a helper appeared with their food.

"There's one more thing," she said after they left. "He wants to have Bella spend the weekend with him. His parents are coming to the island."

The words hung there, heavy and complicated.

London twisted her napkin in her lap, her chest tightening at the thought of Myra. Old wounds still pulsed beneath the surface, memories of sharp glances and unspoken judgments that never fully healed. "I know his dad is kind, but his mother… I don't know if I can fully trust her around Bella yet."

"You don't actually think she'd hurt her granddaughter?" Micah asked.

"No, I don't."

"Give her a chance," Shane encouraged.

"Okay," London responded. "I'll talk to Patrick."

Cia reached for her iced tea and raised it in mock toast. "To small steps."

"To family," Micah added.

She looked around at her brothers and sister and nodded. For the first time in a while, the future felt like something she could face without fear.

Shortly after she returned to the farm and checked in with her staff, London stood in the kitchen, her phone in hand, thumb hovering over Patrick's contact.

She exhaled slowly, steeling herself as she pressed the call button.

It rang once, twice.

"London," Patrick answered, and there was a mix of surprise and hope in his voice that struck a chord deep in her chest.

"Hey," she said, her voice steady but soft. "I wanted to let you know that you can pick up Bella Saturday morning."

There was a pause on the line, then a rush of breath like he'd been holding it. "Really? Thank you. That means a lot."

"She's excited," London added, her thumb pressing into the smooth wood of the kitchen island. "She's been talking about it all week."

"Same here," Patrick said. "We can't wait to spend the day with her. I was thinking of driving across the bridge to Charleston. There's a matinee showing of that new animated movie she mentioned, and maybe we can grab lunch afterward. There's a kid-friendly spot near the water—I checked ahead."

London's chest tightened with something she couldn't name. He sounded…ready. Like he'd already pictured the day a dozen times in his head. The ease of his excitement, the warmth in his voice, it all made her throat close for a moment.

"That sounds good," she said, forcing her voice not to catch.

Patrick must have sensed her hesitation. "She'll be safe with me, London. I promise."

She nodded even though he couldn't see it. "I know."

But knowing didn't quiet the ache in her chest.

When the call ended, London placed the phone down and leaned against the counter, arms wrapped tightly around herself.

Outside, the sound of bees humming around the lavender bush drifted in through the screen door, calming but distant.

It should have been a relief. She was finally letting Bella spend a day with her father and grandparents, but why did it feel like she was giving something up?

She turned and walked to the living room window, looking out over the property. For so long, it had been just the two of them.

Patrick had never seen those first nights, Bella crying for hours, London rocking her until dawn. He hadn't cleaned up scraped knees or walked the floor with a feverish toddler. He hadn't braided tiny puffs of hair or explained why the moon followed them on car rides.

London returned to the kitchen, her hands finding something to do—cleaning up, rearranging, anything to keep her grounded. The truth was she needed to know this wasn't a phase or a guilty reaction to the lost years. She needed to see if he was truly invested—in Bella, yes, but also in them. The three of them.

But more than anything, she couldn't afford to let her heart take the wheel.

Too much was at stake. Bella's joy. Her stability. And London's carefully reconstructed sense of peace.

Saturday would come. Patrick would arrive with that eager smile. Bella would run to him, eyes wide with wonder. And London would wave from the porch, keeping her face calm even if her heart screamed to follow.

She'd stay behind.

And hope that he wouldn't break their daughter's heart.

Or hers.

SATURDAY MORNING ARRIVED on a breeze laced with salt, honeysuckle…and nerves. Patrick's nerves, to be precise.

He'd triple-checked Bella's car-seat installation, practiced his smile in the mirror like a weirdo, and googled *Top 10 things not to forget when hanging out with your kid for the first time*. He wasn't sure what that said about him as a father, but he *was* sure that snacks, wipes, and the ability to not lose a child ranked high.

As he pulled onto the honey farm's gravel drive,

his stomach flip-flopped with something between excitement and *please-God-don't-let-me-screw-this-up* dread.

And there they were.

London, standing tall and composed at the edge of the porch, and Bella—his daughter—bouncing on her toes like a caffeine-powered bee. She wore a yellow sundress with embroidered bumblebees buzzing across the hem and carried a stuffed bee in one hand like a VIP guest.

He barely let the engine finish sighing before he hopped out, camera bag swinging wildly from one shoulder. "Hey, Bumblebee!" he called, crouching low.

She squealed and sprinted toward him like a mini linebacker, launching into his arms with such force that he rocked back a step. "Daddy…where's Nana and Pop?" she gasped.

"They should be at the house when we get there," he said, squeezing her tight.

"I told Mommy I brushed my teeth *twice* today so I could be ready."

"Well," he said, trying not to laugh, "that's… very thoughtful."

London approached, holding out a small backpack like it contained a live grenade.

"Snacks. Wipes. Extra clothes. Allergy meds. Her inhaler. And her backup inhaler, which you should leave in the car."

He nodded solemnly. "Got it. I will guard them like national treasures."

"I mean it, Patrick," she said, eyes steady. "She has a tree-nut sensitivity and asthma. No nuts. Keep her inhaler nearby."

He gave her a look of confusion. "But she eats peanuts…"

"Bella can't eat anything with cashews, walnuts, or pecans. Peanuts are fine for her. Also, she gets hangry. Very hangry."

"Like *bite your hand* hangry or just *verbal destruction* hangry?"

"She once made Kenyon cry," London said without blinking.

Patrick's eyebrows rose. "Noted. Snacks are now priority one."

"Movie!" Bella yelled, pumping her tiny fists in the air. "And lunch and pictures and ice cream and maybe a crab…"

"A crab?" he asked.

"She's been into marine life this week," London said. "Yesterday, she said she's marrying a stingray."

"Well," he said, adjusting the bag and Bella's weight on his hip, "as long as she doesn't elope with a jellyfish, we're good." He turned back to London. "I'll keep her safe. I swear."

London studied him like a puzzle piece she couldn't quite fit. Then she nodded, slowly. "I'm trusting you."

That landed with a thud in his chest. He nodded. "Thank you."

Bella waved her plush bee toward her mom.

"Mommy, don't forget to look at Daddy's pictures when we get back."

"I won't," London said, her voice softer than expected. "Have fun, sweetie." And with that, they were off.

"Why don't dolphins have eyebrows?"

"Can bees do karate?"

"Daddy, why is your car messy?"

Patrick winced. "Because Daddy is an artist. And also, kind of a mess."

They stopped at a drive-through for mini hash browns, which Bella called "breakfast nuggets," and she licked ketchup off her fingers like a lizard. "Mommy doesn't let me do this."

Patrick handed her a napkin and muttered, "Yeah, well...this is Daddy Day. Our rules are pending approval."

They drove back to his place to pick up his parents. Bella had to make a bathroom stop, so they got out the vehicle and rushed inside.

Bella grinned as they settled into the car ten minutes later. "Nana, Pop, guess what? We're seeing a movie today. Daddy says I can get the big popcorn."

"Oh, the *big* one?" Robert chuckled. "You're going to need help finishing that."

"Nope," Bella said proudly. "I'm good at eating popcorn."

Myra laughed, reaching back to squeeze Bella's hand. "I'm just happy we get to spend today and tomorrow with you, sweet girl."

She beamed, her heart full. "Me, too."

At the movie theater, Bella gasped dramatically at every preview and insisted they sit dead center.

During the film, she whispered commentary like a sports announcer.

"Uh oh, she's gonna fall. Oops, see! *Fell!*"

"Nana, that cloud looks like a llama."

"Why's that crab so angry? He needs a time-out."

Patrick was seventy percent sure he missed the plot entirely but didn't care. Watching Bella experience it was better than any storyline.

After the movie, they hit a nearby café with bright umbrellas and overpriced grilled cheese.

Bella insisted they all order "fancy juice," aka sparkling lemonade, and toasted him with a "cheers to bees and dads."

When the waiter asked if they wanted dessert, Bella announced, "We're having ice cream by the water because Daddy says adventures need snacks *and* sweet finales."

He was touched that she'd remembered.

"Take a picture of me and Pop flying!"

"Now take one with me and Nana!"

Patrick snapped away, heart swelling with every frame. Somewhere between shot forty-five and eighty-seven, Bella tugged his hand and whispered, "Daddy, you're doing a good job."

His throat tightened. "Thanks, bee. I'm trying really hard."

She grinned. "Can we go find a crab now?"

Ten minutes later, she had named a hermit crab

Francine and tried to convince Patrick to let her bring it home.

He vetoed that diplomatically by distracting her with strawberry ice cream. She immediately forgave him.

By the time they got back to the cottage, Bella was sugar happy and sun tired. She crawled onto the sofa like a sleepy cat, plush bee under one arm. Leaning her head on her grandmother's shoulder, she fell asleep.

"She's a talker," Myra said with a chuckle. "You were the same way at her age. So curious about everything and a vivid imagination."

Patrick smiled, brushing her curls off her forehead as she dozed.

She was magic.

She was *his*.

He pulled out his phone and took a picture of her curled up peacefully. He knew there would be a thousand more pictures to come, but this one—this first day—would always matter.

A text buzzed from London:

How is she?

He replied:

Perfect. Happy. Asleep. Back at the cottage. No stingrays eloped.

London's reply came with a smiley face:

Tell her I love and miss her.

"I will," he promised.
He stared at his daughter again, heart full.
And then he whispered to himself: "Next time...
maybe a zoo. With maps."

CHAPTER EIGHT

SATURDAY EVENING SETTLED over Polk Island in hues of amber and dusky pink, and London sat at the kitchen table, one hand wrapped around a mug of now-cold tea. The silence in the house felt almost unnatural. She had turned off the television, the radio, even her phone ringer. Everything felt too loud, too sharp, too much. Except the absence. That, she could feel down to her bones.

Bella was with Patrick.

London had smiled as the Jeep drove off, had waved and called out "Have fun!" like it was the most natural thing in the world to watch your daughter go off with the man who hadn't been around for the better part of four years. But now that the sun was dipping low and the hush of twilight settled in, doubt tapped against her ribs.

She missed her daughter. She missed the sound of her little footsteps skipping across the hardwood floor. She missed Bella's constant narrations of life—like she was living inside a very dramatic nature documentary. She even missed her asking for snacks every twenty minutes.

London glanced at the clock. It was almost six. Patrick was keeping Bella overnight since his parents were in town, and he wanted them to get to know their granddaughter. That left her with a long evening ahead and plenty of time for the questions to swirl like a slow-building storm.

Had he remembered to carry the EpiPen?

Did he check every ingredient before feeding her?

Did he buckle her in correctly after every stop?

Was he paying attention or letting his camera distract him?

Did she feel safe?

Did she feel loved?

London stood and wandered into Bella's room, running a hand over the comforter—the one with the cartoon bees and flowers. Her plush toys were arranged in a neat semicircle. The only one missing was the stuffed honeybee.

She smiled, just a little.

The buzz of her phone startled her. Patrick's name lit up the screen, along with the familiar FaceTime icon.

She answered quickly, her heartbeat picking up.

And there they were—her daughter and Patrick, framed in the soft light of what looked like his living room. Bella was grinning, eyes sleepy but sparkling, her sundress a little wrinkled, curls a little wild, like she'd had the time of her life.

"Mommy…" Bella squealed, pressing her face close to the screen. "We saw a crab! Her name is Francine, but Daddy wouldn't let me bring her home. And I did a dance for the seagulls."

London's breath hitched as she drank her in. "Hey, sweetie. Did you have fun today?"

Bella nodded so hard her braids bounced. "Daddy took a hundred pictures. Maybe a thousand. And we had fancy juice and a sandwich that looked like a boat. And I only almost fell in the water one time."

Patrick's voice chimed in from the side. "She tripped. I caught her. No actual danger."

London arched a brow, but her soft smile gave her away. "Good catch." She leaned closer to the screen.

Bella's words spilled out in a breathless rush— the movie, the ice cream, the crab named Francine, the dance for the seagulls, and the mysterious puddle she swore was a mermaid trap.

London laughed through most of it, asking questions, making the appropriately shocked faces. Patrick added the occasional detail, like the time Bella tried to name the waiter Captain Tuna.

When Bella yawned mid-sentence, Patrick gently ruffled her ponytail. "Okay, kiddo. Time to get ready for bed."

Bella's voice softened, sticky with sleep. "Okay… Mommy, will you tell me a story?"

London's throat tightened. "Of course, baby."

After she was dressed for bed, Patrick propped the phone on the nightstand so London could see Bella nestled in bed in her bee pajamas, bonnet slightly askew.

She told Bella a quick story, her voice low and soothing, watching as her daughter's eyes drifted closed, her tiny hand still clutching the honeybee.

When Bella was out, Patrick picked up the phone again and carried it to the kitchen. He held a mug of tea, the tag drooping over the side.

"You made that hours ago, didn't you?"

Patrick shrugged. "It was company for the quiet."

London smiled faintly. "Yeah. I get that."

They sat in companionable silence for a moment.

"I promise I won't let my parents overwhelm her. I just—" his voice cracked a little "—I want them to know her. To love her."

London's gaze softened. She saw it—the hope in his eyes. Not just for Bella. For himself. For family. For healing.

She nodded, and for the first time in a long while, it didn't feel like they were exes navigating a minefield. It felt like they were two parents figuring out how to walk this road—together—for Bella.

THE SUN HUNG high in a pale blue sky, the kind that hinted at the thick heat of summer without yet overwhelming. Cicadas droned in the trees as London turned into the long gravel drive leading to the house that held the echoes of her childhood— a beautiful Charleston-style two-story residence framed by elegant peach-colored roses.

Her gaze lifted to the balcony where large vases brimmed with the same stunning blooms. They seemed to sway and dance in the gentle breeze, their vibrant hues a striking contrast against the white pillars and wide windows of the house. These free-spirit roses were a living, breathing piece of her mother. Radiant and unapologetically free.

London could still picture her mother tending to them with patient hands and a soft hum on her lips, the same tenderness she poured into her family. The story of those roses was stitched into the fabric of their lives—how her father had carefully chosen them for Madelyn's wedding bouquet, enchanted by their bold colors and the raspberry-tipped guard petals that made them unique.

Even now, after all these years, her mother's love for those flowers hadn't faded. They still flourished in her garden, blooming like quiet witnesses to a love that had stood the test of time.

London parked and climbed out, already feeling the press of everything she hadn't said building behind her ribs. She followed the sound of clippers snipping stems to the right side of the yard, where her mother stood amid the rose bushes, pruning with the kind of reverence usually reserved for sacred things.

Madelyn wore her favorite wide-brimmed straw hat, her salt-and-pepper curls escaping at the edges. A lavender-colored apron was tied around her waist, and she hummed quietly to herself as she worked, hips swaying gently like she was dancing with the blooms.

"Hi, Mama," London called.

Madelyn turned, her weathered face lighting with a smile. "There you are. Come keep me company. These roses have minds of their own."

London stepped carefully between flower beds and joined her mother, brushing her hand over the velvety petals. "They look beautiful."

Madelyn snipped another bloom and waited.

"Bella spent the night with Patrick," she announced. "His parents are visiting."

Her mother resumed clipping, each snip slow and precise. "You worried?"

London crossed her arms and glanced up at the pale sky. "I don't know if *worried* is even the right word. I just…" She exhaled sharply. "It's his mother…you know?"

"Well, sometimes things shift when there's a child involved."

"Should they?" London's jaw tensed. "Just because Bella's here now, does that erase how Myra treated me? How she looked at me like I was nothing? I haven't forgotten that."

Madelyn finally turned to face her, brushing her gloved hands against her apron. "You're right to be protective, baby. You've raised Bella on your own. You've made a life for her—a good one. She's safe, she's loved, she knows who she is. That's because of you."

Her throat tightened, but the affirmation settled her heart just a little.

Her mother's gaze softened. "But Bella didn't choose this. She didn't choose Patrick. She didn't choose Myra and Robert. That part of her story was already written before she was born. Now she gets to live it for herself."

London hesitated. "You're right…"

Madelyn reached up and brushed a loose braid from her daughter's cheek. "I think you should give them the chance to love her. And give yourself the chance to see what that looks like. You don't have to forget the past. You don't even have to trust Myra completely. Trust isn't all-or-nothing, sugar. It's built one brick at a time. But if you keep every brick locked away, you'll never know if something good could've come from it."

London's gaze dropped to the worn stone path beneath her feet. "It's not about keeping Bella from them. I just… I remember who her grandmother was to me. And now she wants to be Nana?"

Madelyn's smile was faint, her voice even. "I remember. And I didn't like it either. But people can change. And even if they don't, you're not that same girl you were back then. You're not standing in front of her trying to prove anything. You're Bella's mother. You set the pace. You decide what's safe. And if anything feels off, you don't have to hesitate. You can pull the plug. That's your right."

London exhaled, slow and shaky. "I just can't bear the thought of Bella getting hurt."

"She has you," Madelyn said, her voice warm and certain. "You'll always be her safe place. That won't change."

The garden settled around them in a hush, the breeze picking up just enough to stir the roses. Madelyn clipped another bloom, clean and sure, and handed it to London.

"For strength," she said, as if she knew her daughter would need it.

London held the rose gently, its stem firm, its petals soft against her palm. She glanced toward her car, knowing the day was winding down. Bella would be home soon. "I don't know if I can ever forgive them," she admitted quietly. "Not really."

Madelyn met her gaze, steady and kind. "That's not a one-time decision, baby. That's one you make little by little, when you're ready. But don't let the history you've lived with them rob Bella of the future she deserves to explore."

The words sank deep, settling in a place London rarely allowed anyone to reach. She drew in the familiar blend of roses, salt air, and her mother's quiet wisdom and for once let herself believe that something good was on its way.

PATRICK CHECKED THE time again.

4:10 p.m.

He'd promised London he'd have Bella home by five, and while Polk Island wasn't big, he wasn't about to test the limits of that grace period.

Lunch had come and gone in a blur—grilled chicken, corn salad, Bella chattering nonstop about every detail of the farm. Patrick caught his father's steady, watchful gaze a few times.

His mother's, too, though hers carried more… edge.

She was calculating something. He could feel it.

While Bella napped in the sunroom after they

finished eating, Patrick leaned against the porch railing, watching the sway of the oaks, drinking a glass of lemonade.

Myra joined him quietly. "She's special."

"Yeah," Patrick said, eyes fixed on the trees. "She is."

Neither of them said what they both knew. Time was running short.

"I guess we should wake her up," Myra murmured.

He nodded.

"Patrick, you know…you're her father. You have rights."

"No ultimatums. No pressure. I won't put London through that."

"You've changed," Myra said softly. "I see it."

He glanced back toward the sunroom, where Bella's tiny snores were just audible through the screen.

"I've missed too much already. I'm not missing anything else."

Myra's hand squeezed his briefly before she stepped away. "We'll be here when you get back."

Patrick carried Bella to the Jeep, careful not to wake her, tucking her plush bee into the crook of her arm.

She stirred just as he buckled her in, mumbling sleepily, "Are we going home to Mommy now?"

"Yeah, sweetheart. Right on time."

He pulled onto the road, the sun dipping lower, the ocean breeze creeping in through the open windows.

Patrick made good on his promise, pulling away from the cottage just after four thirty with Bella strapped securely in the back seat, her honeybee plush clutched tightly in her arms.

The ride back toward London's place was quieter than the trip yesterday. Bella's earlier excitement had given way to the soft hum of exhaustion, her small body sagging against the seat belt as she fought to keep her eyes open.

"You hanging in there, Bumblebee?" he asked, catching her nod through the rearview mirror.

"I don't wanna miss anything," she mumbled, her voice thick with sleep.

His chest tightened. "There's plenty more waiting for you, sweetheart. I'll make sure of it."

The words were a vow—one he hadn't fully known he was making until now.

The winding roads passed in a blur of sunlight and shadow until the trees thinned, and London's cottage came into view, its familiar blue shutters and white siding dappled in the late afternoon glow. Bella's tricycle lay tipped over in the front yard, and the sound of waves rolled faintly from the beach beyond the house.

Patrick eased to a stop in the driveway, his pulse hitching in a way that had nothing to do with the clock ticking toward five and everything to do with the woman waiting on the porch.

London stood with her arms folded, gaze steady as she watched them pull in. She wore a pair of cut-off jeans and a loose linen blouse, her braids piled high, tendrils falling around her face.

Bella perked up instantly, wriggling in her seat. "Mommy…"

Patrick barely had the Jeep in Park before Bella wanted free of the car seat. He released her and let her run. He needed a second longer to pull himself together.

London crouched low to catch their daughter, arms wide as Bella barreled into her. Their laughter mixed in the salt-kissed breeze, something pure and steady that rooted him to the spot.

"Did you have fun with Daddy?" she asked, brushing a braid from Bella's damp forehead.

"I did."

London looked up then, meeting Patrick's gaze. Her expression softened, a flicker of something unreadable passing through her eyes. "Thank you," she said quietly.

"I'll call you later," he said, shoving his hands into his pockets.

Her lips parted like she might say more, but then she caught herself and simply nodded back. "Okay."

Patrick watched them disappear into the house, the screen door creaking shut behind them, and stood there for another long moment—long enough to feel the quiet wrap around him, thick with the certainty that he wasn't ready to let them go.

CHAPTER NINE

THE HOUSE WAS QUIET. A rare kind of quiet that usually made Myra Brown uneasy. She stood by the window, arms folded, watching the sun drift lower over the trees that lined Patrick's temporary rental.

Bella had left with Patrick nearly thirty minutes ago. Now it was just Myra and Robert, sitting in a home that didn't quite feel like her son's but had already become infused with the scent of his daughter—fruit snacks and honey from the farm.

Myra turned from the window and sat down slowly, brushing nonexistent lint from her linen slacks.

Robert sat in the adjoining armchair, legs crossed, a can of soda in hand. He raised an eyebrow when she didn't say anything.

"You've been pacing like that since they left," he said, voice calm as a late tide. "Spit it out, Myra."

She looked at him sharply, lips pressed together. Then she sighed.

"London didn't even tell him, Robert. All those years, and she never once reached out. Never once gave him a choice."

His face remained neutral. That was always his way—still waters, deep patience.

"We don't know everything."

"We know enough." Myra's voice tightened.

"That woman kept his child a secret. His child. I know you want to play the peacemaker, but I can't. I won't pretend this is all fine."

Robert finished off his soda, watching her with the same patient eyes he used when fishing or working in the garden.

Myra rose to her feet once more, her heels making a gentle clicking sound on the hardwood floor as she walked over to the fireplace. There sat Bella's photo, captured just yesterday by Patrick, who had caught her candidly enjoying an ice-cream cone, her eyes sparkling with happiness.

She touched the frame lightly. The ache in her chest surprised her. It was that familiar twinge, the one that started when Patrick was barely a teenager and began slipping away from her emotionally.

"I see the way London looks at Patrick. Like she's still holding all the power."

Looking confused, Robert glanced up. "What power?"

"She holds the reins," Myra said softly. "Our son's trying to build a relationship with Bella, and she gets to dictate when, how, and how much."

Robert set the empty can on the end table. "He's her father. That bond will speak for itself."

Myra turned, her voice firmer now. "I don't trust her, Robert. I never have."

There it was—the truth. Not because London had ever done something egregious, but because of what she represented.

"I know," Robert said quietly, reading her

thoughts the way only a husband of thirty-five years could. "She reminds you of your father's wife."

Myra blinked hard. "You mean his mistress? That's all she'll ever be to me."

The words hit like a wave that had been swelling for decades.

"London is that same kind of woman," she whispered. "The kind that makes a man forget his vows. The kind that makes daughters feel disposable."

She hadn't meant to say that. She hadn't even known she still felt that way. But it was true. The woman who stole her father had been young, beautiful, radiant, and bold. Just like London.

"I spent years watching my mother shrink from that betrayal. Watching her wilt in the wake of his absence. I promised myself I'd never let a woman like that near my family again."

"Myra," Robert said softly. "London isn't your father's mistress. And Patrick isn't your father."

Silence hung between them.

But Myra couldn't shake it. That feeling. That deep-rooted fear that Patrick would lose himself, that Bella would become a pawn, that they would all be left chasing after pieces.

"She let him go once," Myra said. "Didn't fight for him. Didn't even tell him she was pregnant. And now—now we're just supposed to trust her judgment?"

Robert stood and crossed to her, placing a hand

on her shoulder. "She's raising a smart, beautiful little girl. Whatever we think of her, Bella loves her mother. And Patrick… Patrick loves them both. We need to give this space to unfold. Don't try to orchestrate it."

Myra pulled away gently. "I don't want to orchestrate anything," she said. "But I also won't sit on my hands while Patrick lets his heart cloud his judgment. He needs to file for joint custody. If she changes her mind one day—if she marries someone else or decides Patrick's too inconvenient—he'll be shut out."

"You've said all that," Robert reminded her gently. "And he heard you."

"He dismissed me."

"He's a grown man. Let him make his own decisions."

Just then, the sound of the front door opening echoed from down the hall. Myra straightened, smoothing the front of her blouse.

Patrick's voice called out. "I'm back…"

"Son, do you have a minute?"

He exhaled, sensing the storm. "Mom, not tonight."

"I just want you to think about joint custody—"

"No." His voice was firm. "Not now."

Her heart squeezed. "I'm only trying to protect you."

"I know." He kissed her temple, but his eyes didn't soften. "But I need space to do this my way."

He walked past her, into the kitchen to grab a drink.

Robert appeared beside her, whispering, "Let it go, hon. Just for tonight."

But Myra Brown had never been good at letting things go. Especially not when it came to family. Especially not when it came to the people she loved most.

She turned toward the window, toward the stars blinking to life over the water. She would try.

For now.

But she wouldn't let her guard down. Not when Patrick's heart—and Bella's future—were on the line.

Not when she still remembered what it was like to be the daughter someone left behind.

Two days later, London sat behind her desk in her home office, sorting through invoices when a knock at the glass-paneled door caught her attention.

She looked up, heart giving an involuntary skip as Patrick stepped inside.

"Hey. Kyla let me in before she headed back to the barn. I know I should've called, but I couldn't wait for you to see this," he said, holding up a manila envelope. His camera bag was slung casually over his shoulder, and the sleeves of his button-down were rolled up to his elbows.

London gestured to the chair across from her. "Is that what I think it is?"

He nodded. "The draft. I wanted you to see it before I send it to the magazine. Photos and copy. Figured you'd want to approve the way your story gets told."

She reached for the envelope, fingers brushing his. A current of awareness danced up her arm. She tucked it away quickly and focused on the contents instead.

Patrick sat quietly, giving her space to read. London scanned the printed pages, her eyes widening as she took in the opening paragraph:

There's something sacred about the way bees move. Industrious, purposeful, and in perfect harmony. London Worthington embodies that same rhythm—gentle yet strong, efficient and full of grace. In the low country heat of Polk Island, she's created more than a business. She's nurtured a legacy.

Her throat tightened. The words—his words—were more than just flattering. They were reverent. And the photographs? One of employees labeling jars in the shade. A wide shot of London standing between the hives, sunlight draping her like a shawl.

She looked up, voice husky. "Patrick, this is…it's beautiful. I love the way you captured my story."

He smiled, but there was a softness in his expression she hadn't seen in years. "It was easy. You shine here."

She blinked against the sudden heat behind her eyes. "Thank you. Really."

"Want to grab lunch?" he asked. "My treat."

London took another glance at the article and nodded. "Sure."

They drove into town, the silence between them companionable.

They ended up at a small seafood shack near the marsh, tucked between weathered docks and swaying reeds.

Patrick ordered blackened mahi-mahi tacos, London opted for a shrimp po' boy, and they sat outside beneath a faded red umbrella.

Seagulls cawed in the distance, and the occasional boat buzzed across the water. Patrick sipped from his sweet tea, his gaze on her over the rim of the cup.

"Where do we go from here, London?"

She paused mid-bite, caught off guard. "What do you mean?"

"I mean with Bella. With us. I want to be in her life. Consistently. Not just for a photo op or when I'm in town for a few weeks."

London looked out at the marsh, the late-afternoon light bouncing off the water like gold coins. "It's hard to know what's right. You being here…it's meant a lot to her. To me. But what happens when the next big assignment comes? When you're off to a conflict zone or a far-off country with limited cell service?"

He didn't answer right away. Just leaned back in his chair, thoughtful. "I'm not taking on any new assignments right now. Not for a while."

London's brows lifted. "Really?"

Patrick nodded. "Yeah. There was a time when I thought I could keep living that way, always chasing the next story. I can't keep doing that. I don't want to do that."

The confession hung heavy in the air. Her heart responded with a flutter, pride and anxiety entwined. "She's going to get used to you being around, Patrick. If you leave again…"

"I won't. Not unless it's something I can't walk away from. And even then, not without talking to you first. And talking to her. London, I've got options. Teaching. Freelancing from here. I'm exploring what that could look like."

London felt herself sway on a precipice. She'd built walls, strong and deliberate, to protect herself from the ache of his absence. But here he was, chipping away at them—not with promises, but with presence.

She toyed with her napkin, voice quiet. "I used to picture this. Us. Together."

He reached across the table, palm up. Not forcing, just waiting.

London looked at his hand, rough and familiar. Slowly, she laid hers in it.

"So did I," Patrick said.

Her breath caught. The wind shifted, carrying the briny scent of sea and forgiveness.

And as they sat there, hands clasped, London realized something terrifying and beautiful—her heart wasn't buried as deep as she thought.

It was waking up.

And it still knew his name.

THE SALTY BREEZE from the Atlantic clung to Patrick's skin as he stepped out onto the back deck of his cottage just a few miles from South Beach. The morning sun gleamed over the marshland, casting a soft golden hue over the reeds. His fingers tightened around the coffee mug in his hand, now lukewarm and forgotten. London's voice echoed in his mind—the gratitude in her tone when she read his article draft, the warmth in her eyes when she saw the photos of herself, her bees, and her team.

Patrick sat down heavily in the wooden Adirondack chair. The wood groaned beneath him, as if sighing under the weight of his thoughts. He closed his eyes.

There it was again. That pull. The undeniable, unrelenting connection he felt with London. Like it had never really left. Like no time had passed.

He saw her face again—not the woman she was now, strong and focused and fiercely protective of their daughter—but the girl she'd been, the one who used to fall asleep beside him while they lay tangled up on a blanket under the stars. He could still hear her laugh from those nights. Back then, everything had felt possible. And then, it hadn't.

Patrick exhaled slowly, setting the mug on the small table beside him. His gaze drifted to the camera bag leaning against the doorframe. Inside it were the images he'd captured of Bella—her joy, her energy, her trust. He hadn't just photographed his daughter; he'd preserved moments that had already begun to heal something broken inside him.

And yet underneath the joy and renewal, a familiar ache settled.

He thought about that conversation with his mother again—or rather, the many conversations. The subtle manipulation. The raised eyebrows when London was mentioned. The way Myra had smiled, thin-lipped, when she reminded him how unpredictable life as a photojournalist could be. *You need someone who can keep up with your pace, Patrick. London is lovely, but you know she's not going to be happy chasing your passport stamps.*

He hadn't seen it then for what it was. Emotional sleight of hand. She hadn't said *Don't be with her.* She'd said *She deserves more stability. You don't want to hurt her, do you?* It had been wrapped in concern. In love. In the language of maternal protection.

And maybe part of him had wanted to believe her. He'd been afraid. Afraid of commitment, afraid of failing at something that mattered that much. So, when his mother had offered a rationale that made his cowardice seem noble, he'd taken it.

Patrick leaned forward, resting his elbows on his knees, fingers steepled over his mouth.

God, how he'd regretted it. The second he walked away from London, something inside him had fractured. He'd thrown himself into his career like a man trying to drown.

Africa. Southeast Asia. The Middle East. He'd chased conflict zones, documented disaster, famine, rebellion. It was important work, but he'd used it as a shield. Each new assignment was proof that he'd made the right choice. But every lonely hotel room, every flight back to nowhere, every email he typed and deleted instead of sending—they all told the real story.

He'd never stopped thinking about London. Not for a single day.

And now Bella.

Patrick rubbed his eyes, trying to still the tremor in his chest. Bella was this little miracle he'd never known to dream of. Smart, talkative, with her mother's sense of mischief and his own deep curiosity about the world. She'd cracked his heart wide open.

His mother's voice came back, less gentle this time. *You need to file for joint custody*, she'd said before they left for home. *You have rights*.

He'd shut her down hard. He knew she was trying to be strategic. Protective. But the truth was he didn't want to fight. He didn't want to create friction with London.

Because this wasn't just about Bella anymore. Not entirely.

It was about that moment on the porch when London laughed at Bella's instructions to look at the photos.

It was about earlier when he showed her the article. The softness in her expression when she read his words, when she saw herself through his lens. And it was about how good it felt to sit across from her again, to laugh with her, to see the walls come down, even if only a little.

He wanted more of that.

But what would it cost?

His career was more than a job. It was part of who he was. The hunger to tell stories, to capture truth in its rawest form—he couldn't deny that part of himself. But he also couldn't pretend he hadn't changed. That the world hadn't changed the second he saw Bella's face for the first time.

Patrick stood and paced the deck, his bare feet silent against the worn planks. He wasn't sure what the road ahead looked like. But there would be his daughter. Her laughter. Her trust. Her little hand tucked in his. And maybe London would be there, too.

CHAPTER TEN

THE SUMMER HEAT on Main Street shimmered off the pavement in waves, the kind of dense heat that pressed down on the sleepy charm of Polk Island like a thick, woven quilt.

London pulled into the angled space in front of the Polk Island Café, her SUV kicking up a whisper of dust from the nearby flowerbeds lining the sidewalk. The little wicker basket on her front seat held four jars of wildflower honey, harvested earlier that week and labeled with her company's delicate bee-and-magnolia-blossom logo.

The bell over the café door jingled as she stepped inside. The space still smelled of cinnamon rolls and strong coffee, just like it had when she was a child visiting with her mother. Wooden booths hugged the walls, and mismatched chairs clustered around round tables in the center of the room. At the back, the display case boasted pies with flaky crusts, cupcakes crowned with swirls of pastel icing, and buttery croissants.

Behind the counter stood Misty, wiping her hands on her apron, her eyes lighting up when she saw London. "Good morning…"

"Morning…these are for Miss Eleanor," London said, holding up the basket.

"Perfect. She'll be so pleased. She's actually here today. She's sitting over there by the window."

London turned to see Miss Eleanor seated at her usual table, a wide-brimmed straw hat perched delicately on her curls, a porcelain teacup clutched between her thin fingers. Her once-brilliant eyes were dimmer now, like the sun through gauze curtains, but they still flickered with recognition when she saw London approach.

"Good morning, Miss Eleanor," London greeted warmly. "I brought you some honey. From my latest batch."

Miss Eleanor blinked slowly. "You look familiar," she said, voice quavering. "Did you used to come in here with your mama?"

London smiled and took the seat across from her. "I did. I'm London. I'm Angus Jr. and Madelyn's daughter."

A flicker of recognition lit Eleanor's eyes before a slow smile curled her lips. "Madelyn's girl. Of course. You always had a sweet tooth for my lemon bars."

London laughed softly, the memory wrapping around her like a hug. "Still do. I tried to make them once, but they didn't taste anywhere near yours."

"The secret," Eleanor said, leaning in with a conspiratorial grin, "is in the zest—and a little patience. Most folks rush a good lemon bar. But I also add a pinch of ground ginger. Just enough to make people wonder."

"I promise not to tell a soul about your secret ingredient."

Eleanor chuckled, her shoulders loosening as she reached for one of the jars of honey London had set on the table. "This is so thoughtful of you. Rusty and I adore this honey. We swirl it in our tea, drizzle it over fruit and muffins… My husband even brushes it on grilled chicken—I swear it makes the meat taste like summer." She gave a playful wink. "These jars never last long in our house."

A slow warmth spread through London's chest, unexpected and humbling. Something about hearing her say they *adore this honey* made the work of tending hives in the heat and checking jars in the quiet hours feel…sacred.

"I'm so glad to hear that," London said softly. "Making honey is a labor of love for me."

Eleanor nodded, her gaze drifting just a little before it settled again on London's face. "How are your parents doing? I can't remember the last time I saw Angus Jr."

London's smile faltered, just for a second—so quick, it might have been missed if someone wasn't looking for it. But inside, it felt like the ground shifted beneath her feet. The mention of her father's name, so casual and sweet, sent a sharp pang through her ribs.

He'd been gone almost five years.

She swallowed. Hard.

"Mama's still stubborn as ever," she said gently, forcing a small smile.

Eleanor patted her hand, beaming. "That's Madelyn for you."

London nodded, her throat tight, the ache of loss mingling with affection and something heavier, grief that still crept up and caught her off guard. Eleanor meant no harm. She never did. But the gaps in her memory were growing wider, and this one had cut through London like a paper-thin blade.

Still, she held her smile. Because Eleanor was still here. And that mattered.

They talked for a few moments, mostly about the weather and the honeysuckle blooming near the church.

Miss Eleanor occasionally slipped into silence, her mind wandering, but her politeness never faded.

As London stood to leave, Misty came to her side, gently placing a hand on her arm. "Thank you for coming. It really helps. Some days she remembers everyone. Some days no one at all. But she loves the honey. She says it reminds her of her father and how he used to steal honey from the bees."

"She's still got that same grace," London said softly. "Even when her memory doesn't catch. She asked about my dad. I didn't tell her that he was gone. The last time I told her, she cried."

Misty nodded, eyes misting. "She loves this island and the people. I'm just doing my best to keep this place going the way she would've wanted."

London offered her a warm smile, then turned to head toward the door.

That was when the bell rang again.

She looked up—and saw Patrick.

He paused in the doorway, blinking at her like he wasn't sure he believed what he saw.

His camera bag hung over one shoulder, and he wore a soft blue T-shirt over jeans that were dusty, and his boots looked like he'd been tromping around the honey farm again.

"Hey," he said, offering a slow, surprised grin. "Didn't expect to see you here."

London blinked at him, her heart giving an involuntary skip. "I could say the same. What have you been up to?"

Patrick glanced down at his jeans and brushed at the layer of red dust clinging to the fabric. "Oh, I was in Charleston this morning at the Slave Mart Museum and the old Gadsden's Wharf site." Something softened in his expression, something almost reverent. "It felt…important to stand there. To see it. To capture it right."

Her throat tightened. "That dust tells on you."

He chuckled, stepping inside. "Yeah, well. Some places stay with you. Get under your skin."

Their eyes met, the weight of his words lingering between them.

London smiled, just a little. "Yeah. Some places do."

"I was going to grab a bite. Want to join me?"

She nodded. "Sure."

They took a booth near the window, one table away from Miss Eleanor. Patrick slid into the seat across from her, setting his camera bag gently on the floor.

"I took some pictures yesterday over at the marsh walk. There was a blue heron nesting near the bridge." He gave her a wry smile. "I could've used Bella's excitement. Birds seem to love her."

London laughed. "She does have a way with all creatures."

Their food arrived—grilled shrimp tacos for him, a spinach-and-strawberry salad for her—and conversation flowed easily. They talked about Bella's sudden obsession with dragonflies, how she insisted they were just bees in disguise. They laughed about the time she'd tried to teach her a friend's cat to fetch, and they marveled at how fast she was growing.

As they finished lunch, Patrick leaned forward slightly. "I've been thinking," he said. "*About us.*"

London froze, fork halfway to her mouth. "Us?"

He smiled, but it was tentative. "I'd like to take you out. On a proper date. Just you and me."

London stared at him.

He continued, "There's a movie premiere in Charleston this Saturday night. One of my friends directed it—it's a documentary about coastal communities and climate change. There's a little celebration afterward. Nothing fancy, just good people, good conversation."

London's mind spun. "Bella's already got plans with my mom and Cia," she said slowly. "So, I'm free."

His grin widened. "So that's a yes?"

She hesitated, but only for a breath. "Yes."

They left the café together, the afternoon sun catching in her long braids, bouncing off his camera bag. He walked her to her car, his hand grazing hers as they paused at the driver's side door.

"Thanks for lunch," she said softly.

"Thanks for saying yes."

She slipped inside, heart fluttering. As she drove away, she watched him in her rearview mirror, standing on the sidewalk, hands in his pockets, watching her go.

And for the first time in years, London felt that same thrill she'd felt at twenty-four, when she believed that anything was possible.

This time, maybe it was.

THE GOLDEN HOUR had begun to spill over Polk Island like a warm secret, and Patrick adjusted his lens as he moved through the island's historic district. Time clung to this place. The skeletal remains of houses belonging to the first settlers lined the narrow street, their tabby walls—made from lime, oyster shells, and water—weathered by salt air and softened by creeping moss. Most had been abandoned after the cyclone in the late 1800s, their families relocating to the south side of the island, leaving behind these hushed, hollowed shells.

But not the Polk Island Praise House.

It stood, small and defiant, at the end of the road, like a survivor. Built by hand by brothers Hoss and

Polk Rothchild, the one-room church had outlived the storm, the exodus, and the years. The whitewashed walls had long faded to soft gray, the tabby foundation still solid beneath it. Its steeple, though leaning slightly now, still pointed skyward.

The Praise House looked simple from the outside, but Patrick could feel the weight of what it held—generations of worship, of foot-stomping praise, of whispered prayers that had never left these walls.

He crouched low to capture the angle of the cracked steps, the way wildflowers poked up defiantly through the foundation. The warped stained-glass window caught the slanting sun, casting fractured ribbons of color across the doorway. Vines, thick and patient, curled around the bell tower as if nature itself was cradling what remained.

Patrick adjusted his lens and clicked through a series of shots, but his thoughts weren't on exposure or framing. They drifted, as they had been doing lately, to London.

To the life he wanted to build.

To the roots he was finally ready to sink deep.

He didn't just ask her out on a date for nostalgia's sake. It wasn't some sentimental play. It was intention. Real. Tangible. Deliberate. He wanted a future with her. With Bella. He wanted to rewrite a past he'd let slip through his fingers.

Patrick straightened and shifted his gaze toward what was left of Polk Rothchild's house.

Only the stone outline of the foundation remained, but the chimney still stood like a sentinel in the middle of a wildflower patch.

He walked toward it slowly, the camera lowered at his side.

Why now? That was the question that had haunted him for weeks.

He'd spent years traveling the world, telling stories with his lens. But none of it had ever filled the hollow he felt when he looked back and realized what he'd left behind.

London.

He remembered the day he left her as sharply as if it had happened yesterday. The fight had been quiet, full of unsaid things. His mother had made her opinions known.

And he'd listened.

Not because he didn't love London. He did. Ferociously. But because he was afraid. Afraid that love would make him small, that it would anchor him when he needed wings.

Now, standing on the ground the Rothchild brothers built with bare hands and stubborn dreams, Patrick could see the flaw in that logic. Love hadn't made Polk small. It had made this island possible.

He raised his camera again and took a photo of the chimney. Through the lens, he imagined what the house must've looked like when it was whole. A family sitting around a fire. Children laughing. A man holding a woman's hand and saying, *We did this together.*

Patrick lowered the camera. A breeze carried the scent of honeysuckle and distant saltwater.

He had asked London on a date because he needed to start something real. Not just repair what they had. Not just apologize. He needed to show her he was ready to be present.

Accountable. Invested.

He thought of Bella's smile, the way she had curled into his side during their movie night. How she had picked a flower at the honey farm and insisted it was for her mommy. And how London had blushed when he handed it to her.

Patrick moved toward Hoss's homestead. It was more intact, its porch still holding strong, although the interior had long been reclaimed by nature. He stepped inside the threshold, careful where he walked. This house had hosted generations. He imagined it filled with voices. With hope.

This was legacy. And for the first time in his life, Patrick wanted to create his own.

He didn't know if London would say yes to more than a movie premiere. He didn't know if her heart could open to him again fully, or if he even deserved that.

But he was done pretending he didn't care.

The sound of a shutter clicking echoed as he took one last photo of the doorway, framing it so the golden light spilled across the threshold.

His way forward.

That evening, as the sun dipped low and painted

the sky in pinks and oranges, Patrick packed away his camera gear and walked back to his Jeep.

He paused one more time to look at the church and the two old homesteads that once held the dreams of Polk Island's founders.

He whispered under his breath, as if confessing something to the land itself.

"I want to belong somewhere, too."

He slid into the driver's seat, and before he turned the key, he pulled out his phone.

A text to London lit the screen:

Thanks for agreeing to Saturday night. Can't wait to see you.

He hit Send. His thumb hovered for a moment before he added one more message.

I'll pick you up at 6.

The road ahead wasn't easy. Rebuilding trust never was. But it was worth every step.

And Patrick was ready to walk it.

SATURDAY ARRIVED WRAPPED in sunlight and the soft hush of waves beyond the marsh. London stood in front of the mirror, smoothing the front of her deep emerald cocktail dress, the color rich against her warm brown skin. The dress was sleeveless with a modest V-neckline and a subtle high-low hem that flowed when she moved. It cinched at the waist, accentuating her curves, and sparkled faintly at the shoulders with a scatter of delicate beadwork.

She had her locs styled in a bun at her nape with a few left loose to kiss her cheekbones. Gold hoops glinted at her ears, and her makeup was soft, just enough shimmer on her eyelids and gloss on her lips to reflect her mood—curious, cautious, and a little bit excited.

Patrick was due to pick her up at six, and though she'd never admit it aloud, she'd been ready by five thirty.

When the doorbell rang, she gave herself one last glance, her heart fluttering for reasons she pretended not to examine, and opened the door.

Patrick stood on the other side, looking entirely too good in a tailored charcoal blazer over a crisp white shirt, open at the collar, and dark jeans that fit like they'd been custom-made for him. His loafers were polished, and his camera hung from one shoulder out of habit more than necessity. But it wasn't just what he wore—it was how he wore it. Confident. Easy. Like he belonged anywhere he stepped.

His eyes swept over her, warm and appreciative, and for a second, London felt like that twentysomething woman again, the one who used to sit across from him in coffee shops and kiss him under streetlamps.

"Wow," he said, his voice quiet. "You look… amazing."

She smiled, holding on to composure even as a

flurry of butterflies took flight in her chest. "You clean up pretty well yourself."

The ride across the bridge into Charleston was smooth. The sky had begun to streak with coral and lavender, casting the water below in soft, glowing hues.

Patrick drove with one hand on the wheel, his other resting on his thigh, occasionally glancing her way, as if still surprised she was really there.

The event was being held at a historic venue near the waterfront. The building had brick walls, oversized windows, and twinkling string lights looping across the ceiling beams. Inside, there was a buzz of music and conversation, people gathered in clusters sipping cocktails and laughing.

Patrick introduced her to colleagues, fellow photographers, and a few magazine editors. London found herself surprised at how easily she moved among them, laughing at jokes, engaging in conversation, and accepting compliments on her dress.

"So, this is the honey queen?" one of the editors teased after Patrick proudly told someone she owned and ran the most sought-after honey company on Polk Island.

Patrick chuckled, slipping his hand briefly to the small of London's back. "She's not just the queen— she's the whole hive."

London shot him a playful look. "Don't make me regret this date, Patrick Brown."

He grinned, unbothered. "Not a chance."

They watched the short film together—beautiful visuals of Low Country life and culture, narrated with poetic reverence. Patrick's friend had captured the soul of coastal living, much like he had captured the soul of London's honey farm in his photos.

Afterward, there were hors d'oeuvres, soft jazz from a live band, and a few more introductions. London sipped wine and let herself enjoy the night, aware of Patrick's nearness, his subtle glances, the way his hand occasionally found hers without fanfare.

It was romantic. It was unexpected.

It was dangerous.

Because each smile he sent her softened something inside her she'd worked hard to guard. And each time he laughed, it reminded her of the years when his laughter was her favorite sound. When his arms had felt like home.

They left the party a little after ten, walking to the Jeep beneath the moonlight. Charleston pulsed gently around them—laughter spilling from restaurants, carriage wheels rolling down cobblestone streets, live music slipping through open doors.

"Thank you for coming with me," Patrick said as he opened the car door for her.

"Thank you for asking," she replied, settling into the seat.

The drive back to Polk Island was quieter, more contemplative. The radio hummed a soft tune, and their hands brushed once on the center console, neither of them moving away.

When they pulled up in front of her house, the porch light glowing in welcome, London turned to him. "It was a lovely evening."

Patrick cut the engine but didn't get out immediately. He looked at her, something tender and hesitant in his eyes. "Can I walk you to the door?"

She nodded.

At the porch, they lingered. The cicadas sang in the distance, and the sweet scent of jasmine curled around them like a whisper.

Patrick stepped a little closer, his voice low. "Tonight…felt like more than just a night out."

London's heart pounded. "It did."

He reached up, brushing a strand of hair that had escaped her updo. "London…"

She didn't know which of them moved first. Maybe it didn't matter. What mattered was the sudden softness of his lips against hers. Gentle, searching.

She didn't pull away. She didn't stop to think. Her eyes fluttered shut, and for a few seconds, time rewound itself to those late summer nights years ago, when love had been simple and the world hadn't yet demanded so much from them.

When the kiss ended, it left her breathless and blinking beneath the porch light.

Patrick stepped back, searching her eyes. "Good night, London."

She could only nod as he walked down the steps, got into his car, and drove off.

Once inside, she leaned against the door, fingertips pressed to her lips.

CHAPTER ELEVEN

Sunday mornings used to mean airport lines, international datelines, and the hum of adrenaline before chasing another story. But this Sunday, Patrick Brown was elbow-deep in glitter glue and construction paper.

Bella sat cross-legged on the living room floor, brow furrowed in concentration as she glued Popsicle sticks into what he assumed was either a bridge or a sunburst. Maybe both.

He'd stopped asking for clarification—Bella's art didn't follow logic. It followed joy.

"Daddy, this one's for Grandma," she said solemnly, holding up the glittery creation. "She said her favorite color is peach like her roses, so I made the heart peach. I'm gonna make one for Nana, too. Only hers is pink."

Patrick smiled. "She's going to love it."

She beamed up at him, her puffy ponytail bouncing. Something inside him cracked a little every time she called him Daddy. The title felt both foreign and natural, like a favorite song you hadn't heard in years but somehow still knew all the lyrics to.

Earning London's trust hadn't been easy. He didn't expect it to be. And yet every small moment like this—every picture he helped color, every dance party in the kitchen, every time Bella asked him to tuck her in—felt like another brick laid in the foundation of something lasting.

At first, London had hovered. She was never unkind but guarded, protective in a way that made sense. Patrick had walked away from her. From this life. From a daughter he hadn't known about but now couldn't imagine living without.

But he was here now having spent the night at his place. Fully. And determined to prove that commitment wasn't just a word he tossed around like a travel itinerary.

He cooked breakfast for Bella every morning he had her. French toast had become their Sunday ritual, always cut into heart shapes. He learned how she liked her apples peeled but her oranges whole. He memorized her bedtime stories—particularly *Goodnight Moon* and the one about the ladybug who lost her spots. He discovered that she hated loud noises, adored ladybugs, and had inherited London's stubborn chin and quick wit.

And through it all, Patrick kept showing up.

Not just for Bella, but for London, too.

It wasn't always easy. London didn't let her guard down often. She was kind, but there was a steel beneath that kindness, forged by years of raising Bella on her own.

Patrick respected that. He admired it. And sometimes, when they shared those quiet glances over Bella's head or exchanged brief touches of hands when passing plates across the dinner table, he dared to hope that the steel was softening.

Now Patrick was sitting in the backyard, watching Bella chase butterflies with a net far too big for her. The sun was dipping behind the marshes, golden light glinting off the water.

"It's time to go inside, Bella," he announced.

"I want to stay out here," she responded with a shake of her head.

She could be stubborn at times. Patrick had seen glimpses of it during each of her visits. "If you want to watch a movie before bedtime…we need to go inside and prepare dinner."

"No," Bella said, an expression of defiance on her face.

Patrick studied her, the way her arms folded tightly over her chest, the stubborn tilt of her mouth. A part of him felt the flicker of a smile—she was testing him, pushing at boundaries the way children did. But another part of him, the one that had been holding everything together for weeks now, felt the weight of her resistance.

He reminded himself she wasn't trying to be difficult. Bella was still adjusting—still making sense of why her world felt different. Stubbornness wasn't just defiance, sometimes it was armor. Still, dinner needed cooking, bedtime routines mattered, and boundaries had to hold.

Straightening, he kept his voice even. "Bella, I'm not asking again. We'll have time to sit out here tomorrow. Tonight it's dinner first."

Her eyes narrowed, but the flicker of uncertainty

betrayed her. Patrick stayed steady, letting her see that his decision wasn't going to waver.

"Okaay…" Bella uttered.

She made no effort to mask her reluctance, and Patrick could read her displeasure as easily as if she'd spoken it aloud. Still, he hoped that once they sat down to dinner, the edge in her mood would soften, replaced by the warmth he knew she carried beneath the pushback. That night, Bella brought out her *Daddy* box—a shoebox she had decorated in stickers and filled with every drawing they'd made together, little notes he'd written her, even a napkin from their first ice-cream outing. She pulled it onto the couch and snuggled beside him.

"I want you to always be here," she whispered. "Even when I grow up."

His throat tightened. "Me, too, baby girl. Always."

She fell asleep in his arms.

London came later than usual. Her face was tired, but when she saw Bella tucked against him, her lips lifted into something soft.

"She asked if she could stay over here next visit," Patrick said, brushing a strand of Bella's curls off her cheek.

"She did?"

He nodded. "I'd love that. If it's okay with you."

London hesitated and then slowly nodded. "I think that would be good."

Something in him expanded. Grew roots.

After she left, Patrick stepped outside and looked up at the stars.

He missed his camera sometimes. Missed the chase. The rush. But this—this was a different kind of rush. A steady, anchoring one. Every bedtime story, every painted rock, every hug from his daughter grounded him in a way he hadn't known he needed.

He was building a life here.

TUESDAY DAWNED SOFT and golden, the kind of early afternoon that asked for quiet reflection. As London rinsed the last of the dishes from lunch, she felt something crack open inside her. Something she hadn't dared touch in years.

Hope.

Patrick had joined them for lunch, settling into the rhythm of their day like he belonged there. He brought over new paints for Bella's art projects, remembered her favorite bedtime stories, even learned the names of her stuffed animals. It wasn't just the gestures—it was the consistency. The quiet, steady way he wove himself into their days. Into their routines. Into their lives.

"Mommy, look..." Bella's voice rang out from the patio.

London dried her hands on a dish towel and padded barefoot outside. Bella stood proudly beside a sprawling finger-painted mural stretched across a drop cloth Patrick had laid down to protect the bricks. He'd thought of everything.

Bella beamed in a pair of old, paint-splattered overalls, her curls pulled up into a high ponytail and her hands streaked with color.

"Daddy helped me," she announced.

London's breath caught, but she quickly found her smile. The painting was a joyful swirl of blues, greens, and yellows—a garden scene with a sun wearing sunglasses and a bumblebee dancing in a bright pink tutu.

"It's beautiful, baby," she said, crouching beside Bella.

"Daddy said it should go on the fridge."

London smoothed a hand over her daughter's curls, her heart tightening in the sweetest way. "Then that's exactly where it will go."

And somehow, in that quiet moment, she realized that maybe Patrick wasn't just visiting their lives.

Maybe something was taking shape here. With them.

That night, after Bella had fallen asleep with her new bedtime story resting against her chest, London sat on the porch with a blanket wrapped around her shoulders.

The night air was cool, fragrant with jasmine and marsh grass. Stars scattered across the sky in patterns she'd never learned to name.

Her phone buzzed softly beside her, and she saw that Patrick had texted her: Did she like the book?

She fell asleep halfway through it.

That's a win.

She smiled, typing back slowly: Thank you. For everything.

A beat passed before the reply came: I'm where I want to be, London.

She didn't respond right away. She tucked her legs beneath her, pulled the blanket tighter. Her heart was racing. She could still remember the ache of him leaving. The hollow days after she'd learned she was pregnant. The fear. The anger.

And now here he was.

Patient. Present. Persistent.

London closed her eyes and let herself feel it. The longing that had never really left. The quiet comfort of his voice, the familiar cadence of his laugh. The way Bella glowed when he walked into a room.

She hadn't just wanted a partner. She'd wanted *him*. She looked at the glowing screen again.

I want to believe you.

His reply came immediately.

Then let me show you. One day at a time.

THE DAYS THAT followed fit together like pieces of a fragile puzzle slowly coming to life. Patrick embraced each moment with a quiet resolve—

he wanted to be the kind of father he himself had longed for as a boy.

His father had been a man of discipline and duty, a military man whose life was stitched together with deployments and travel. The man had loved his family—Patrick knew that. But love wasn't enough to erase the hollow spaces left by absence.

There had been birthdays without him, school plays where the empty seat was a glaring reminder, bedtime stories told by someone else. Patrick had understood why his father was gone so often, but he hadn't understood why that absence left a permanent ache inside him.

He never wanted Bella to grow up feeling that way.

So, when Bella skinned her knee in the backyard, Patrick knelt beside her and carefully placed a butterfly Band-Aid over the scrape—a small but sacred ceremony of presence. It wasn't just about fixing a scrape; it was about showing her that he was there. That he saw her. That he wouldn't leave.

At the farmers' market, Patrick arrived early, coffee in hand, offering London a quiet smile as he carried her honey jars without a word. These small acts of service were more than polite gestures— they were promises made with actions, the way his own father had failed to deliver.

Patrick was determined not to repeat that pattern.

He watched London with a tenderness that cut through his own doubts. She moved through the kitchen with care, brushing flour from Bella's nose as they baked cookies. She endured Bella's impromptu living room concerts in full princess regalia without distraction or complaint. Her attention was absolute, unwavering—a kind of love Patrick both admired and feared.

Because he knew how hard it must have been for her, too.

Sometimes when their eyes met over Bella's messy play, Patrick glimpsed the weight London carried—the past heartbreak, the quiet walls she'd built to protect herself and their daughter. It wasn't lost on him that trust was fragile. But that made each shared glance, each quiet smile, feel like a breakthrough.

After Bella was asleep, they'd sit together in the dim light, the silence heavy with unspoken memories and new hopes. Patrick's hand would drift toward hers—gentle, tentative, offering rather than demanding. And when London's fingers sometimes found his, it was like a soft balm for both their wounds.

This wasn't just about rekindling an old flame. It was about rewriting a story—his story—one where he didn't walk away again. Where he was a father who showed up, who stayed, who fought to be part of every ordinary, extraordinary moment.

Because the ache of an absent father still echoed in him.

CHAPTER TWELVE

The next afternoon was sweltering and humid. London and Cia sat at the table with the ice in their lemonade gradually melting between them.

Her sister always had a way of cutting straight to the bone. "You're not sleeping," she said bluntly, watching her with narrowed eyes over the rim of her glass.

London blinked. "What gave it away?"

Cia tilted her head. "The dark circles and the fact that you've been pushing that piece of lettuce from one side to the other for five minutes."

"Busted."

"What's going on?"

She and Cia were close—had always been—but some truths still felt too fragile, like a porcelain bowl with a hairline crack that might shatter if handled too roughly. London lowered her gaze. "Patrick being here…" she said quietly, "it's a good thing, but it's also harder than I thought it would be."

Cia didn't say anything at first. Just nodded, letting the silence expand like a safe place to land.

"I thought I had everything figured out," London said after a beat. "I had our life in this neat, manageable rhythm. And then Patrick walked back in, and everything feels so…so different."

Cia reached across the table and squeezed her hand, wordless.

"I don't want to need him," London whispered, her voice cracking. "I don't want to look forward to him knocking on the door or catching him smiling at Bella as if she's his whole world. I don't want to remember how it felt when he loved me. Because I think… I think some part of me never stopped."

The admission was a weight lifted and a wound opened all at once.

Cia sat back slowly, giving her a long, assessing look. "Is it that you don't trust *him*? Or you don't trust *yourself*?"

London blinked. The question pierced her in a place she hadn't even been guarding.

"I trust him," she said, the words falling out in a rush. "And that's the scariest part. Because the last time I trusted him, he walked away. He left without knowing I was carrying his child, and yes, that was on me, too, but he still left. And I told myself I would never let someone have that kind of power over me again."

Her throat felt tight, the tears stinging just beneath the surface now.

"I kept things safe. I kept us safe. But now he's back, and he's doing everything right. And Bella loves him already. He's folding himself into her life like he's always been there, and she doesn't even question it. But I do. I question everything."

Cia softened. "Because you remember what it felt like to be abandoned."

London nodded, swallowing. "And I know what it would do to Bella if he left again. That's the part I don't think he understands. This isn't just about him and me anymore. This is about her. Her heart. Her trust. If he disappears again…"

She didn't finish. She couldn't.

Cia let the silence hang for a moment before she spoke again. "Do you think he will?"

London opened her mouth. Closed it.

She wasn't sure. She *wanted* to believe he wouldn't. Everything about the way Patrick moved in this second chance—his patience, his gentleness, the way he looked at Bella like she was a miracle he'd been gifted after years in the desert—it all whispered *stay*.

But there was still a wound inside her that hadn't fully healed. The part of her that remembered the voicemail he left, the silence that followed, the ache of having and raising their child alone.

"I don't know," she said finally. "And that's what keeps me up at night."

Cia stood and walked around the table, wrapping her arms around London from behind. "You don't have to know today. You're allowed to take your time. You're allowed to ask him to earn it."

London leaned into the embrace, letting her sister's steady warmth anchor her. "Yeah," she whispered. "I just don't want to fall for him again and find out it's still not enough."

Cia kissed the top of her head. "Maybe this time, he falls for you harder. Maybe he already has."

She smiled faintly, tears catching on her lashes. "Wouldn't that be something?"

London sat there in the stillness, clinging to the fragile hope she hadn't dared voice out loud.

That maybe—just maybe—this wasn't the beginning of the end.

Maybe it was the beginning of something real. Again.

Something worth trusting.

Something worth risking everything for.

Later that night, the house was quiet. Bella had finally fallen asleep after demanding four stories, three sips of water, and an emergency check under the bed.

London hadn't fought it. She'd crawled under the covers with her, held her little girl close, and let the rhythmic rise and fall of her daughter's breath calm the storm still churning inside her.

She recalled Cia once saying, *sometimes strength means being brave enough to open the door.*

London padded down the hallway barefoot, the floorboards cool beneath her feet. She hesitated when she reached the living room. The lamp by the window was still on, casting a soft, amber glow.

Patrick sat on the couch, one ankle propped on his knee, flipping through one of Bella's picture books. He wasn't reading, not really. Just turning pages, lost in thought.

He looked up when he heard her.

"I didn't want to leave without saying good

night," he said. His voice was low, careful. Like he could feel the shift in the air, too.

She nodded and crossed to the chair across from him, curling her feet beneath her. "She likes having you here," London said quietly.

"I like being here," he replied without hesitation. "More than I can put into words."

There was a beat of silence. Patrick set the book down on the coffee table, then leaned forward, resting his elbows on his knees.

"I know I wasn't around in the ways you needed," he said, eyes steady. "And I won't insult you by pretending I can undo the years I missed. But I'm not going anywhere now."

London looked down at her hands, twisting the ring she always wore on her thumb. "You say that so easily."

"It's not easy," Patrick said. "It's the hardest thing I've ever had to face. Not because I don't want it—but because I know I don't get to ask you to believe it until I earn it."

She glanced up at him. "Then why keep showing up? Why try at all? You've rebuilt your life, Patrick. Why come back into ours now?"

He drew in a breath, and for a long moment, he didn't answer.

"When I was growing up," he said finally, "my dad was…there, but not really. Military. Then after he retired, he jumped into a consulting job that took him overseas all the time. He was a good man. Provided for us. Never raised his voice. But he wasn't present."

He looked away, staring out the window like he could still see his father's shadow out there somewhere.

"I spent a lot of time waiting for him to notice me," Patrick continued. "Waiting for him to show up to games. Waiting for him to ask about the song I wrote or the drawing I made. And when he didn't, I learned how to be fine without him."

London's breath caught.

Patrick met her gaze. "I didn't even realize how much that absence shaped me until I met Bella."

Emotion laced his words now. "I refuse to let Bella grow up without me."

Her throat tightened. "It's not just about showing up, Patrick. It's about staying."

"I know," he said gently. "And I will. Even if it's messy. Even if it takes time. Even if you don't take my hand every night. I'll be here."

London stared at him, her heart aching with equal parts fear and longing. The wall she'd spent years reinforcing had a crack in it now, just wide enough to let in the possibility of something more.

She didn't say yes. Not yet. But she stood and walked over to the couch.

Patrick watched her carefully, unsure.

She sat beside him—not too close, but close enough that their shoulders brushed. And then, without a word, she reached for his hand.

Their fingers threaded together, quiet and warm.

"I'm scared," she whispered.

Patrick's thumb brushed her knuckle. "Me, too. But I'm here anyway."

And in that silence, thick with things unspoken, London let herself believe that this time could be different.

THE WARM LIGHTING of the private dining room at Southwinds cast a soft glow over the elegantly set table. Patrick stood at the doorway, adjusting the cuff of his shirt as he glanced around the room. It was London who had invited him to the Worthington family dinner, and though the invitation had been casual—almost offhand—he knew it meant something. He didn't take it lightly.

This wasn't just a meal. This was entrance into a circle.

He caught sight of London arranging her purse on the back of her chair, her fitted navy dress hugging her figure in a way that had made his breath catch.

Now, though, she was busy making sure Bella's curls were in place and that her daughter knew how to behave at the grown-up table. Her smile when she saw Patrick was soft but sure. A silent reassurance. She was glad he came.

Bella clung to his hand, and Patrick noticed she didn't let go when they walked toward the table.

Kenyon, the eldest Worthington sibling and head chef at Southwinds, had the night off but held court at the far end of the table. London's brother

Aiden sat beside his wife, Tami. Shane and his wife, Ace—pregnant and radiant—held their toddler son, Shane Jr., on their laps, alternating who wrangled the little ball of energy. Cousin Oliver and his wife, Emma, had their daughter nestled between them, while Cia sat beside their cousin Louella and her husband, Noah, who managed their lively twin daughters, Kelly and Kadence. Bella sat between London and Patrick. It was a full table. Loud, warm, alive.

And yet there was a palpable space at the table where Angus Worthington Jr. once sat. As soon as they were all seated and mocktails—bright and fizzing—were served, conversation drifted toward the man who had been the center of this family.

"I swear, if Daddy were here, he'd be the first one trying to sneak one of those stuffed shrimp rolls before the rest of us said grace." Kenyon chuckled, his deep voice rich with fondness.

"Mama would've smacked his hand away, and he'd still wink at us like he got away with something," Shane added with a nostalgic grin.

"I sure would," Madelyn interjected.

"He loved food. And he loved seeing all of us around the table," Louella said softly, lifting her glass. "To Uncle Angus. Four and a half years gone, and not a day goes by I don't think of his laugh."

Tami placed a hand on Aiden's arm as she raised her glass, too. "To the patriarch."

Everyone echoed the sentiment, their glasses

raised, the clink of crystal not loud enough to mask the emotion swimming in their eyes.

Patrick felt the weight of the moment. This was a family who had lost their anchor but refused to drift. They gathered. They celebrated. They remembered.

London's gaze met his across the table. There was something raw in her expression—grief, yes, but also gratitude. Maybe for the strength her family had found in each other. Maybe because she felt safe enough to share this moment with him.

Dinner was passed around in heaping platters—roasted chicken, creamy seafood pasta, charred asparagus, and cheesy cornbread.

As conversation drifted from food to childhood memories to work stories to kids and back again, Patrick noticed how natural it all felt. How right.

Aiden cleared his throat, drawing attention. "Tami and I have something to share."

Tami laughed as everyone turned to her expectantly. "We're having a *baby...*"

Cheers erupted. Chairs scraped. Hugs were given across the table. Even Shane Jr. clapped his tiny hands.

Patrick leaned close to London. "Big night for your family."

She smiled. "They don't do anything halfway."

"No," he said, studying her profile in the candlelight. "They don't."

Her hand brushed against his. Neither pulled away. Not immediately.

Later, when dessert was brought out—warm peach cobbler with vanilla-bean ice cream—Patrick found himself in a quiet conversation with Aiden.

"You coming back into London and Bella's lives," he stated, "that's not something we take lightly."

Patrick nodded. "Neither do I."

"Just make sure you're here to stay."

"I am," Patrick said. And he meant it.

London caught his eye again, and this time the corner of her mouth lifted.

There was no question anymore.

Something had shifted.

Not just in him.

In her, too.

CHAPTER THIRTEEN

MYRA STARED OUT the window of the downtown Charleston café, her fingers wrapped tightly around the stem of her water glass. She wasn't nervous. She didn't get nervous. But there was a tightness in her chest, a coil of tension that had settled the moment she reached out to her old college roommate, Olivia Haynes, a well-respected family law attorney.

The meeting wasn't about her. It was about Patrick. It was about protecting him—from mistakes, from sentiment, and, most importantly, from heartbreak.

Olivia breezed in right on time, a crisp navy pantsuit hugging her frame, her graying hair pulled back into a no-nonsense twist. She still had the same commanding presence she did back in undergrad, the kind that made you sit straighter in your chair.

"Myra Brown. Haven't aged a day."

Myra offered a smile; one she reserved for reunions and formal occasions. "Flatterer. Thank you for meeting me. I know Sundays are usually family days."

Olivia waved off the comment. "When you said it was about your son and a custody situation, how could I say no?"

Myra nodded, carefully weighing her words.

"Patrick…he recently discovered he has a daughter. She's four."

Olivia's brow rose. "Four? That's a long time to be kept in the dark."

"Exactly," Myra said, tone clipped. "The mother never told him. And now, suddenly, she allows him into the child's life like it was always part of the plan."

Olivia leaned forward. "Is he listed on the birth certificate?"

"No. But he's started the process to get it amended."

Olivia scribbled something into her notepad. "That changes things. A lot. So, what does he want to do? File for legal custody?"

Myra hesitated, then took a small sip of water. "He's still processing everything. But he's building a bond with the little girl. She adores him. And I—we—want to make sure that no matter what happens between him and the mother, he doesn't lose that relationship."

Olivia studied her. "Myra. Has Patrick asked you to investigate this?"

Myra's smile returned, this one tight and practiced. "Not in so many words. But I know my son. He's overwhelmed. And frankly, I don't trust this woman not to turn the tables if he doesn't dance to her tune."

Olivia sat back. "Well. Here's the good news. South Carolina favors biological parents having relationships with their children. The bad news? If there's no formal custody order, it's a free-for-all."

"So, she could keep him from seeing Bella. Just...like that."

"Technically yes. Unless he petitions the court for custody or visitation and establishes paternity."

"He did a test," Myra said quickly. That wasn't true, despite her insisting he have a DNA test done. "Privately. It's his child. There's no doubt."

"Good. Then the next step would be to file a petition to establish paternity formally with the family court. From there, he can ask for visitation, even shared custody if he wants."

Myra leaned in. "Could he sue her? For not telling him? For keeping his daughter a secret?"

Olivia blinked. "Sue? Not successfully. There are moral implications, sure, and it might sway a judge in a custody hearing. But there are no legal damages unless he can prove that being deprived of that knowledge harmed him in a quantifiable way."

Myra frowned. "He missed four years. First words. First steps."

"And a judge may be sympathetic to that. But you can't win damages for emotional loss in this kind of case."

"Still," she murmured, eyes narrowing, "it says something about her. About her judgment. Doesn't it?"

"It can," Olivia said carefully. "But Myra, I need to ask. What does Patrick want? Not *you*. Patrick.

Does he want shared custody? Full custody? To fight her in court?"

She hesitated. She knew what Patrick wanted. He wanted peace. He wanted the family he never thought he'd have. He wanted London.

And that terrified her.

Myra let out a slow breath and admitted what she hadn't even told herself fully. "Olivia, I just know that London isn't the right woman for my son."

Olivia blinked but said nothing, allowing her the space to go on.

"This woman kept something so monumental from him. Something that could've changed the entire trajectory of his life. And now? Now she wants to act like she didn't take that choice from him. How can I trust her not to make another decision that excludes him? Or, worse, hurts Bella?"

"You think she's dangerous?"

"Not in a physical sense," Myra admitted. "But emotionally? Yes. She's reckless. And my son is vulnerable right now. He wants to do the right thing, and she knows exactly how to use that against him."

Olivia studied her carefully. "Well, if you truly want to help him, then the best thing you can do is make sure he has legal standing. Paternity. Visitation. Custody arrangements. Once those are in place, she can't just cut him off without a court's involvement."

Myra nodded slowly, her gaze drifting back to the window. "That's what I want. To make sure

Bella has her father. And Patrick has a voice. No matter what happens with… London."

They made polite conversation after that, but Myra's mind buzzed. She barely heard Olivia's updates about her law firm. All Myra could think about was London—and how neatly she'd inserted herself back into Patrick's life.

It wasn't that Myra didn't believe in second chances. But she knew her son. Knew how deeply he felt. He had inherited that from his father. One moment of softness, and he'd throw himself into something headfirst.

He was vulnerable now. Vulnerable in a way he hadn't been since college.

She had tried to protect him once before, urging him to focus on his career, to put space between himself and a relationship that would tie him to one place too soon. She hadn't done it out of malice. She had done it out of fear.

Fear that he would give up everything for a woman who might not stay.

Now the stakes were higher. A child was involved. And if London's feelings changed? If she met someone else? If she decided to cut Patrick out?

No. Myra wouldn't allow it. Her son deserved stability. Deserved rights. Deserved protection.

Even if he didn't ask for it.

Even if he resented her later.

She would make sure the path he walked wasn't clouded by emotion.

She would handle this.

Because mothers—the good ones, the strong ones—didn't wait to be asked.

They acted.

THE QUIET HUM of the dishwasher and the low melody of an old R&B record set the rhythm for the evening. The kitchen light cast a warm glow over the countertops, where remnants of dinner—a roasted chicken, mashed potatoes, steamed green beans, and garlic bread—sat cooling in the pans.

London leaned against the sink as she watched Patrick pour two glasses of wine.

Her home felt different with him in it.

He handed her a glass. Their fingers brushed, and her pulse jumped. "To quiet nights and simple joys," he said.

London clinked her glass to his, eyes never leaving his. "To us."

She had loved this man since college. Since their long, meandering conversations beneath campus oaks. Since the nights he walked her home after library study sessions, always stopping a few feet from her door like he wasn't sure if he was allowed closer. She had loved him even when she let him go.

Tonight, watching him move around her kitchen with ease, laughing about how he always burned the garlic bread no matter how hard he tried, she realized how deep that love still ran. How the years hadn't dulled it. If anything, time had carved it into her more deeply, leaving it permanent.

"You didn't burn it tonight," she said, smiling as she leaned against the counter.

"Miracles happen," he replied with a grin.

They ate together at her dining table, knees brushing beneath the surface. The conversation was light at first—Bella's sleepover, her new obsession with unicorn puzzles, Patrick's work drama. But as the plates emptied and the wineglasses refilled, the air between them shifted.

London studied him as he talked. The curve of his jaw, the way his eyes crinkled when he smiled, the faint shadow of a scar near his temple from a college bike accident. She knew his stories, his laugh, his silences. And still, being near him felt new.

"You know," she said softly, running her finger along the rim of her glass, "I used to imagine nights like this. You and me, sharing dinner, the quiet kind. Not rushed or scheduled. Just…here."

Patrick looked at her, eyes softening. "I used to imagine that, too."

Silence settled between them, not uncomfortable but full. Full of what had been missed.

Full of what might still be.

"We were different then," she said. "Scared. Unsure. And then life happened."

"Yeah," he said, his voice low. "Life."

London stood slowly, carrying their plates to the sink. She felt him behind her before she heard him. His hands came to rest on her hips, gentle but grounding. She leaned back against him.

"I think about the time we lost," she whispered. "All the ways I should have told you about Bella sooner."

Patrick turned her gently in his arms. "I was hurt. Not gonna lie about that. But I understand. You did what you thought was best."

Tears pricked at her eyes. "I don't want to lose this again."

He cupped her face, his thumb brushing her cheek. "Then we won't. We take it slow. We figure it out."

She nodded, swallowing the lump in her throat. "I can do that."

His lips met hers in answer, tender at first, then deeper, more certain. The kiss was years in the making—sweet with longing, fierce with promise.

Later, they curled up on the couch, wrapped in the soft throw blanket that had once belonged to her mother. London rested her head on his chest, listening to the steady beat of his heart.

"This feels so perfect," she murmured. "You and me like this."

Patrick kissed the top of her head. "It is."

And for the first time in a long while, London believed it.

She didn't want to move. The weight of his arm draped across her back was grounding, the steady cadence of his breathing syncing with her own. The record had ended, leaving behind a soft hiss and the ticking of the clock above the mantel. It was late, but neither of them seemed in a hurry to chase sleep.

He reached up and tucked a curl behind her ear, his fingers lingering on her cheek. "We can't reclaim those lost years, but we have this moment. Right now. And maybe more tomorrows."

She leaned in and kissed him gently, savoring the moment.

Nestled in his arms, she finally allowed herself to relax. It was the kind of relaxation that came when love was no longer just a distant dream but a life rediscovered.

London shifted slightly, her cheek brushing against the soft fabric of Patrick's shirt. She felt his chest rise and fall, the rhythmic motion as soothing as waves lapping against the shore. For a long time, they remained silent. They didn't need words.

Their hearts spoke for them.

PATRICK STOOD IN the center of his cottage, one hand resting on the back of the couch, the other clutching a bottle of water that had long gone warm. Outside, a soft drizzle pattered against the windowpane, painting streaks over the skyline of Polk Island.

The weight of realization settled into Patrick's bones.

He loved her.

He still loved London Worthington.

It wasn't a sudden epiphany. It was the kind of truth that had been slowly blooming under the surface, subtle but relentless, winding itself through the moments they'd shared since reconnecting. From Bella's delighted giggles as they baked cookies to the quiet glances between him and London across dinner tables and playground benches. From the tension that once marked their interactions to the softness now shaping their time together.

He'd thought he'd moved on. Tried to. Dated casually. Focused on work. Poured himself into everything except the aching space she'd left behind. But nothing fit. No one filled it. And now being back in her world, to find London waiting with a hesitant smile and honest eyes—he couldn't deny it any longer.

He wanted more.

Not just co-parenting. Not just friendship.

He wanted them.

The thought made his pulse quicken. It wasn't about rushing. It wasn't about fixing what had gone wrong with a grand gesture. It was about honoring what had always been true.

He needed a ring.

The decision felt enormous and grounding all at once.

The following Saturday, Patrick found himself in the historic South End district of Charleston, the cobblestone sidewalks slick with rain. He walked past the galleries and cafés until he reached the corner boutique he'd read about online—Sasha & Fields Jewelers. Small, family-owned, known for custom work and thoughtful service. It felt like the kind of place where a choice like this was taken seriously.

The bell above the door chimed as he stepped inside. A wave of warmth greeted him, along with the soft scent of sandalwood and the gleam of glass cases lined with velvet. An older woman with silver-streaked braids and wire-rimmed glasses looked up from behind the counter.

"Welcome in," she said, her voice gentle. "Looking for something special?"

Patrick nodded, removing his cap. "Yeah. I think I'm ready to propose."

Her smile widened. "Then we better find something that speaks for you. I'm Sasha. You can call me that. And you are…?"

"Patrick. Patrick Brown."

"Nice to meet you, Patrick." She studied him kindly. "Tell me about her."

He didn't hesitate.

"Her name's London. We met in college. Reconnected after…a lot of time. She's smart, strong. Protective. But she's got this soft heart. She's the mother of my daughter, and… I've loved her for longer than I care to admit."

They spent the next hour exploring settings and stones. Patrick bypassed the more traditional cuts—London wasn't flashy—and focused on elegant, timeless designs. Something that would feel like her. Eventually, Sasha pulled out a vintage-inspired setting with a salt-and-pepper oval-cut diamond on a slim platinum band, accented by two inlaid baguettes.

"This one," he said, breath catching.

Sasha nodded. "Understated but stunning. Just like she sounds."

He asked to hold it.

As the ring sat between his fingers, Patrick saw more than just a proposal. He saw Bella's face lighting up when he told her, the way London's eyes might well with tears. He saw holidays, late-night talks, ordinary mornings, laughter in the kitchen.

He saw home.

"Wrap it up," he said, voice hoarse. "I want to take it with me. I notice you also do custom wedding bands."

"We do," Sasha confirmed.

He told her his vision for their wedding bands.

"I'll send over some graphics for your approval."

Patrick smiled in gratitude.

Back in his truck, parked beneath the steady mist of the afternoon rain, the small black box sat on the passenger seat like a secret, like a promise.

He wasn't proposing tonight. Patrick knew that.

But the ring was a symbol of intent. A step forward. He wasn't just trying to win London back. He wanted a future—one shaped by love, patience, and the truth they'd danced around for years.

He glanced at his reflection in the rearview mirror. There was a steadiness in his eyes he hadn't seen before.

Whatever came next, he was ready.

For her.
For Bella.
For all of it.

THE RHYTHMIC HUM of the dryer and the faint chatter of birds outside filled the quiet of the laundry room as London methodically folded a stack of Bella's tiny T-shirts. Her hands moved out of habit—fold, smooth, stack—while her mind wandered, untethered and insistent.

She could hear them through the open window—Bella's bright laughter carried on the breeze, Patrick's deeper voice trailing close behind as he pretended to be the monster chasing her around the yard. The sound of them, together, had become something she'd grown used to. Something she'd come to depend on.

And maybe that was what scared her the most.

London pressed her palm over the warm cotton of a freshly dried towel and let her eyes fall shut for a beat. She'd been here before, hadn't she? Letting him in, letting herself believe that the ground beneath her feet was steady. That love could be safe.

But the past had taught her otherwise. Love could crack open the floor, send you plummeting into a free fall with nothing to catch you at the bottom.

She'd spent years building walls, carefully stacking every stone to protect what was left of her heart. Even when Patrick first came back, even when he smiled at Bella like she was the sun and the sky, London had told herself to be careful.

Her hand stilled over a pair of Bella's polka-dotted leggings, the fabric soft beneath her fingertips, and she thought about all the ways Patrick had chipped away at her defenses—not with grand declarations or sweeping gestures, but with the quiet, consistent rhythm of showing up.

He hadn't missed a single lunch with Bella, even when work tugged at his attention. He knew which stuffed animal Bella couldn't sleep without, and which bedtime story needed three full readings before she finally closed her eyes.

And it wasn't just what he did for Bella. It was the way he saw London, too. The way he defended her when his mother's sharp comments tried to burrow under her skin. He didn't ask London to excuse it. He didn't expect her to bend or to shrink to make anyone else comfortable.

And she realized now, sitting cross-legged on the laundry room floor with a half-folded towel in her lap, that she had been waiting for Patrick to fail.

For him to back away.

For him to love their daughter but not love her enough.

But he hadn't.

Each day, he pushed his roots a little deeper into their lives—the morning coffees he brought without asking, the way he reorganized her linen closet because he knew she couldn't stand a messy stack, the small, quiet ways he told her repeatedly that he wasn't going anywhere.

London swallowed hard, her chest tightening

against the truth that had been building for weeks, maybe longer.

She still loved him.

Not in the cautious, tentative way she thought she might, but in the fierce, breath-stealing way she had years ago. And this time, she wasn't waiting for him to choose her.

Because he already had.

Her walls had been falling, slowly, deliberately, brick by reluctant brick, and somehow—between finger-painting afternoons and family breakfasts— he'd walked right into the center of her life again.

She reached for one of Patrick's T-shirts that had found its way into the laundry pile, worn soft and familiar. Pressing the fabric to her chest, London closed her eyes, allowing herself—just for a moment—to lean into the weight of what she felt.

She didn't have to hold her breath anymore.

He was here. And she believed him now.

Believed in the steadiness of him.

Believed in the shape of the family they were becoming.

A tear slipped down her cheek, unbidden but not unwelcome. She hadn't realized how tightly she'd been gripping her fear until it began to loosen, until the possibility of loving him fully no longer felt like a risk but like a refuge.

Patrick had earned his place—not by demanding it, but by patiently building it.

The dryer buzzed, a gentle reminder that life was still moving forward, still unfolding.

London set the folded towel aside and exhaled, slow and steady.

She was done bracing for impact.

She was ready to love him without the weight of the past pressing against her ribs. Ready to stop measuring his commitment against old wounds. Ready to believe that this time, it wasn't temporary.

Because some people didn't just come back.

Some people came home.

And as she rose to her feet, gathering the last of the laundry, London realized she wasn't waiting for the other shoe to drop anymore.

She was ready to live. To love. To let him in completely.

For the first time in a long time, she folded that truth carefully, tenderly, and tucked it away—not as a guarded secret, but as something she intended to give him, fully and without hesitation.

She smiled softly to herself as she carried the basket toward the bedroom, the weight of her fear finally, blessedly, left behind.

CHAPTER FOURTEEN

THE AUGUST SUN filtered softly through the blinds of Madelyn Worthington's sunroom, casting golden streaks over the elegantly set table. The space, filled with the scent of peonies and warm lemon scones, buzzed with laughter and warm chatter as family members gathered to celebrate Ace and the upcoming arrival of her and Shane's second baby.

London paused at the threshold of the room, her hand grazing the doorway as she took it all in. The table was covered in ivory linen and adorned with soft peach and blush florals. A charcuterie board the size of a small canoe rested near the center, overflowing with vibrant fruit, cheeses, and delicate crackers. Madelyn, regal as ever in a linen dress and pearls, fluttered around the room like a benevolent queen bee, making sure everyone had tea, mocktails, or prosecco in hand.

"London…c'mon in, sugar," her mother called, waving her over with a smile. "Ace insists on sitting by you."

She smiled and crossed the room to where her sister-in-law sat, radiant despite her gentle protests about all the attention.

Ace wore a pale blue wrap dress that hugged her baby bump, her curls pinned up in a loose crown that made her look like a goddess in repose. Her son, Shane Jr., currently preoccupied with stacking sugar cubes with his cousin Kadence at the kid's table, glanced up and beamed at London.

"Hey, London," Ace greeted warmly. "I'm so glad you came."

She leaned down and hugged her, then settled into the chair beside her. "Of course I came. You tried to pretend this baby didn't deserve to be celebrated, and I couldn't let that slide."

Ace gave a sheepish smile. "You know how it is with the second. I figured one big shower the first time around was enough."

"Well, your mother-in-law clearly didn't agree," London teased, giving Madelyn a wink.

"Not one bit," Madelyn called from across the room. "Every baby deserves to be welcomed with love."

As women from both the Worthington and Martin sides of the family mingled—Louella, Emma, even a cousin who'd driven in from Raleigh— London found herself slowly relaxing into the rhythm of the afternoon. It was a kind of rhythm she hadn't always allowed herself to enjoy in recent years. Not with everything that had happened. But today felt different.

Maybe it was the way Ace kept resting her hand over her belly with unconscious tenderness. Or how Tami—glowing in her own right now that her pregnancy was official—kept sneaking salted crackers when she thought no one was looking. Or how her mother sat back during the meal, pride shining in her eyes as she watched her daughters-in-law chat and tease one another.

London couldn't help but feel the ache of something both old and new. The kind of ache that whispered of belonging and distance in the same breath.

"You okay?" Ace asked quietly, breaking through her thoughts.

London blinked and smiled. "Yeah. I'm just… taking it all in. It's a beautiful day."

Ace nudged her gently. "You're allowed to love again, even if it scares you."

She looked at her sister-in-law, a startled expression on her face. "What do you mean?"

Ace shrugged, her expression soft. "I see the way Patrick looks at you. And the way you look at him when you think no one notices."

"I thought we were here to celebrate you."

"We are," Ace stated. "But truth is truth."

Before London could respond, Madelyn rose with a tinkling of her glass. "Ladies, if I may have a moment. I just want to say a few words about why we're here today."

The room quieted. London glanced around at the sea of faces—her family, by blood and by love—and felt the emotions swell in her throat.

"Ace," Madelyn began, turning toward her daughter-in-law with warmth, "you've given so much of yourself to this family. You've brought joy, strength, laughter, and a fierce protective heart for this family."

A round of soft chuckles followed.

"But more than that," Madelyn continued, her voice dipping into something more tender, "you reminded us of all what it means to build love. To show up for it. Not just in the big gestures, but in the small, everyday things. The way you love your husband and your son. The way you care for this family. That's worth celebrating. Every time. Every child. Every moment."

London glanced down at her lap, feeling a wave of emotion. Tears were on the brink of spilling over. Perhaps it was the speech or the way Ace reached out to hold her hand beneath the table. Or maybe it was just being surrounded by women who cherished love, family, and the importance of being present.

As the applause faded and everyone raised their glasses in a toast, London felt something shift deep in her chest.

Later, after the plates were cleared and the lemon tart had been devoured, London stood by the bay window, sipping on her ginger-peach mocktail, watching as the children played outside. She sensed someone approaching before she heard the voice.

"You look like your thoughts are loud."

She turned to find Tami beside her.

London gave her a small smile. "I didn't mean to get all in my head. Just…this is a lot. A good kind of lot."

Nodding, she responded, "I get it. Every new chapter comes with echoes of the last one."

"I used to wonder if I was ever allowed to write a new one. If I deserved it."

Tami looked at her then, with a kind of knowing that only sisters-in-law who'd become sisters could share. "You're not the same woman you were back then, London. While I don't really know Patrick, I get the sense that he's not the same person either. But the love—that didn't disappear. It just got buried. And now it's rising again. Don't be afraid to let it."

London swallowed hard, the emotion caught in her throat. She glanced down at her hands, fingers wrapped around her glass. "I do love him, Tami. These past few weeks have been perfect."

The room filled with laughter again as someone told a story about Angus Jr., their late patriarch. London looked up, her heart squeezing.

"He would've loved this," she whispered.

Tami nodded. "He's still here. In all of this."

And somehow, London believed it. In the joy, the teasing, the shared memories and open hearts—Angus Jr.'s presence lingered. And maybe, just maybe, there was space for something new to grow. Something whole. Something lasting.

As the luncheon wound down and everyone began hugging their goodbyes, London felt Ace squeeze her hand once more.

"When love shows up," Ace said softly, "let it."

And this time, London nodded. "I am."

She was ready to try.

Patrick sat in his home office, the morning sun filtering through the blinds. The place was quiet—the kind of quiet that made you think too much, feel too much. His laptop was open, but he hadn't touched the keys in twenty minutes. His phone sat face-up beside it, the screen dark, reflecting the furrow in his brow.

He picked it up, thumb hovering over the name of his agent, Miriam Dorsey. He exhaled and tapped the screen.

"Patrick Brown," Miriam answered, her voice brisk, polished as always. "I was just about to call you. You got the new contract, right? It shows that it was delivered at eight sixteen this morning."

Patrick leaned back in his chair, dragging a hand over his face. "Yeah, I got it."

"And? It's a generous offer. This is a good deal, Patrick."

"It is," he said slowly, choosing his words with care. "But I'm not taking it."

There was a beat of silence on the other end. "Come again?"

"I meant what I said when I told you that I'm stepping back. Taking some time off."

"Patrick."

He could hear her sit up straighter, even through the phone. "Do you even realize what you're walking away from? You've been granted exclusive access to the Sahel-conflict corridor. The *real* story. Not the sanitized wire reports. You'd be embedded with nomadic tribes caught between warlords, terror cells, and the encroaching desert. No one else is getting in, Patrick. This is career-defining. People would kill for this chance."

"I know." His voice was low, almost regretful. "The last untold story. The one that could change everything."

"Exactly."

He rubbed his chest, feeling the familiar ache settle there. "But right now, I'm not the guy to tell it. I can't chase ghosts in war zones when I haven't even faced my own."

She was quiet, then said, more gently, "Is everything okay?"

"I want to spend time with my daughter. With London."

He could practically hear her blink. Miriam had always been supportive, but she was also pragmatic. A strategist. She measured everything in terms of career trajectory.

"Bella's four," he said. "I missed the first few years of her life, Miriam."

She let out a slow breath. "This industry moves fast, Patrick. Taking time off now could mean losing momentum."

"Then let it. If I lose momentum, I'll get it back. I'm not walking away forever. Just for now."

There was a long silence, then: "You sound certain."

"I am."

He ended the call with a strange sense of relief and unease intertwined. Setting the phone down, he stared at the screen for a few seconds before closing the laptop altogether.

But as certain as he'd sounded, Patrick knew there was a sliver of doubt lodged deep inside him. Not about Bella. Never about her. But about London. About them.

He was so close to proposing.

The ring was in a box, hidden at the back of his sock drawer like some vulnerable secret.

But every time he reached for that box, something inside him pulled back.

They hadn't really talked about the future. Not clearly. Not with timelines or definitions. London welcomed him into her home. Into her life. They laughed, cooked, watched documentaries and movies. But was she ready for forever?

Was she just adjusting to co-parenting? Was she still learning to trust him again?

He didn't want to assume. He didn't want to take a beautiful, fragile thing and pressure it into permanence before it was ready.

So, he waited.

Later that afternoon, he found himself at a park near London's place. It was the one with the huge oak trees and the turtle pond Bella loved. She was at preschool, and London was working, but Patrick needed to walk, to think. He watched a father push a stroller down the path while holding his toddler's hand, and something inside him stirred—longing, peace, fear.

He sat on a bench and closed his eyes.

The prayer wasn't fancy. It wasn't even fully formed. Just a breath, a reaching.

I want to do this right. I want to be a good man. For Bella. For London. For myself. But I don't know what comes next.

He didn't expect an answer. But a quiet sense of relief washed through him.

When he got back to his cottage, he took the ring out of the drawer and held it in his palm. The stone caught the light, throwing shards of light onto the ceiling.

"Not yet," he whispered. "But soon."

He placed it back carefully.

And then he picked up his phone and texted London.

Made a decision today. Hope I can tell you about it over dinner tonight.

Her reply came quickly.

I'd like that. Just me, or should I bring our favorite third wheel?

Just you. I want you to myself for a bit.

As he cleaned up his kitchen and pulled out ingredients to cook, Patrick realized something.

He might not have all the answers. But he was learning how to ask the right questions.

And for now, that was enough.

LONDON ARRIVED JUST after seven, dressed in jeans and a lavender top that brought out the warm undertones in her skin. Her locs was swept up in a loose bun, and she smiled as soon as Patrick opened the door.

"Mmm…something smells amazing," she said, stepping inside.

"Garlic-butter salmon and lemon risotto," Patrick said, ushering her in. "I figured I needed to pull out a little culinary charm since I'm stealing you away tonight."

She grinned. "I have to confess that the way to my heart is definitely through a well-cooked meal."

They settled into the small dining nook, the soft flicker of candles casting warm shadows between them.

Patrick watched her, feeling the weight of what he needed to say pressing against his ribs.

"I spoke with my agent earlier today," he said finally, breaking the quiet.

London looked up, her wineglass paused midair. "Yeah? About what?"

He exhaled, resting his forearms on the table. "She offered me this assignment. Big one. Career-making."

London set her glass down, curiosity sparking in her eyes. "What kind of assignment?"

"They were sending me into the Sahel. It's this stretch in Africa where villages are literally getting squeezed to death. The desert's creeping in from one side, and on the other, you've got warlords, terrorists, human traffickers—just layers of violence and poverty that most people don't even know exist." He rubbed the back of his neck, the enormity of it still sitting heavy on him. "Nobody's been able to get in. Not journalists, not aid workers. They were going to embed me with some of the nomadic tribes still moving through the region. I would've been the first to document it up close."

London's eyes widened, her wine momentarily forgotten. "That sounds...huge. Dangerous, but huge."

"Yeah," he said, voice low. "The kind of story people spend their whole lives chasing. The kind that changes how the world sees things."

She leaned in, searching his face. "So, when are you leaving?"

"I turned it down."

Her lips parted in surprise. "You *what*?"

"I know," he said quickly. "It doesn't make sense on paper. I've spent years running toward stories like that, but something shifted. I don't want to just *document* life anymore. I want to actually *live* mine."

London sat back, her expression softening as the weight of his words settled between them. "Are you sure about this, Patrick?"

He nodded, a small, almost relieved smile tugging at his lips. "I'm ready to choose a different story now—this one with you and Bella."

She didn't speak right away, just turned her palm to meet his, fingers lacing through his.

"I want to be here," he said.

Her eyes glistened, and for a second, he worried she might cry. But then she smiled, soft and sure.

They ate slowly, talking about little things—Bella's preschool art project, London's new customer, a grocery store in Charleston. But under every word was a current of something deeper. Something lasting.

After dinner, they moved to the couch. Patrick held her close, her head resting on his chest.

"Do you ever think about…what comes next?" he asked.

"All the time," she said softly.

"And?"

"And I think we're writing it one moment at a time."

Patrick kissed her temple and whispered, "I like that."

Later, after she'd gone and the dishes were washed, he went back to the ring.

Not yet, he thought again.

But soon. Very soon.

Because now, he believed in the promise the ring held—not just of forever, but of a love rooted in presence, in patience, in possibility.

And Patrick was ready for all of it.

CHAPTER FIFTEEN

MYRA SAT AT the window of her Savannah brownstone. Outside, the Spanish moss swayed in the breeze like ghosts whispering secrets through the oak trees. She had lived here nearly thirty-five years, but something about this night felt different. Heavier. More decisive.

She was expecting Olivia to show up any moment with the papers. Custody papers. Joint physical custody, drawn up with expertise and surgical precision, ensuring that Patrick would never again be shut out of his daughter's life.

She hadn't told him yet.

This was a mother's preemptive strike.

Myra sighed and pressed the wineglass to her lips, then set it down without drinking. Her nerves wouldn't allow it. She stood and crossed the room, the rustle of her silk blouse the only sound as she moved to the fireplace where a photo of Patrick—fresh-faced, grinning in his high school graduation gown—stood framed in antique silver.

He had been brilliant that day. Bright with promise. She remembered the way he hugged her afterward, so tightly it had hurt, whispering, *Thank you for believing in me*.

And she had. Every step. Even when he'd left Savannah for college. Even when he'd dated a woman she hadn't approved of. Even when he moved to New York.

But what London had given Patrick—what she'd given Bella—was grace. And stability. And Myra had seen something bloom in her son since reconnecting with the mother of his child. A quiet joy. A steadiness.

Still, she worried.

Not about London's character anymore, but about her choices. About the weight she carried as a mother, a business owner, a woman who had raised Bella largely on her own. Myra knew how hard it was to let go of control once you'd been the only anchor. And while London had made room for Patrick in Bella's life, that room wasn't yet cemented by the law.

Which was why Olivia had drawn up the papers.

The doorbell rang, breaking her reverie. Myra moved to answer it, her heels clicking against the polished floor.

"You're early," she said as Olivia stepped inside, a leather portfolio under her arm.

"Traffic wasn't as bad as I thought," Olivia replied. She kissed Myra's cheek. "And I figured you could use the company."

They settled into the parlor, and Myra poured a glass of wine for Olivia. The envelope remained untouched on the table.

"He's going to be angry," Myra said softly.

Olivia arched a brow. "Patrick?"

"Yes. He'll say I overstepped."

"Did you?"

Myra didn't answer right away. She stared out the window, watching as dusk began to settle.

"I'm his mother," she said finally. "And I've seen what it's like when fathers are left on the outside. I saw it with my brother. He withered. Never recovered from being sidelined in his kids' lives after the divorce. I won't let that happen to Patrick."

Olivia sipped her tea. "Do you think London would actually block him out again?"

"No," Myra admitted. "I don't. But feelings change. Life gets messy. And if something ever happened to her…or if she got scared and decided Bella was better off in one place…this gives Patrick legal standing."

Olivia studied her. "You're doing this out of love. But if he refuses to file them, are you prepared to let it go?"

Myra hesitated. "I'll cross that bridge if we come to it."

They sat in silence a moment before Olivia reached into her portfolio and pulled out a second set of papers. "I brought an alternate version, too. One that simply affirms shared custody as it currently stands, without the joint physical requirement. It's less aggressive, more collaborative."

Myra nodded, grateful for her friend's foresight.

Later that night, long after Olivia had gone and the crickets had begun their nightly song, Robert had gone to bed already, but she wasn't sleepy. Myra sat alone with the documents spread across the dining table. She read each clause carefully, weighing not just the legality but the emotional impact.

Patrick was finally grounded again. He was doing the right things and asking the right questions, even if he hadn't yet asked the big one Myra knew was coming—the one that involved a ring and a lifetime.

However, she prayed fervently that it wouldn't come to that. She didn't want London as a daughter-in-law. Myra just wanted Patrick to protect his role as Bella's father.

She pulled out a sheet of stationery and began to write a note to him. Not an ultimatum. Not even a plea. Just a mother's heart on paper.

Dearest Patrick, I know you may not agree with the way I've handled this, but I pray you can understand the spirit behind it. My only concern is you—and Bella. You are her father. Not by chance, not by convenience, but by blood, by devotion, by every sacrifice you've made to show up for her. That bond is sacred, but it also needs to be protected.

Patrick, I need to believe you're not considering marrying London just to keep your place in Bella's life. You don't need to tether yourself to a woman who, despite her charm, has always kept her own interests at the forefront. Let's not pretend otherwise—London's company is thriving. She's built something impressive, and the courts will see her as stable, successful, and capable. Add to that her deep family roots here. The Worthing-

tons practically have Polk Island written in stone. They've owned the Polk Island Hotel for generations, they've built their name here, their history is baked into this place. Whether you like it or not, that carries weight.

And you, my son, may not get a fair shot if you aren't careful.

This is not about control. It's about legacy. About ensuring Bella always knows where she comes from, that her father's place in her life is secure and unquestionable—not something she'll have to fight to understand later.

Please don't let fear—or guilt—push you into a choice that could cost you more than you realize.

With all my love, Mama

She folded the letter and tucked it inside the envelope with the less aggressive version of the custody agreement. Then she sealed it and addressed it to Patrick.

Tomorrow she would mail it to him.

She sat back, closed her eyes, and let the sound of Savannah's night winds wrap around her like an old hymn. She had done what she could.

The rest was in his hands now.

PATRICK STOOD IN the kitchen of his cottage, sleeves rolled to his elbows, hands deep in a mixing bowl. He could've hired a chef or taken London to the fanciest rooftop restaurant in Charleston, but none of that felt right. This had to be intimate. Personal. Them.

He tasted the sauce simmering on the stove, adjusted the seasoning, and smiled.

Everything needed to be perfect tonight. He'd set the table himself with fresh lilies—London's favorite—candles flickering softly, the playlist cued up with the soundtrack of their college years and new songs they'd discovered together more recently. Bella was spending the night with Shane and Ace, giggling about slumber-party plans when Patrick dropped her off.

He needed this evening to be about just the two of them.

For a week now, he'd been holding back. He'd had the ring tucked away like a secret too fragile to bring into the open. There had been doubt. Not because he didn't love her—he loved her more now than he ever had before—but because he didn't want to misread the space they were in. He wanted to propose, but he wanted it to mean something lasting. Not a bandage. Not a promise too early. But something rooted. Something real.

And now he knew it was the right time.

Not because things were perfect. But because they were honest.

It had been the little things. The way London made space for him in her home—not just physically, but emotionally. She left him notes sometimes, just a quick *You're a great dad* or *Dinner was amazing.*

She didn't guilt him for time missed with Bella, but she encouraged every new moment he took.

He caught her watching him sometimes when he was playing with their daughter, and her expression was soft, wondering.

She trusted him again.

That trust was what sealed it for him.

The buzzer rang, and his heart leapt. He wiped his hands and buzzed her in.

When he opened the door, there she was, a vision in blue, hair pinned back loosely. She smiled when she saw the candles behind him and the table set for two.

"What's all this?" she asked, stepping inside.

He leaned in and kissed her gently. "Dinner. And maybe the start of forever."

She blinked, startled but touched.

They ate slowly, talking about Bella's new fascination with dinosaurs, about Ace's upcoming delivery, about the random things that made up their everyday. Patrick kept watching her, memorizing the curve of her smile, the way her eyes crinkled when she laughed.

When dinner was over, he didn't rush. They moved to the couch, wineglasses in hand, soft music playing in the background. She curled into his side the way she always used to in college, and it hit him how far they'd come. From dorm room debates to co-parenting a four-year-old to rebuilding something they once believed they'd lost.

"London," he said quietly, drawing back just enough to look into her eyes.

"Hmm?"

"I need to ask you something. Something important."

She sat up slightly, sensing the shift in his tone.

He stood, heart hammering, and reached into his pocket. He dropped to one knee.

Her hand flew to her mouth.

"Patrick…"

"Let me say this…" he began, steadying his voice as his heart pounded. "I've loved you since college. Even when we drifted apart, even when life pulled us in different directions, I've always carried you with me. And now…now we have Bella. We have something tangible, something precious I don't ever want to lose."

He pulled out the ring box and opened it between them, revealing the salt-and-pepper diamond ring that caught the candlelight and shimmered with quiet elegance.

London gasped, her eyes lighting up instantly, her hand flying to her chest. "Patrick…you remembered."

Of course he remembered. Years ago, when they were young and dreaming about futures they couldn't yet see, she'd told him she loved the imperfect beauty of salt-and-pepper diamonds. She'd said they looked like they'd already survived something.

Patrick's throat tightened, but he pressed on. "You've shown me grace, London. You allowed me to find my way back to you. You let me be a father to Bella. You made room for me in the life you built—without ever making me feel like an outsider. You laugh with me. You challenge me. You inspire me to be better."

His voice softened, vulnerable now. "I have to ask you…do you still love me?"

Tears shimmered in her eyes as she nodded, her voice trembling. "Yes. I never stopped."

He took her hand gently, sliding the ring onto her finger. "Then marry me. Let's create something our daughter can be proud of. Let's build it together. As a family."

"Yes," she whispered, her smile breaking through her tears. "Yes, I'll marry you."

He stood up, and their embrace was tender, the salt-and-pepper diamond sparkling between them as soft music and candlelight wrapped around the moment.

Patrick knew, without question, he'd made the right choice.

Not because it was flawless.

Not because it followed some perfect plan.

But because it was real. Hard-earned. Fought for. Proven.

It was love that had weathered storms and still chose to stay.

And this time, it was forever.

LONDON WOKE TO soft morning light slanting through the curtains of her bedroom. For a long moment, she lay still beneath the pale sheets, listening to the quiet rhythm of the house, the occasional creak of settling floorboards, the distant hum of traffic. It was the kind of morning that whispered of peace, of a world just waking up.

Her eyes drifted to her left hand, resting near her face on the pillow. The ring caught the light immediately.

Her breath caught.

It hadn't been a dream.

Patrick had proposed.

She rolled onto her back slowly, hand resting on her chest now, staring at the ceiling while tears welled in her eyes. She didn't cry often. Not like this. But something about the way her heart ached and bloomed at the same time felt too big for her chest to contain.

She remembered every second of the night before—the way Patrick had lit candles around the backyard patio, soft jazz playing through the speakers. The way he'd made her laugh over dinner.

And then he spoke.

No fancy speeches. No sweeping declarations. Just Patrick, steady and sincere.

He had loved her in college. He had loved her in memory. But last night, he told her he loved her now. The version of her who had survived heartbreak and disappointment. The woman who had carried their daughter alone and never once used that to shame him. The woman who had let him back in without conditions.

He had looked her in the eye and asked if she still loved him.

She had.

She did.

More than she ever thought possible.

London pressed her hand to her lips, her fingers brushing the ring as she blinked away fresh tears. It wasn't just about the proposal. It was the timing. The patience. The man who had once let fear keep him away was now stepping up with a quiet strength that didn't ask for applause.

This time he had chosen her.

She slipped out of bed, the ring glinting as she pulled on her robe.

In the bathroom mirror, her eyes were still soft from sleep, her curls a bit wild around her face. But her smile—her smile was unmistakable.

Joy.

She ran a hand over her belly, where Bella had once grown. She thought of the long nights, the aching loneliness, the prayers whispered through exhaustion. And then she thought of now.

Of Patrick.

Of their future.

Not just co-parents. Not just friends navigating an awkward reconciliation. But partners.

She let out a laugh, surprised at how light it sounded. How free. This love had taken the long way around. It had weathered silence, pride, absence, and the deep wound of betrayal. But it had returned anyway.

London went into the kitchen; the hardwood

floors cool beneath her feet. The sunlight hit her plants just right, making the leaves glow.

A coffee mug waited by the sink. She picked it up, heart full, thinking of how Patrick had stood in this very spot the night before, washing dishes like it was the most natural thing in the world.

He fit.

Here. With her. With Bella.

Her phone buzzed on the counter.

Morning, beautiful. You awake yet?

She typed quickly: Been staring at this ring for ten minutes. Still not over it.

Good. Because I plan on giving you a million more reasons to stare at it.

She bit her lip, grinning.

Come over.

Be there in ten.

She put the phone down, the ring catching the light again as she reached for the coffee pot.

Today the world looked different. Brighter.

Not because it was perfect.

But because she wasn't doing this alone anymore.

She was loved.

Chosen.

CHAPTER SIXTEEN

PATRICK ARRIVED AT London's house mid-morning. The moment he saw London's smile when she opened the door, that familiar warmth inside him stirred. She was wearing a comfortable sweater, her long locs loosely tied back, the kind of casual beauty that made him catch his breath.

"Hey," she said softly, stepping aside to let him in.

"Hey," he replied, stepping inside. The smell of fresh coffee greeted him, mingling with the faint scent of cinnamon from something baking in the oven. The kitchen was cozy and inviting, the table set simply but thoughtfully with two plates, a small vase of fresh flowers, and cloth napkins folded neatly.

They moved around each other in quiet rhythm— London cracking eggs while Patrick buttered toast and sliced avocado. The sounds of their small kitchen dance—the clink of cutlery, the soft sizzling from the pan—felt like music after so much silence between them.

Patrick's eyes kept drifting to the ring on London's left hand, the diamond glinting in the morning light. His chest swelled with a mix of pride and relief. He hadn't rushed into this; he'd waited until he was sure—until he'd seen the way London held

Bella, the way she looked at him with steady, unwavering trust.

This was the right time. The right step.

But even as he soaked in the quiet intimacy of the morning, his mind drifted to the future—how would his parents take the news? Would they be supportive or skeptical? And London's family? They had their own history, their own expectations.

Most importantly, what about Bella? She was the heart of this decision. How would she feel knowing that her parents were committing to a life together, a family fully united? He hoped she'd be excited, but he knew children sensed more than words sometimes, and he wanted to protect her from any confusion or hurt.

As they sat down with their breakfast, London's eyes caught his. "It's still surreal," she murmured, tracing the edge of the napkin. "I never thought... I mean, after everything..."

Patrick reached across the table, his fingers brushing hers. "Me neither. But here we are."

Before they could say more, the doorbell rang.

Patrick got up to answer it, and Ace stood there with a bright smile and Bella in tow.

"Morning," Ace said softly, her gaze flickering to London's hand. Patrick saw the subtle catch in her breath, the way her eyes widened almost imperceptibly. "London, that ring—"

She gave a small, shy smile. "Thank you, Ace. But please, keep it quiet for now. We want to tell the family together."

Ace nodded, stepping inside. "Of course. Your secret's safe with me."

Bella's energy filled the room instantly, her laughter bubbling. "Daddy," she exclaimed, running into his arms.

Patrick scooped her up, spinning her around before setting her gently on the floor. The joy on her face, the way she reached for both, filled Patrick with a fierce protectiveness.

As they settled back around the table, the conversation naturally turned to Ace's pregnancy.

"So," London began, smiling warmly at Ace, "how are you feeling? Only a few weeks left now."

Ace rested a hand on her belly, her eyes shining with anticipation. "It's been…a lot. But good. We can't wait to meet this little one."

"My brother and Ace didn't want to know the sex beforehand," London told Patrick.

"It feels more special that way," Ace contributed.

He nodded, impressed. "That takes patience."

She laughed softly. "We've got three more weeks to go. Hopefully the baby stays put until then."

London leaned forward, genuinely interested. "Have you thought about names yet?"

Ace shrugged with a grin. "A few ideas, but nothing set in stone. If it's a girl, we have a short list. Shane's been clear he wants a little girl. If it's a boy…well, we'll figure it out."

Patrick glanced at London, noticing how her face softened with each family story Ace shared. There was a gentle lightness in her expression, a deepening smile that made him believe even more firmly this was the life he wanted. Messy, unpredictable, full of love and laughter—unfolding one perfect morning at a time. Yet underneath it all, the questions and hopes about how this new chapter would truly settle in the lives of those he loved lingered in his heart, urging him forward but reminding him to tread gently.

LONDON WATCHED AS Bella twirled around in the living room, her small hands clutching her favorite stuffed bunny, eyes wide with curiosity and innocence. The sunlight filtered through the curtains, casting a warm glow that softened the edges of the moment—a moment London knew would mark the beginning of something new, something important.

Patrick sat on the couch nearby, his posture relaxed but his eyes alert, attentive to every little movement Bella made. London's heart squeezed with a mix of hope and nerves. Today they would have the talk—the conversation that felt enormous even for a tiny girl who saw the world with such simple clarity.

"Bella," London began gently, lowering herself to the child's level, "can we sit together for a little bit? I want to talk to you about something special."

She stopped twirling, her gaze flickering to her mom, then to Patrick. Bella nodded seriously, setting the bunny down and settling on the floor between them.

London took a deep breath. *How do you ex-*

plain family to a four-year-old? How do you explain that sometimes family looks different than what she might see at school or in the playground? That her daddy, who has sometimes been away, is now planning to be with us—not just sometimes, but most of the time?

"It's okay to ask questions, sweetie," London whispered, brushing a stray curl behind her daughter's ear.

Bella's big hazel-colored eyes searched London's face. "Mommy, why does my friend Emily's daddy live with her every day, but my daddy don't live here with us?"

London glanced at Patrick, who smiled softly, then turned his full attention to Bella.

"Bumblebee," Patrick said, his voice calm and warm, "I love you and your mommy so much. My job would sometimes take me far away, but for now, I'm going to be home. I promise."

"I want my daddy to be home all the time."

Patrick's voice lowered to something tender, hopeful. "Bella, I'm glad you said that because I have something very important to tell you. I'm going to marry your mommy."

Bella's eyes went wide, sparkling with delight. "You're going to marry Mommy?"

"Yes, baby. I love her very much. And we'll live in the same house—I'll be home with you."

"Yeah…" A giggle bubbled from Bella's lips. "That means I get to be the flower girl again. Remember when I was the flower girl at Uncle Aiden's wedding?"

London smiled through tears. That memory was still so fresh—a tiny Bella, tossing petals down the aisle with pure joy, not knowing how much her world was about to change again.

"Yes, sweetheart, you were the most beautiful flower girl."

Bella bounced excitedly. "I want to wear my flower crown again."

London's heart ached with happiness and hope. This was the family they were creating—one full of love, patience, and the kind of magic only children could see.

As Patrick and Bella talked and laughed, London sat back quietly, letting herself feel the full weight of the moment. She was nervous, of course—wondering how all of this would settle in their hearts and the hearts of those around them—but above all, she felt certain.

This was right.

This was home.

PATRICK SAT BACK in the living room after their conversation with Bella, watching her curl up on the couch with London, her small hand tucked into her mom's as if holding on to a lifeline. The soft murmur of their quiet voices filled the room, a lullaby of safety and love. For a moment, Patrick let himself breathe in the warmth of the scene, the peace he had yearned for but seldom allowed himself to claim.

He flexed his fingers, still feeling the faint weight of Bella's small hand in his own. That simple touch grounded him, more than any ring or promise ever could. It was real—this was real.

But underneath that peace, a familiar undercurrent of unease tugged at the edges of his mind.

What if he wasn't enough?

The question wasn't new, but now it felt heavier, sharper. He had seen so many relationships crumble, heard too many stories of promises broken under pressure. Was he prepared for this? To be the husband London deserved, the father Bella needed? Could he balance the demanding, unpredictable work that often pulled him away with the home life they deserved?

He swallowed hard, pushing the doubts down where they wouldn't poison this moment.

No. Not now.

Not when London's smile still lingered in his mind, bright and unyielding. Not when Bella's laughter echoed in the corners of the room like a fragile, beautiful song.

He remembered how London's eyes had searched his during the talk, full of hope and trust. How she'd looked at Bella with so much tenderness it made his chest ache.

This was the family he wanted—not some idealized version, but the messy, complicated, imperfect kind that meant showing up every day, even when it was hard.

He glanced down at the ring on London's finger, the simple band gleaming in the sunlight. He'd agonized over it, wondering if it was enough to say *I'm all in.* But as he looked now, he knew that the ring was just a symbol. The real promise was the one he was making in his heart—to be present, to fight for them, to build something that could withstand storms.

He leaned forward, elbows resting on his knees, and let his thoughts flow.

How would his parents react? His mom, always so quietly hopeful for his happiness but cautious after all the years he'd spent trying to find his footing…would she embrace London fully or hold back like she sometimes did with things she didn't understand right away?

And London's family—their fierce loyalty, their protective instincts—how would they respond to the news? Would they see him as the man he was now or as the one who'd made mistakes in the past?

And most importantly, Bella.

Bella, with her little hands and big questions, who deserved the kind of childhood filled with stability and love. Would she feel safe with him as her dad? Could he be the anchor she needed, or would his job always pull him away?

The doubts circled again, but this time Patrick breathed through them instead of fighting. He reminded himself of the moment Bella had asked if he'd marry London, her face lighting up with joy. The way she'd talked about being a flower girl again, imagining a future full of celebrations and family memories.

That was the future he wanted.

He straightened up and stood by the window, watching the world outside—a mix of quiet streets, neighbors going about their days, and the steady hum of life moving forward. It was a different world from the one he'd lived in during his years on the road, in hotel rooms and airports, always chasing deadlines and danger.

Now the road ahead looked different. It had London's laughter, Bella's bright eyes, and the promise of home.

Patrick ran a hand through his hair and let himself smile. He could still feel the weight of uncertainty, but it no longer felt like a chain. It was a challenge, a call to be better, to rise higher.

He stepped away from the window and found London sitting quietly on the couch, watching Bella with a softness that made his heart ache with love. He sat beside her, slipping his hand into hers, feeling the steady pulse of connection.

"We did good, didn't we?" he said quietly.

London nodded, her smile small but full of meaning. "We did. So, how do you think your parents are going to take the news of our engagement?"

Patrick sank into the couch as London's question hung in the air between them. He looked at her, the soft morning light catching the edges of her face—hope, concern, and trust all mingled there. It wasn't a question he'd avoided; he'd been wrestling with it himself.

"They'll be surprised," he said honestly, voice low and steady. "I don't think Mom's expecting this, not so soon. She's always been careful about me rushing into things." He paused, thinking about the cautious warmth she usually offered. "But I believe she wants me to be happy, and I think when she sees how serious I am about you—and Bella—she'll come around."

London's eyes searched his, and he could tell she wanted more—more than reassurances, she wanted the truth, the fight she knew he was willing to bring.

"I'm ready to fight for us," Patrick continued, voice firm with conviction. "For you, for Bella, for this family we're building. I've carried a lot of responsibility in my job—long hours, travel, tough calls—but this…this is different. This is personal. This is everything I want."

He leaned forward, clasping her hands in his. "I'm driving to Savannah on Saturday morning. I want to tell them in person. Face to face. I want them to see who you are, who we are together. I want to give them no room for doubt."

London's lips curved into a tentative smile, the kind that held relief and a flicker of excitement. He squeezed her hands gently.

"We'll get through it, London. Together."

And for the first time in a long time, Patrick felt the weight of fear ease—replaced by the fierce, determined hope of a man ready to claim his future.

CHAPTER SEVENTEEN

PATRICK HAD BARELY stepped out of the Jeep before Myra was handing him a printed schedule and gesturing toward the street of manicured homes nestled just outside downtown Savannah.

"This one just came on the market yesterday," she said briskly, nodding toward the wide porch and tall windows of a stately colonial-style house. "Great school district, close to the park. I've got three more for us to see this afternoon."

Patrick took the paper without really looking at it. The sun beat down, humid and unrelenting, as cicadas buzzed lazily in the distance. Savannah always had a way of feeling timeless—until moments like this, when time and pressure pressed down on him all at once.

"Mom—"

"I know you said this wasn't a final decision," Myra continued, as if he hadn't spoken. "But it doesn't hurt to look, and if we find something that feels right, we can put in an offer quickly. These houses don't last long."

"Mom," Patrick said again, sharper now. She stopped walking and turned, eyes bright with expectation.

Robert stood behind them, quiet but observant, hands in the pockets of his slacks. His silence made

Patrick's heart thud louder. He hadn't come here to look at houses. Not really. He had come for something far more personal, and as difficult as he knew this conversation might be, he owed it to them— and to London and Bella—to say it plainly.

"I'm engaged," Patrick said, steady and clear.

Myra blinked. "*You're what?*"

"I asked London to marry me. And she said yes."

There was a moment—a breathless, suspended moment—before Myra's face shifted. The joy she had worn just moments before melted into a look of confusion, then disbelief.

"Patrick…you don't have to marry her to be a father to Bella."

His stomach dropped. He had known it wouldn't be easy. But hearing the words out loud still hit like a sucker punch.

"That's not why I proposed. I love her. I want to spend my life with her. This isn't about obligation— it's about family."

Myra gave him a look that was too practiced, too measured. "Sweetheart, I know you think this is what's best, but it's a big decision. You've been back in Bella's life for what, a few months? You're still adjusting. You don't need to lock yourself into something just to prove a point."

Patrick's jaw clenched. "It's not a point, Mom. It's my life. And I didn't come here for house hunting. I came to tell you both in person because this matters to me. You matter."

Robert stepped closer, brows drawn. "Son, she's

just saying we want you to take your time. You don't want to regret rushing into a marriage."

Patrick shook his head, a bitter laugh catching in his throat. "I didn't rush anything. We've been through hell together. We've done the work."

Myra exhaled, reached into her bag and pulled out a cream-colored envelope. Without speaking, she handed it to him.

Patrick looked down. His name. Typed. No return address. He opened the flap and pulled out several pages—custody papers.

"What is this?"

Myra didn't flinch. "Olivia helped me draft them. I was going to send them to you earlier. Joint physical custody. So you could have a legal claim to Bella, no matter what happens."

He stared at her, stunned. "You went behind my back? You talked to Olivia about this without telling me?"

"I was trying to help," she said, her voice rising slightly. "You've been talking about wanting to be a father to Bella. This is a way to protect your rights. To protect her."

"This isn't protection. It's control," Patrick snapped. "You don't trust me to make my own decisions, so you decided to get the law involved before I even knew it. Do you have any idea what this would've done to London if she got served custody papers out of nowhere?"

Myra's face twisted, hurt flashing in her eyes. "I wasn't trying to hurt her. Or you. But she walked away from you once, Patrick. She kept Bella from us. I just wanted to make sure—"

"That it didn't happen again," he finished bitterly. He looked to his father. "Did you know about this?"

Robert hesitated, then nodded. "She showed them to me. I told her it was a little...premature."

Patrick paced a few steps, fury and heartbreak warring inside him. He had expected hesitation. Even concern. But not this. Not betrayal. Not from the people he had always leaned on.

"You say you want what's best for me," Patrick said, turning back to them, voice low but fierce. "Then start believing I know what that is. I love her. I love Bella. And I'm going to marry London because she's the best thing that ever happened to me."

Myra folded her arms. "I don't doubt your feelings. But love doesn't always fix things."

"No, it doesn't," Patrick said. "But trust does. And if you can't give me that—if you can't trust me to choose what's right for my own life—then maybe we need to rethink what being a family means."

Silence followed. Heavy. Condemning.

Myra's eyes glistened, but she said nothing.

Patrick took a breath, the ache in his chest growing. "I've changed my mind. I'm going back home."

"Son..."

He glared at his mother and shook his head. "You know... I really wanted you and Dad to be part of this, to celebrate with us. But I won't let anyone—not even you—undermine my relationship with London and Bella."

Patrick turned and walked away, leaving the envelope on the coffee table, unread and unnecessary.

Behind him, the street was quiet except for the cicadas—still buzzing. Still pressing. Still persistent.

Just like him.

MYRA SAT AT the breakfast table, her fingers wrapped around a porcelain teacup gone lukewarm. The soft clink of china echoed as she set it back onto the saucer, the silence in the room pressing in from every side.

Robert was reading the paper, but his eyes hadn't moved over the text in minutes. Myra knew he was still thinking about the scene earlier.

Patrick's goodbye had been brief, restrained, and it stung more than she expected. He hadn't looked at her the way he used to—not with trust, not with affection. There had been something hard in his eyes, something distant. And it was all because she had tried to protect him.

She turned to Robert, her voice brittle around the edges. "I don't understand why he's so angry with me. I was looking out for him. I always have."

Robert folded the paper slowly, setting it aside. "You were trying to control him, Myra. There's a difference."

Her brow furrowed. "I was not. I was making

sure he didn't make a mistake. He's not thinking clearly. He's so caught up with that girl and the child—"

"That girl? That child? You mean his fiancée and daughter?" Robert's tone was sharper now, the calmness giving way to frustration. "Myra, he's not moving to Savannah. He's not buying one of these houses you've been dragging him to. He told you clearly—he's staying on Polk Island because that's where London and Bella are. That's his family."

She straightened, her lips tightening. "He doesn't have to marry her to be a father to Bella. I told him that. I even had Olivia draw up joint custody papers. He could've been a present father without tying himself to a woman who—"

"Who what? Who loves him? Who gave birth to his child and raised her without bitterness? I know why you don't like London, but what has she done to earn your contempt, Myra?"

She felt her cheeks burn. The shame crept in quietly, behind the wall of her defensiveness. "She's not the woman I imagined for him. She's not—she doesn't understand him the way we do."

Robert shook his head. "No one will ever understand him the way you do, and that's the problem."

Myra blinked, caught off guard. "Excuse me?"

"You don't want anyone to be good enough. You never have. From the moment he brought girls home in high school, you nitpicked them all. And now you're doing the same with London. But he's not a boy anymore. He's a man. A father. About to be a husband. He doesn't need you orchestrating his future."

"I was trying to help," she whispered.

"Help is when someone asks you for support, not when you impose your vision over their life and call it love."

The words hit harder than she wanted to admit. Her gaze dropped to the envelope on the coffee table—the custody papers. She originally planned to mail them but decided it was best to give them to him in person. Patrick had seen them and looked at her like a stranger. Like she'd betrayed him.

"He's always been mine to protect," she said softly, her throat tightening. "I've always wanted him to feel safe and loved…that he was cherished by his parents."

Robert stood and walked to her side, his tone gentler now. "He still is, Myra. But protection doesn't mean possession. If you keep trying to shape his life, he'll pull away. You've already started to lose him."

She looked up at him, pain etching deep lines in her face. "I just wanted him to have the best life."

"Then trust him," he said, placing a hand on her shoulder. "Because right now, that life is on Polk Island. With London. And Bella."

But Myra's mind didn't quiet. As Robert turned away, she stared at the envelope again.

She picked up the torn halves, as if reconsidering. Letting go didn't come easily—not for her.

No, she thought bitterly. She wasn't ready to surrender just yet. Patrick was her son. She had invested too much, loved too fiercely to let him throw his life away on a woman who had already broken his heart once.

London Worthington had her hooks in him. And Myra wasn't about to stand by and watch it happen again. She would simply have Olivia print out another set. Just in case.

Because a mother didn't give up. Not when she knew—truly knew—what was best for her child.

Not yet.

London heard the familiar creak of the screen door before the latch clicked shut. She glanced up from the small stack of paperwork she was sorting through at the kitchen table. Her eyes lit up with a soft flicker of surprise, and then joy, as Patrick stepped inside.

"I thought you weren't coming back until Sunday night," she said, her voice holding a gentle curiosity. The sight of him standing there in his jeans and button-down shirt, sleeves rolled up, gave her that familiar ache in her chest—the one that always bloomed when he came home.

Patrick dropped his overnight bag by the door and offered her a smile that didn't quite reach his eyes. "I changed my mind. Thought I'd come back early."

She tucked a curl behind her ear and set her pen down, rising from the chair to cross the room. Her arms wrapped around his waist, and she pressed her cheek against his chest. He held her a little tighter than usual, as if grounding himself.

"Everything okay?" she asked, pulling back just enough to search his face.

He nodded too quickly. "Yeah. I just missed you. Missed being here."

London didn't press him right away. She reached for his hand and led him to the couch, settling in beside him as the early evening light poured through the front windows. His fingers laced with hers, and for a while, they just sat in silence, listening to the ticking clock and the faint hum of the island wind outside.

"So," she said softly, "did something happen? I know you said you were staying through the weekend. I'm sure your mom made plans for y'all…"

Patrick exhaled, a slow and steady breath that made his chest rise against her shoulder. "Yeah, she had plans all right. But I got some edits back on the article—the one about your honey farm. Thought I might as well come back and work from here. Figured Bella would be happy to see me, too."

London's heart warmed at the mention of Bella. Her daughter had been asking when Patrick would be back, and London had felt the pang of that growing bond between them—both comforting and terrifying in its permanence.

Still, she wasn't convinced that editorial notes had brought him back early.

She glanced up at him, her voice quiet but steady. "You sure that's all?"

He met her gaze then, and she could see the shadows behind his eyes—thoughts he wasn't ready to voice. But he gave her a soft smile, kissed her forehead, and said, "Yeah. That's all."

She nodded, though her chest felt tight. She knew him too well. There was something else. Something heavier. But if Patrick had taught her anything over the past year, it was that he would talk when he was ready. Not before.

So instead, she leaned into him and said, "I'm glad you're home."

He wrapped his arms around her, burying his face in her hair. "Me, too, London. Me, too."

And in the quiet of the living room, as the sun dipped lower over Polk Island, London let the silence speak for them, offering space for the truth to come—whenever Patrick was ready to share it.

Patrick was upstairs reading with Bella, their voices a soft murmur that made London's heart swell. It was these quiet moments she cherished—the ones that didn't require grand gestures or words. Just their presence, woven into the rhythm of her day, made everything feel more complete.

Still, the knot in her chest lingered.

She couldn't stop thinking about the way Patrick had come back early from Savannah. He'd smiled, kissed her, even made a joke about article edits needing his immediate attention. She hadn't pushed him.

But her gut—well, her gut told her there was more.

And she couldn't help but wonder if the tightness around his smile had anything to do with his mother.

London sighed and turned off the burner, setting the pot aside. She wasn't someone who jumped to conclusions. She tried—honestly tried—not to read too much into the conversations that never happened, the looks that never lingered. But she had noticed something when they'd gone to Savannah together months ago, a tension beneath Myra's polished politeness. A wariness. A silent assessment that never quite ended.

And Patrick hadn't said much about how the visit had gone. He'd mentioned dinner, a few errands. Nothing about his parents' reaction to the engagement.

London walked out to the screened-in porch, letting the sea breeze tug at the hem of her robe. She stared out toward the marshlands, trying to slow her thoughts. Worry wouldn't help anything.

Still…she could feel it.

Myra hadn't been thrilled.

And that knowledge scraped something raw inside her. Not because she needed Myra's approval. She didn't. But because it would've meant something to Patrick. She wanted that for him. For them. For Bella.

London leaned against the porch railing. They'd come so far, her and Patrick. Through misunderstandings, through the ache of time lost, through the reality of a child born into silence. They had clawed their way to this—love, honesty, forgiveness. She wasn't going to let one disapproving parent dim that light.

Not now. Not ever.

A breeze swept across the porch, lifting strands of her hair. She closed her eyes and breathed in deep.

She would not live her life for the approval of others. Not even for someone as important to Patrick as his mother. Myra didn't know their story—not the nights London had wept over Bella's crib, not the way Patrick had held her hand at the ocean's edge when she was afraid to trust again, not the joy in Bella's voice every time she said *Daddy*.

Myra didn't have to see it.

London did.

And that was enough.

The door creaked open behind her. She turned to find Patrick stepping out onto the porch, his hair tousled, a lazy smile on his lips.

"She's finally asleep," he said softly. "But she insisted on reading the flower girl book twice. Said she needed to practice in case our wedding is sooner rather than later."

London chuckled, feeling the weight in her chest ease a little. "She's taking her role seriously."

"She's not the only one," Patrick said, stepping close and sliding his arms around her waist.

She tilted her head back, resting it against his chest. "How are you feeling today?"

He kissed the top of her head. "Better."

London hesitated, her voice quiet. "Was Savannah hard?"

He paused. Just for a beat before responding, "It made me surer of what I want."

London turned in his arms to face him. "You didn't answer my question."

He met her gaze with a tired smile. "No. I didn't."

And that was that.

London nodded slowly, brushing her fingers along the edge of his jaw. "Okay."

Patrick's brow furrowed slightly, but she shook her head before he could speak.

"I trust you," she said. "When you're ready to talk, I'll listen. But just so we're clear…" Her voice steadied. "I'm not going anywhere. Not because of your mom. Not because of anything or anyone else. I choose this. I choose us."

He exhaled deeply and pulled her closer, holding her like a man who needed anchoring.

"I love you, London."

"I love you, too."

They stood in silence, the hush of the island wrapping around them.

Later, she would tuck away the ache she carried and plant it somewhere deeper, somewhere quieter. For now, she let herself rest in his embrace, knowing that some battles didn't need to be fought all at once. Some things—like trust—had to unfold at their own pace.

And London had finally learned the difference between waiting in fear and waiting in faith.

She would wait. She would love. She would build.

Because this was her family. And she was done questioning whether she belonged.

CHAPTER EIGHTEEN

THE LATE-AFTERNOON sunlight streamed in through the wide living room window of the cottage, gilding the hardwood floor in amber and shadows. Patrick stood frozen in the center of the room, a manila envelope clenched in his hand. His jaw worked as he stared at it, pulse ticking at his temple like a metronome out of sync.

The return address on the envelope had been enough to make his stomach clench: *Crawford & Millner, Attorneys at Law. Charleston, SC.*

He opened it.

There it was.

His hands trembled as he unfolded the document and scanned the dry legal language. The deeper he read, the colder he became. Words blurred together—*Petitioner: Patrick Brown, Respondent: London Marie Worthington, Minor child: Arabella Worthington.*

Patrick sank onto the edge of the couch, the papers slack in his grip. He let them fall to the coffee table beside his laptop with a soft flutter, like the sound could somehow echo louder than the fury building inside his chest.

What was she thinking?

He pressed his hands against his face, digging his fingers into his scalp. His heart beat a little too fast, too loud. He couldn't think straight, couldn't catch his breath. This wasn't just some meddling comment at Sunday dinner or a disapproving look when his mother thought London wasn't watching. This was betrayal. Legal. Intentional. Deliberate.

His mother had always been strong-willed. Controlling. She masked it in manners and homemade biscuits and fundraisers, but underneath all that Southern charm was a woman who didn't like being told no.

Patrick had tried, for years, to keep the peace. He'd bitten his tongue through her passive-aggressive remarks, through her opinions about his career choices, his friends, his bachelorhood. And now through this new chapter with London and Bella, he'd hoped— *prayed*, even—that his parents would give him room to work on his relationship with London.

But this? This wasn't just disapproval.

It was war.

He moved to the kitchen, needing something to do. He opened the fridge, stared at the rows of labeled containers London had stocked for him— leftovers from her honey-citrus chicken, a few jars of her homemade yogurt, a bag of freshly picked blueberries. She did things like that without asking. Without expecting anything in return.

He closed the fridge door and leaned against the counter.

His mother didn't see London. Not really.

To her, London was a problem to be managed. A mistake he hadn't fully reckoned with. A woman who'd kept Bella from them, from him, from *their* family.

But London was his family now.

Patrick ran a hand across his head, exhaling hard. He didn't know how to fix this. Didn't know how to protect both the woman he loved and the parents he'd grown up believing he could trust.

But he knew one thing for sure: He had no intention of filing the custody paperwork his mother had drawn up. He wasn't about to let her make decisions for him.

His chest ached.

How dare his mother think she could march into their life with legal documents and force her way in.

She hadn't been the one who stayed up all night with Bella when she had the flu. She hadn't been the one who had to learn how to braid tiny curls without tugging. She hadn't been the one to hold London when she broke down crying, terrified she was doing it all wrong.

Patrick had been there.

He had earned this family.

The tears surprised him. They came hot and sudden, stinging the backs of his eyes before he could wipe them away. He sank into the couch again, the papers in his lap, and let himself feel the weight of it all.

The grief. The rage. The sadness.

Because he had wanted his mother to like London.

Not just tolerate her. Not just smile for appearances. He'd wanted Myra to see what he saw when he looked at her—a woman of strength, of fierce love, of resilience. A mother who had protected their daughter with everything she had, even when the world hadn't protected her.

But maybe it had been too much to ask.

Maybe Myra only ever saw what she wanted to see.

Patrick looked down at the documents again and then shoved them aside, letting them slide off the table onto the floor. He stared at the ceiling, at the faint water stain in the corner where the roof had probably leaked in some forgotten season.

He couldn't ignore this. He knew that.

But he also couldn't bring it home to London. Not yet.

He needed to think, to figure out what to do. How to respond. How to keep this from wrecking everything.

His phone buzzed. A text from London.

Just checking in. Everything okay?

He stared at the screen, then typed slowly.

Yeah. Just needed a little air. I miss you.

Miss you, too. We saved you some cornbread.

His throat tightened.

Patrick set the phone down, picked up the petition again, then laid it on top the envelope. He wouldn't burn it. Not yet. But he sure wasn't going to let it decide their future.

Right now, he needed to hold on to what was real.

And London Worthington was real.

Their love was real.

And he wouldn't let anyone—even his own mother—tear it apart.

THE SUN STREAMED through the slats of the barn, casting golden shafts of light across the wooden floor and illuminating the floating dust particles like flecks of glitter. The scent of warm hay mixed with the faint sweetness of beeswax and lavender.

London stood at the workbench near the open window, her sleeves rolled up and her hands sticky with honey as she worked beside Kyla, carefully spooning amber-colored liquid into rows of sample jars.

They'd already completed three dozen and were halfway through the fourth tray. Each small jar had a kraft paper label that read *Lavender Honey* in London's neat script, followed by the harvest date.

Kyla was lining up the completed jars into boxes padded with burlap, humming under her breath as she worked. A low playlist of mellow music spilled softly from a Bluetooth speaker balanced on the edge of the window.

"I think it should be outdoors," Kyla said, her voice dreamy. "The wedding, I mean. You and Patrick should get married right here, between the garden and the orchard. You know, have it at golden hour with those twinkly string lights everywhere. Maybe a hay bale or two for the rustic vibe."

London smiled, her fingers steady as she twisted a lid onto another jar. "Hay bales? That sounds itchy."

Kyla laughed. "You know what I mean. Farm chic. Elegant country."

"I don't want fancy," London replied, her tone softer. "I want something…honest. Just us, close friends, family. Simple flowers. No ballroom. No drama."

"That sounds like you." Kyla stopped to wipe her hands on a towel. "Patrick on board with that?"

London gave a small nod. "He said whatever makes me happy. I know he likes the idea of keeping it small, too. Something about not wanting to share me with too many people." She gave a wistful chuckle and twisted another lid into place.

Kyla smiled, but it faded slightly. "You think his mom's going to come around?"

Her hands stilled for a moment, her fingers resting on the glass. She didn't look up right away. "She pretty much had some other vision for Patrick's life. So, I don't know."

"Still," Kyla said gently, "she's got to see how happy he is. And he clearly adores you."

London let out a breath and finally looked over at Kyla. "He does. And I adore Patrick. That's what matters. The rest… I'll learn to live with."

Kyla reached for another spoonful of honey, but

before she could scoop, London's phone buzzed from the shelf above the workbench. The vibration rattled lightly against the wood.

London wiped her hands on a towel and reached for it, glancing at the screen. "It's my mom."

"Better answer," her assistant said, giving her a look.

She slid her finger across the screen and lifted the phone to her ear. "Hey, Mama."

"Ace is in labor," Madelyn announced. "She and Shane just got to the hospital. I'm here with them now."

London's breath caught in her throat. "Oh goodness…"

Her mother sounded breathless and excited. "Yes, her water broke an hour ago. It's all happening fast. Shane is pacing like he's the one giving birth."

She laughed; her voice caught between glee and surprise. "How is Ace?"

"She's doing fine. A little nervous, but calm. She asked for you."

London turned away from the workbench, eyes wide as she looked out the barn window, her heart thudding in her chest. "Tell her I love her and that I'll be there soon. I need to check in with Patrick… see if he can stay with Bella."

"I'll keep you posted."

The call ended, and London lowered the phone slowly, still gripping it tightly. Her breath came a little faster, her emotions all tangled up inside—surprise, happiness, a touch of worry, but mostly awe.

"What is it?" Kyla asked, already wiping her hands again.

London turned, her eyes shining. "Ace is in labor."

She gasped, a hand flying to her chest. "How exciting..."

London nodded, her mouth lifting into a smile that wouldn't stop. "Yes. Shane and Mama are at the hospital with her."

Kyla practically jumped in place. "Girl, go... Why are you still standing here?"

"I need to call Patrick."

"I can stay with her until he gets here."

"Kyla, thank you."

London laughed, hurrying to untie the apron from around her waist. Her heart was racing now, her thoughts already spinning toward her sister-in-law, toward the hospital room, the moment that was unfolding.

She turned back to the workbench for a second and looked at the rows of honey jars. They sparkled in the low light, beautiful and golden and full of labor and care. This place, this life she envisioned—it all felt right. And now her family was growing.

"We'll finish these later," she said, grabbing her phone and keys.

Kyla nodded. "Keep me posted. And give Ace a kiss for me."

London didn't wait. She bolted from the barn

with joy swelling in her chest, the scent of wild honey and summer air following her into the evening light.

Patrick sat cross-legged on the living room floor, a tea set spread between him and Bella. Her stuffed animals circled around them in a semicircle of fluffy guests, each balanced delicately on child-sized chairs she'd insisted they needed. A stuffed unicorn with a crooked horn, a well-loved teddy bear, and a floppy-eared rabbit all stared back at him with button-eyed intensity.

Bella poured imaginary tea into each of their cups, sticking out her tongue in concentration. "Mr. Fluff gets two sugars," she said with the seriousness of a queen officiating court. "Because he's fancy."

Patrick chuckled, grateful for the distraction. "Of course. Nothing but the best for Mr. Fluff."

She smiled up at him, cheeks glowing, then tipped the tiny teacup toward his mouth. "Your turn, Daddy."

He pretended to sip and made a satisfied sound. "Mmm…delicious. You're quite the chef, little miss."

She beamed and turned to the unicorn. "Your turn, Sparkle." Bella put the teacup down. "Can we go outside now?"

He looked at the clock. Still plenty of light out. "Of course, Bumblebee. Let me clean up this royal banquet first."

She giggled and began gathering stuffed animals into a basket, her little feet padding across the hardwood floor.

Outside, the sun dipped just low enough to cast everything in golden hues. Bella danced across the backyard, chasing bubbles Patrick blew in her direction. Her laughter carried on the wind, light and high like chimes.

He sat on the steps, bubble wand in hand, letting her joy wrap around the hollowness that still gnawed at him. His mother's betrayal was still fresh. Her attempt to use the legal system to force some kind of wedge between him and London was still a weight on his chest.

He'd left the papers sitting on the coffee table, untouched since he read them. He couldn't bring himself to throw them out, but he couldn't look at them again either.

Bella collapsed on the grass, arms outstretched like a starfish. "I'm tired," she announced.

Patrick set the bubble wand aside and walked over, lowering himself onto the grass beside her. "That was quite a show you put on. You deserve a rest."

She rolled toward him, eyes half-closed. "Will Mommy bring the baby to our house?"

He smiled, brushing a strand of hair from her forehead. "Not tonight. But soon, I bet."

Bella nodded, satisfied. Then after a beat, she asked, "I hope it's a baby girl. Uncle Shane wants a little girl. Auntie Ace says she don't care."

They lay in silence for a moment, the warm

breeze brushing over them, the sounds of birds in the trees above. He could almost pretend that everything in the world was settled. That there were no unresolved conversations. That his mother hadn't tried to weaponize the courts against the woman he loved. That he didn't feel this constant tension between his past and his future.

London had sensed something was off. He could see it in her eyes, the way she didn't ask questions when he said he wanted to spend a day at the rental to think. She'd just nodded, touched his chest gently, and told him she loved him.

She hadn't pushed. That was what he needed most. Time. Space. Grace. London gave him all three.

As the sun dipped further, he scooped Bella into his arms and carried her inside the cottage. She rested her head on his shoulder, arms looped lazily around his neck. Inside, he got her changed into pajamas and let her pick out a bedtime story.

She chose a book titled *I Love to Sing and Dance*, then curled up beside him as he read. His voice was soft, steady, even though the words blurred a few times as emotion welled in his throat.

Bella drifted off to sleep before they reached the last page.

He gently closed the book and watched her for a while. His father's words echoed in his mind, reminding him that clinging too tightly could push away the very people he wanted to protect. That was something his mother failed to grasp.

Patrick was no longer a child; he didn't require supervision. What he needed was trust, respect, and the freedom to create the family he envisioned.

He tucked Bella in, switched off the light, and then heard a car door shut outside.

London felt like home.

As he stepped into the hallway of the cottage and heard the faint jingle of her keys, Patrick understood that home wasn't a location—it was the sound of her returning.

CHAPTER NINETEEN

LONDON HADN'T EXPECTED to feel this drained—emotionally full since the arrival of her new niece, yet physically exhausted as she made the drive to Patrick's cottage to pick up Bella. She loved her family, loved that sweet baby already, but the weight of the long day clung to her shoulders, and all she wanted was to get home and collapse.

She didn't have a key to Patrick's place—something they'd joked about but never fixed—so she rapped gently on the door and waited, her arms crossed tightly against the cool evening air.

The door swung open a moment later, Patrick's easy smile softening at the edges when he saw her.

"Hey," he said. "You okay?"

"Yeah," she exhaled, stepping inside. "Just tired. Today was a lot."

"Ace have the baby?"

London nodded. "A little girl. Shane is over the moon at having a daughter."

"I know the feeling."

She eyed Patrick and grinned. "Where's Bella?"

"She's asleep," he answered, his voice. "She's in bed."

London's eyes followed him to the bedroom. Bella lay, bundled in a light blanket, her tiny chest rising and falling in the rhythm of deep sleep. The sight tugged at her heart, easing something tight inside her.

"She's out cold, huh?" London murmured, moving closer to her daughter, brushing a stray curl from Bella's cheek.

"Wore herself out," Patrick said, his voice warm. "We played hard today."

"She's comfortable here," London said, her tone soft, grateful. "But I'm looking forward to you moving to the farm after the wedding."

His grin broadened, as if he'd been waiting for her to voice it. "Me, too. I'm already considering which room to convert into my office."

They'd discussed it often—what it would be like to create a home together, how they'd make room for each other beyond just their schedules. Now it felt tangible. Almost within reach.

Gesturing to the far side of the house, Patrick said, "Bella left her backpack in her room. I'll grab it."

Her eyes caught on something on the coffee table—legal-sized documents, crisp and neatly arranged.

Initially, London thought it might be another article or something related to his freelance work. But as she moved closer, she noticed the title at the top of the document.

Petition for Custody.

Her stomach clenched.

Her hands shook as she reached out to pick up the papers. Each page pierced her with implications. Terms. Legal jargon. Her name. Bella's name. Patrick's name.

Her breath hitched. The room seemed to spin.

He had said nothing.

All this time. He hadn't said a word.

"London…"

She turned at the sound of his voice.

Before she could ask, Patrick's voice found her. "I was going to tell you about that."

She looked over her shoulder, waiting.

"My mother's lawyer," he said with a sigh. "She did this without telling me."

London's jaw tensed. "Your mother?"

"I haven't filed anything. I would never—London, I would never try to take Bella from you. I was furious," he said, stepping closer.

London nodded slowly, trying to collect the cyclone of thoughts roaring in her head. She believed him. She did. But the deeper ache was harder to ignore. "I don't want anything to do with your mother."

Patrick's shoulders fell.

"*I mean it*," she said. "I have done everything I could to include her, to respect her, even when she made it clear she didn't approve of me. But this? This is unforgivable."

"You won't have to," he said firmly. "I told her that already. I won't let her near you or Bella unless you want it."

London crossed her arms, unsure if she wanted to scream or cry. "Here we are again…"

Patrick moved closer, voice thick. "Don't say that. Don't compare this to then. I'm not that man anymore. I'm not letting anyone—not even my mother—stand between us."

She looked at him, this man who had grown so much. Who had proven his love in a thousand small ways. And yet…

"You can say that," she said, voice cracking, "but you can't control her. And deep down, Patrick, I'm not sure you ever will."

Silence stretched between them.

Patrick swallowed hard. "I may not be able to change her, but I can choose you. Every day."

London turned away, pressing the heels of her hands into her eyes. "I love you. But I don't want to walk into a marriage constantly looking over my shoulder, wondering what she'll try next."

He stepped behind her, voice low, desperate. "I'm not going to lose you. I won't. I'll do whatever it takes to make this right."

She nodded, tears slipping down her cheeks.

He reached for her hand. She let him take it, but her heart was wrapped in caution.

London looked at the man she loved. And deep down, she hoped he was strong enough to protect what they had.

But she wasn't so sure.

London brushed a hand across the white muslin curtains in the nursery, letting the soft fabric flutter through her fingers. Sunlight streamed through the windows, painting warm golden stripes along the hardwood floor. The room smelled like fresh paint and lavender—Ace's signature scent—calming and bright.

Every detail had been arranged with such love: the hand-sewn quilt folded over the crib rail, the basket of organic lotions and tiny diapers near the changing table, the mobile made of clouds and stars twirling lazily overhead. London smiled, imagining tiny Sage lying beneath it, fist curled tight around one of her own dark curls.

"She's going to love this," London said aloud, even though the room was empty. Her voice was hushed in reverence.

From the hallway, Cia called out, "London, come downstairs! Micah's almost done putting up the welcome banner, and your man just walked in with three bags of groceries."

London chuckled and gave the room one last appreciative glance before heading out. She passed a collection of family photos on the stairwell wall: one of Ace and Shane at their beach wedding, arms around each other and beaming; another of the entire Worthington clan, taken last Christmas.

Downstairs, the house was bustling. Balloons in pale pink and mint green bobbed from the dining chairs, and streamers curled over doorframes.

Patrick stood by the kitchen island, sleeves rolled up, talking to Shane about last-minute errands. London caught his eye, and he grinned.

She walked over, accepting his quick kiss on the cheek.

"Hey, beautiful. How's the nursery looking?"

"Perfect. They're going to cry when they see it."

"Good. That's the goal. Emotional overload." He winked.

Tami came bustling in from the backyard, holding a tray of muffins. "Okay, tell me someone made coffee. I've been up since six baking these, and if one of y'all doesn't hand me a cup, there's going to be a muffin casualty."

Her husband, Aiden, reached for the pot. "You want cream and sugar or just a straight IV drip?"

Tami smirked and accepted the mug. "You're lucky I love you."

Patrick leaned against the counter, surveying the room. "We doing anything formal for the welcome home, or just chaos and hugs?"

London reached for a dishtowel and started wiping down the counter. "I think Ace will just want everyone here, happy and relaxed."

Cia inquired, "When are y'all going to let me throw you an engagement party?"

London laughed, shaking her head. "We haven't even set a date yet."

"Exactly why now is perfect. It's like a pre-prelude. You're already family, but it's time to celebrate that rock he put on your finger."

London instinctively looked down at her hand. The ring caught the light and glittered, its warmth matching the flutter in her chest.

"Have you at least thought about a venue?" Tami asked.

"The farm," London responded. "String some lights, hire a jazz trio, order food. Classy but chill. Nothing stuffy."

When she and her sister were alone in the kitchen, she said, "I'm not inviting his parents to the wedding."

"I get that they haven't treated you right," Cia said quietly. "I do. But…they're still his parents."

Patrick entered the kitchen. "My parents made their own choices."

London leaned back against him, breathing in his warmth. "I want you to be completely honest with me. Do you want them there?"

He was quiet a long moment. "I don't know. I want them to be the kind of people who could show up and support us. But I don't trust them to do that."

Cia stepped back. "Sis, there's your answer. If there's even a chance they'd ruin the day, they stay home. The Worthington family will be there. In full force. Loud and proud and slightly overwhelming, but one hundred percent supportive."

Patrick kissed her temple. "Then it's settled."

London laughed through the lump in her throat. "*Overwhelming* is right. One of my cousins cried when I told her about the engagement."

Nodding, Cia said, "That's Shonda. She cries at dog food commercials."

They all laughed, and the tension lifted a little.

London smiled, allowing herself to imagine it:

the way the lights would twinkle overhead, the sound of laughter and music, the people who loved them most gathered in one place. It wouldn't be perfect. But it would be theirs.

PATRICK ADJUSTED THE strap on his camera and moved through the narrow alley behind the outreach center in Charleston, careful to keep his body language open and respectful. He wasn't here to exploit anyone. He was here to understand.

The light was good—soft and golden, just shy of evening. It cast long shadows on the pavement and brought out the quiet resilience in the faces of the people he photographed. Men and women with cardboard signs and sun-worn skin, with tired eyes and layers of clothing that couldn't possibly protect against winter's bite.

He spoke to a woman named Doris, who wore a pink baseball cap and carried her belongings in a rolling suitcase. She'd once worked as a nurse, she said, before her hospital closed and rent prices doubled. Her voice cracked when she talked about her grandchildren.

Patrick offered a quiet, empathetic nod, taking mental notes alongside his audio recordings. This project wasn't just about capturing images. It was about telling stories that mattered.

But as he thanked Doris and moved toward a small cluster of tents pitched behind a vacant warehouse, his phone vibrated in his pocket.

Myra.

Patrick stilled. The name on the screen felt like a cold slap. His jaw tightened. He didn't answer.

The phone buzzed again. A voicemail this time. Then a text.

Patrick, please call me back. I want to talk.

He slipped the phone back into his jacket and forced himself to focus.

Later, he promised himself. Right now, he had a purpose.

It was past dusk when Patrick arrived back at London's house.

He parked behind her car, letting his muscles unwind for the first time in hours. The emotional weight of the day had been heavy but fulfilling. He felt raw, reflective, and deeply aware of the privileges he often took for granted.

Inside, the scent of lavender and honey met him at the door. Warm light spilled from the kitchen, where London stood barefoot, stirring something on the stove. Bella was at the table, coloring with intense focus.

London looked up and smiled. "Hey, you."

"Hey," he said, grateful for the normalcy of her. He set down his camera bag and crossed the kitchen to kiss her cheek. "Smells amazing in here."

"Pasta. With a honey glaze. Don't laugh. I'm experimenting."

"I would never laugh at your brilliance."

Bella piped up. "Mommy let me taste it. It's sweet and weird. But good weird."

Patrick chuckled, tousled Bella's hair, and turned back to London. "Mind if I shower before dinner?"

"Go ahead. You look like you walked through half of Charleston."

"I practically did."

After dinner, once Bella was tucked into bed and the dishes were done, Patrick and London curled up on the living room couch. She rested her head on his shoulder, her fingers laced with his.

"Cia wants to throw us an engagement party," she said softly. "At the hotel, but something small. Well, *smallish*. You know how she is. I told her I'm okay with the engagement party at the hotel, but I really want the wedding here on the farm."

She grew quiet for a moment, then asked carefully, "Are you sure you're okay about them not coming to the engagement party? Cia wants to be sure before excluding them off the guest list. I told her that I'd check with you one more time."

He didn't answer right away. His gaze shifted to the coffee table, where a bouquet of dried wildflowers sat in a honey jar. "I know things are still… tense," he said after a moment. "I wouldn't blame you if you didn't want them around."

"Patrick, look at me…" London met his eyes. "If you really want them there, I'll be okay with it."

He exhaled slowly. "I'll talk to my parents, and I promise you…my mother will be on her best behavior."

London gave him a soft look. "I know she loves you. I just don't understand why she doesn't trust me."

He wrapped his arm tighter around her, drawing her close. "I don't either. But I won't let her create division between us. Not again. Not ever."

His voice trembled slightly, and he hated that it did. But the pain was still fresh. He hadn't told London about the voicemail or the text. He wasn't ready. And he didn't want to spoil this moment.

"You and Bella are my family," he said. "My real family. And I'll protect that with everything I have. Even if it means setting boundaries with my parents."

London reached up and cupped his cheek. "I don't want to come between you and them, Patrick. But I won't pretend to be okay with how your mother has treated me either."

"You shouldn't have to."

He rested his forehead against hers. "All I want is to have something solid with you. Something real. A home. A life. We're so close. We're already doing it."

She nodded. "Then let's celebrate it. Let Cia throw her party. Let your parents come if they want. But just know—I won't let anyone ruin what we have either."

His heart swelled with pride and gratitude. "That's one of the million reasons I love you."

They sat in silence after that, a quiet pact forged between them. Outside, the night deepened. The moon rose high, casting silver light over the honey fields beyond the house.

Patrick knew that the conversation with Myra would have to happen. He couldn't ignore her forever. But tonight, here with London in his arms and their future shimmering just within reach, he chose hope.

And for the first time in days, he felt peace.

CHAPTER TWENTY

THE GRAND BALLROOM of the Polk Island Hotel shimmered with candlelight, every corner of the space transformed into a lush, romantic vision of celebration. Warm amber hues bathed the cream-colored walls, and strings of delicate fairy lights wove through garlands of greenery and soft white blooms. A live string quartet played softly in the background as guests mingled, sipping champagne and exchanging stories under the soft hum of conversation.

London stood near the edge of the ballroom, taking in the beauty of it all. The vision had been Cia's, but the love behind it was shared by every Worthington who had rallied to make this night perfect. Tami had insisted on planning the dessert table; her mother, Rachel Rose, helped arrange the floral centerpieces. Everything felt like home, like family.

And yet her gaze kept drifting toward the heavy double doors, the ones she knew would soon open for Patrick's parents.

She inhaled deeply, grounding herself.

"You look like you're preparing for battle," Tami said, slipping up beside her with a flute of champagne.

"Maybe I am," London replied, offering a smile that didn't quite reach her eyes.

Tami nudged her. "You've already won. He's here. You're here. This is your life now. Don't let anyone make you feel like you don't belong."

London nodded, the comfort of her sister-in-law's words wrapping around her like armor. But the knot in her stomach refused to loosen. She loved Patrick, deeply. But love didn't make his mother any easier to deal with.

It wasn't long before the doors opened again, and in walked Myra and Robert Brown, elegantly dressed and impeccably poised. Myra wore a pale turquoise sheath dress and a string of pearls so perfect it might have been commissioned by royalty. Her expression was one of polite approval, but her eyes were as calculating as ever.

Patrick noticed the shift in London before he saw them himself. He crossed the room quickly, wrapping an arm around her waist. "Hey," he murmured. "You okay?"

"They're here."

He turned, saw his parents, and stiffened. "Stay close. I'll handle them."

London nodded. "I know. Just…be ready. I'm pretty sure she's not here to play nice."

He pressed a kiss to her temple. "Neither am I."

The greetings were civil but cool. Myra offered London a smile that could slice glass. "This is quite a charming setup, dear. Very…rustic elegance."

"Thank you," London replied evenly. "We wanted something warm and welcoming."

"Well, you certainly achieved that. Though I imagine planning an event like this must be a challenge when you're managing a full-time farm."

London kept her posture relaxed. "It helps to have a lot of family who love us."

Robert gave a curt nod. "Congratulations again. We wish you both well."

It wasn't long before Myra pulled Patrick aside.

London watched from across the room as his mother leaned in, her words quiet but firm. Patrick's jaw clenched. Whatever she was saying, it wasn't a blessing.

London turned her attention to Cia, who had stepped up to the microphone to thank everyone for coming. Her voice, always vibrant, echoed over the guests, offering a toast to love and new beginnings.

London smiled, grateful for her sister's joy and generosity.

But then Myra reappeared.

"May I speak with you, London? Just for a moment."

She didn't flinch. "Of course."

They stepped into a quieter alcove near the ballroom's side entrance. The hum of music and laughter faded.

"I admire your strength," Myra began, tone syrupy. "I truly do. Raising a child, running a farm, maintaining a relationship—it's commendable."

London arched a brow. "Thank you."

"But *commendable* isn't the same as *sustainable*."

London crossed her arms. "Say what you came to say."

Myra smiled tightly. "Patrick has been offered an executive position in New York. A position that would afford him and Bella every comfort imaginable. Private schooling, a trust fund, stability beyond what a honey farm could ever offer."

London's heart thudded. She kept her voice even. "That decision belongs to Patrick."

"He's loyal to a fault," Myra continued. "But you—you could make this easier. You could encourage him to choose what's best for Bella."

London took a step forward. "What you really mean is I could step aside."

Myra didn't deny it. "You may love him. But love doesn't pay for a child's future."

London leaned in, her voice steel. "You don't get to decide what's best for Bella. Or for Patrick. This farm, this life we have—it's not flashy, but it's built on love, not leverage. You don't scare me, Myra. And I'm not walking away."

Myra tilted her head. "We'll see."

They parted without another word.

London returned to the ballroom with her chin high and spine straight. Patrick saw her and moved quickly, concern etched across his features. "What did she say?"

"That you were offered a job in New York."

His face darkened. "I told her I wasn't interested. Weeks ago."

London searched his eyes. "Why didn't you tell me?"

"Because it wasn't worth our time. I knew I was saying no the moment it came in."

Before she could reply, Myra approached again. This time, in front of a small cluster of guests.

"Patrick," she said, tone light, "we should discuss the offer again. A future in New York is nothing to dismiss lightly. Bella deserves the best."

Patrick turned fully toward his mother, his voice loud enough to hush the nearby conversation. "The best for Bella is stability. Love. A home where she knows she's safe and wanted. That's what London and I give her every day. You want to help? Then start by respecting our family. *This family*. Not the one you wish I had."

Gasps echoed nearby, but Patrick didn't stop.

"You gave me a choice, Mom. And I'm making it. I choose London. I choose Bella. I choose a life that we build together, not one you buy."

Myra stood frozen, her facade cracking.

London slipped her hand into his. He squeezed back, never looking away from his mother.

"We're done here," he said.

The silence was heavy until Robert placed a hand on his wife's arm. "Let it go, Myra."

She blinked, once, then turned and walked away.

Patrick pulled London into his arms, his voice

trembling now. "I won't lose you. I won't let her ruin this."

She touched his cheek. "You didn't waver. That means everything."

"I keep thinking about what love really means," he said quietly. "And I think…it's what we just did. It's not about the party. It's not about the promises. It's about standing up. Choosing each other. Over and over."

London rested her head against his chest. "Then we're doing just fine. Now it's time to enjoy this party—we're celebrating our engagement."

In that quiet moment, surrounded by the remnants of celebration and the echo of hard-won victory, they knew.

What they had was something real.

And they weren't going to let anyone tear it down.

PATRICK TOOK A slow breath. The time had come.

He turned slightly and gestured behind his mother. "Look behind you, Ma."

Myra blinked, puzzled, and turned.

Her spine went rigid. The color drained from her face.

Standing a few feet away, just inside the ballroom doors, was a man in his late seventies. Distinguished, well-dressed, and holding the hand of a woman whose soft features and wide eyes mirrored London's own so clearly it silenced the surrounding chatter.

Patrick watched the realization crash into his mother.

"Daddy?" Myra said, breath catching.

Her father nodded gently. "Myra."

The woman beside him smiled, hesitant but warm. "Hello, Myra."

"What is this?" she whispered. Her voice shook. "What are you doing here? And you brought this woman with you. You don't have a right to be here—"

"I invited them," Patrick interjected quietly. "Because it's time we laid the past to rest."

Myra turned on him. "You had no right."

"*No?*" Patrick asked. "Like the papers you had drawn up behind my back? You think I haven't noticed? The way you treat London, the contempt, the subtle jabs. And for what? Because she reminds you of your stepmother?"

"Don't," Myra hissed. Her voice trembled now, eyes wide, furious.

"London has done nothing but love me. Love Bella. She has nothing to do with what happened between you and your father."

"That *woman*," Myra snapped, pointing toward her stepmother, "ruined our family."

"That woman," Patrick said, voice rising slightly, "loved your father when he was broken. Just like London loves me. Even with everything I came with. And you can't punish her because of old wounds you refuse to heal."

Myra's lips pressed into a thin, bloodless line.

"I didn't understand at first, but now I do. You don't like London because she resembles your stepmother."

"Don't you dare call her that," Myra uttered. "That woman is a homewrecker."

"Every time you look at London, you're seeing the past. You're trying to rewrite my future because you never got closure on your own. But I won't let you project your pain onto my life. Not anymore."

"I gave you everything," she said, her voice small. "I fought for you. For your life to be better than mine."

"And I appreciate that," he said, stepping closer. "But better doesn't mean richer. It doesn't mean a penthouse in Manhattan. It means fuller. It means love. It means waking up beside someone who makes the world make sense. That's London. And if you can't accept that—"

Myra turned on her heel and walked away.

Her father started to follow. "Myra, please…"

But she brushed past him, refusing to look back.

A heavy silence fell over the room. London appeared at Patrick's side, her hand finding his. "Are you okay?"

He exhaled slowly. Then nodded. "I am now."

Patrick looked at the guests still lingering around them, saw the stunned expressions slowly melting into admiration. He could feel something shift, not just in the air but in his spirit.

The final chain had broken.

He stepped onto the small stage reserved for speeches and cleared his throat.

London followed.

"Thank you all for being here tonight. It means more than I can say. But before we continue celebrating, I want to say this."

He lifted his glass. "To new beginnings, to love that stands the test of time, and to a future we choose for ourselves."

A wave of applause swept across the room. London's eyes glistened with tears as she squeezed his hand.

"I love you," she whispered.

Patrick leaned in and kissed her forehead. "I love you more."

They stood side by side, bathed in the glow of the chandelier, surrounded by family—the one they were born into and the one they built together. And in that moment, Patrick knew that they had finally won.

Their love had been tested, but this time, they fought for it.

And this time, they weren't letting go.

MYRA STOOD ALONE in the hallway just outside the Grand Ballroom, her arms crossed tightly over her stomach as if trying to hold herself together. The hum of voices, music, and laughter drifted from inside, but it all sounded distant now. Muted. Like it was happening in another world she wasn't part of.

Her father had shown up. With his wife.

And London—London, with her gentle eyes and quiet dignity—had borne the face of the woman Myra had spent her life trying to forget.

It wasn't just the resemblance. It was the way London carried herself. The way Patrick looked at her like she was the center of his universe. The way Bella had clung to her side, safe and warm, without question. And it stirred something in Myra that she hadn't wanted to name, hadn't dared to acknowledge—not until now.

Shame.

The word pulsed through her like a dull ache, low and constant. Her breath caught in her throat as she leaned against the wall, pressing her fingers to her temples. She'd spent so long hiding behind control, behind precision and poise. She'd built an entire identity on being untouchable, unshakable.

But tonight—tonight had shaken her to her core.

The door creaked open behind her. She expected it to be her husband or Patrick—maybe even her father, coming to explain. But it wasn't.

It was London.

She hesitated in the doorway, wearing a soft golden gown that shimmered in the low light, her curls pinned up, her eyes kind but unreadable.

Myra braced herself for a confrontation.

For judgment. For fury.

But instead, London stepped forward slowly. Calmly.

"Are you all right?" she asked, her voice low.

Myra blinked at her. "You're asking *me* that?"

London offered a slight smile. "You looked like you needed someone."

The words landed with more force than Myra expected. She swallowed hard, her throat suddenly dry. "I didn't expect him to be here. And certainly not with her. Why would my son do this to me?"

London nodded. "Patrick didn't know about this until earlier today. It was Robert who invited your father. He said he thought you needed to see them. Patrick agreed."

Silence settled between them for a beat.

Myra looked away, unable to hold London's gaze.

"I owe you an apology," she said finally, her voice quieter than usual. "For everything. The things I said. The way I treated you. It wasn't fair."

London's expression didn't change. "I appreciate that."

"I told myself that you were all wrong for him. That this was about your honey farm," Myra continued, words tumbling now. "That you weren't stable. But it wasn't that. Not really."

London waited.

"I saw *her* in you. My stepmother. The woman my father left us for." Myra paused, her throat tightening. "I was thirteen when he walked out. One day he was mine—ours. Then he was *hers*. She was warm and sweet and soft in the ways my mother wasn't. And I hated her for it."

London listened without interrupting. Myra felt that small mercy like a balm.

"My mother never recovered. She clung to control the way I did. She wore bitterness like armor. And I… I became her. I thought I was protecting Patrick. I thought I was preserving some legacy, some dream. But really, I was still trying to make someone pay for what my father did to us."

The words hung there between them, raw and painful.

"I'm sorry," Myra said again, voice cracking this time. "Not just for what I did to you. But for making Patrick choose between us."

London stepped closer and, to Myra's surprise, took her hand. Her grip was steady and warm.

"You're not the first mother who's struggled with letting go," London said softly. "But Patrick and I—we hope one day that you'll be a part of our life—our family. I want you to be part of it. So does Bella."

The mention of Bella undid her. Myra's eyes welled up.

"I love that little girl."

"She loves you, too," London said. "She sees what's good in people."

"I don't deserve that."

"Maybe not yet," London admitted gently. "But you can earn it."

Myra nodded, her throat tight with emotion. For the first time in a long time, she felt something like hope flicker in her chest.

"Will you come back in?" London asked.

"I don't know if I can face him. Or her."

"You don't have to face them," London said.

"They are willing to give you space. Just come back to Patrick. To Bella. To your family."

That word struck her harder than the rest. Family. Not obligation. Not reputation. Family meant love.

She inhaled slowly, wiped her eyes, and straightened her posture. "Yes," she said quietly. "Yes, I'll come back."

They walked into the ballroom together, the doors swinging open with a gentle whoosh that barely disrupted the laughter inside.

A string quartet played in the corner. Glasses clinked. Someone was giving a toast.

But Myra didn't hear it. All she saw was Patrick, holding Bella on his hip, laughing as London approached.

His gaze flicked to his mother. Surprise registered first, then something softer—something like gratitude.

Myra met his eyes, then Bella's. The little girl clapped her hands and reached toward her.

"Nana… I thought you left."

Patrick's mouth twitched into a small smile. Myra walked forward and took Bella in her arms, holding her tight against her chest.

The little girl giggled.

"I'm here," Myra whispered. "I'm finally here."

And for the first time in years, she meant it.

Patrick raised his glass again, his voice rising above the din. "To healing. To family. To love that endures."

And this time, Myra clinked her glass with theirs.

She still had a long way to go.

But she wasn't walking it alone anymore.

CHAPTER TWENTY-ONE

THE NIGHT AIR was warm as Patrick held the car door open for London, the sounds of the engagement party still echoing in his heart. The ballroom at the Polk Island Hotel had been a whirlwind of music, laughter, speeches, and love. But now, as the door clicked shut and they were finally alone, Patrick felt the weight of the evening settle on him in a different way.

He started the car but didn't drive just yet. The silence wrapped around them like a soft blanket. London turned toward him, radiant even in the soft glow of the dashboard lights, her dress catching bits of starlight.

"Thank you," he said quietly.

London raised an eyebrow, a smile already playing at the corner of her lips. "For what?"

He let out a slow breath. "For the way you handled my mother. For your grace. Your compassion. You didn't have to go check on her, London. After everything she said to you tonight, no one would've blamed you for leaving her alone. But you didn't. You went to her anyway."

London looked down, brushing an invisible wrinkle from her dress. "She was hurting, Patrick. And I know what it's like to feel like someone chose someone else over you. I've never experienced it in the way she has, not with a parent walking away, but I could feel the wound in her. It didn't excuse what she said, but it made me understand it."

Patrick watched her, heart swelling. Every day he fell for her all over again, but tonight it was different. Tonight it was her strength wrapped in softness, her willingness to love even when wounded that pulled him deeper into the place where she lived inside him.

"You could've walked away from all of it," he said again, his voice low with wonder. "But you chose to walk toward her. To offer her peace. Do you know how rare that is?"

London reached for his hand. "Maybe. But I didn't do it for her approval. I did it for us. I love you. And that means I want peace with the people you care about, even when they make it hard."

He turned her hand over and kissed her palm. "I think part of me always worried that my mom's pain would cast a shadow over our future. That she'd never be able to see you for who you really are because of her past. But tonight…you helped her begin to see. And you helped me see her differently, too."

Patrick paused, then glanced toward the hotel in the distance. "I hope she can forgive him one day. Her father, I mean. I saw how she looked at him. Shocked. Furious. But there was something else, too. Hurt. So much hurt. I never realized how deep it ran until tonight."

London nodded. "Hurt turns into armor when we

don't deal with it. She's been carrying that armor for a long time. But she took a step tonight. It might take more time, but that door is open now."

Patrick gave a small smile. "I think I want to get to know him. My grandfather. He looked at me like he saw more than just a face—like he saw a connection. I want to know what kind of man he is. Why he left. What he learned. Maybe hearing his story will help me understand my mom better, too."

"That sounds like a good place to start," London said. "Maybe he needs to be heard, too. Maybe he's been carrying his own kind of hurt."

Patrick shifted in his seat, finally putting the car in gear. He pulled away from the hotel slowly, glancing over at her again. "Do you think she'll really be okay with us? After everything?"

London smiled gently. "She doesn't have to be okay all at once. But tonight, she saw that we're strong. That we're not going anywhere. That we love each other in a way that can't be shaken by passive-aggressive remarks or subtle threats. And I think that scared her. But it also might have earned her respect."

He laughed softly. "She did look a little startled when I made that toast."

"A toast that made me fall for you all over again," London said, eyes twinkling.

"Yeah?"

"You showed everyone who we are. You made it clear that love isn't a negotiation or a business deal. It's a choice, every day. And you chose me, Patrick. I will never forget that."

He reached over and intertwined their fingers. "Always you."

They drove in silence for a while, the road stretched out before them, lit by moonlight and the soft glow of streetlamps. The hum of the tires on pavement became the rhythm of a night they would always remember.

"You know," London said, breaking the silence with a warm laugh, "we threw a pretty great party."

Patrick grinned. "We really did. That ballroom was stunning. The flowers, the food, the music—everything felt like a dream."

"Cia went all out. I could tell Shane and Kenyon had a hand in it, too. And don't even get me started on the cake. I think Misty should do our wedding cake, too."

Patrick laughed. "I caught Shane sneaking a second slice when he thought no one was watching."

"Typical," London said. "And the dancing… I haven't laughed that much in ages. Did you see my Uncle Terrence try to keep up with Bella?"

"That little girl has moves. I think she gets them from you."

"She gets her sass from me," London said proudly. "But her rhythm is all you."

Patrick's heart warmed at the thought of Bella, spinning in circles, giggling with pure joy. "She loved every second of it. And watching you two together…it felt like home."

London's gaze softened. "That's because we are your home, Patrick."

He nodded. "I can't wait to marry you."

Her fingers tightened around his. "Me neither."

They talked more about the wedding as they neared her place—about colors and flowers, guest lists and vows. But beneath all the plans was a quiet, sacred certainty: They were erecting something lasting.

Patrick pulled into the driveway and turned off the engine. For a moment, neither of them moved. The silence wasn't heavy now. It was full. Of love. Of promise. Of everything that lay ahead.

He turned to her, eyes full of emotion. "I know it won't always be easy. We might face more storms. But if I get to face them with you, I'll be okay."

London leaned in and kissed him softly. "We're stronger than any storm, Patrick. And we have something better than money or security. We have each other."

He smiled against her lips. "To love that stands the test of time."

She echoed it back with a kiss. "And to a future we choose for ourselves."

London stood in front of the grand three-paneled mirror, her reflection framed by delicate lace and soft satin. The Charleston bridal boutique was sunlit and serene, with floral arrangements in every corner and the gentle hum of classical music playing in the background.

She took in her image slowly, reverently—a woman transformed.

The pale gown she wore was everything she never dared to dream of…peach crepe hugging her body with a grace that whispered elegance. Off-the-shoulder sleeves gave way to floral appliqués that trailed down her arms like a delicate wisteria vine. The train spilled behind her like a story yet to be written. Her hands trembled as she smoothed the bodice, her fingers brushing over the row of tiny buttons that sealed her future.

She had never been this happy.

Not just for herself, but for Bella. Her daughter's laughter floated through the boutique as she played with a satin ribbon near the fitting pedestal. Bella had spent too many years caught between questions and heartbreak. But now? She would grow up knowing what love looked like when it stayed. When it chose you, over and over again.

"I don't think she's breathing," Cia whispered to Madelyn, watching London as if afraid to interrupt the moment.

Madelyn, elegant as ever in a pink blouse and wide-legged slacks, gave a misty-eyed smile. "I'm still surprised by the color. I really thought she'd choose white or ivory… I remember the first time London wore a white formal gown. She was five. For the church pageant. Thought she was marrying Jesus himself."

Cia snorted. "Really, Mama…"

London laughed through her tears. "Y'all are ridiculous."

"You look radiant," Madelyn said, stepping forward and smoothing a strand of hair from her daughter's temple. Her voice was thick with emotion. "Like joy itself dressed you this morning."

London caught her mother's eyes in the mirror. "I feel it. I really feel it."

She had always known how to work. How to fight. How to rebuild what others had broken. But this? This was new. Letting herself want happiness. Letting herself keep it.

The door chimed, and the shop attendant stepped in, smiling. "Just confirming your final appointment for the custom adjustments. And would you like to bring the veil next time, or shall we match it here?"

London turned, gown sweeping in a soft whisper. "I'm not wearing a veil, but I'd like to find a beaded rhinestone headpiece. I want everything to feel like today. Like this moment."

Cia tilted her head. "You really mean that, don't you?"

"Every word."

They had come so far. From the college campus where she first met Patrick to stolen kisses under Carolina stars to heartbreaks that tried to pull them apart. And now here she stood, a few months from becoming his wife.

"He still texts me random bee facts every morning," London said with a soft smile, brushing a hand over the silky fabric of her gown. "You know he had our wedding bands designed with a bee motif?"

Madelyn chuckled. "It's called effort, honey. That man loves you something fierce."

London nodded. "I know. And I love him back just as fiercely."

She stepped down from the pedestal and scooped Bella into her arms, her daughter's cheek pressing against her shoulder.

"Do you like Mommy's dress?" she asked.

Bella giggled. "You look like a fairy queen."

Tears pricked again, but London held them at bay. "Then I guess you're my fairy princess."

Cia walked over and touched her forehead to London's. "I can't believe we made it here. After everything."

London thought of Myra. Of the confrontation that had nearly undone the engagement party. But she also thought of the moment Myra came back. The apology. The quiet reconciliation. Patrick's hand finding hers in the middle of chaos.

"We didn't just make it," London said. "We earned it. Every step."

They stayed in the boutique longer than they meant to. They tried on headpieces and jewelry, narrowed down shoes, and finally shared glasses of celebratory champagne in the lounge.

Outside, the sun cast long shadows as it prepared to set, and London stepped out onto the quiet patio with Bella in tow. The ocean breeze kissed her cheeks. Patrick would be here soon to pick them up.

Bella twirled in her own little tulle dress. "Mommy?"

"Yes, baby?"

"Will I get to walk down the aisle, too?"

London crouched down. "You sure will. Right before me. You're the most important part."

Bella grinned. "Okay. I'll be brave."

London touched her cheek. "You already are."

Headlights pulled into the lot, and Patrick stepped out, looking every inch the man who had walked through fire to be here. He held a bouquet of wildflowers and a bag of Bella's favorite cookies.

"How'd it go?" he asked, leaning in to kiss London's cheek.

She beamed. "I found *the one*."

Bella squealed and jumped into his arms, her little hands grabbing the cookies immediately.

As they drove back to Polk Island, London leaned her head against Patrick's shoulder, feeling the gentle curve of the road and the rhythm of the future unfolding ahead.

Their wedding would be at the honey farm. A canopy of string lights, soft music, and everyone they loved close by. The scent of sweet clover and beeswax in the air. A new beginning rooted in everything they'd fought for.

Patrick reached for her hand in the dark, threading their fingers together.

"Ready?" he asked.

She looked out at the horizon, the ocean glowing with the last of the day's light. "More than ready."

And she meant it.

Because the best kind of love stories weren't the ones that avoided the storms. They were the ones that danced through the rain, hands clasped, hearts open, never looking back.

EPILOGUE

Three months later

THE AIR CARRIED the crisp promise of fall, laced with salt from the nearby marsh and the sweet, earthy perfume of leaves shifting from green to gold. The island was glowing beneath an overcast sky streaked with filtered sunlight, every pine and live oak rustling in gentle celebration.

Patrick stood near the altar beneath the grand oak draped with Spanish moss, his heart thudding in rhythm with the wind.

The honey farm had been transformed into something out of a dream.

Long wooden benches lined the clearing, floral arrangements in burnt orange, rust, and deep burgundy lining the aisle. Lanterns flickered with soft amber light, even in daylight, casting a warm glow beneath the canopy of trees. Pumpkin vines, eucalyptus, and scattered acorns marked each table set up for the reception, with copper accents twinkling in the soft light. It was intimate. Rustic. Wholly them.

And in a few short minutes, she'd walk toward him.

Patrick adjusted his collar and took a deep breath, steadying his nerves. It wasn't cold, but it was cool enough that he could smell the wood smoke from one of the fire pits already crackling nearby. A slight breeze teased the hem of the aisle runner.

The sound of Bella's giggles floated from the farmhouse porch, where she was being kept from peeking before her moment as flower girl.

Everything was exactly as it should be.

When Patrick turned his head slightly, he saw his grandfather sitting in the front row across from Madelyn and London's siblings and their wives. His mother, Myra, was seated with them, her hands folded neatly in her lap. There had been tension in the months since the engagement party, but slowly, something had softened between her and London—especially after Myra opened up.

Today, though quiet, she wore a look of peace Patrick hadn't seen in her in years.

He was grateful. For all of it.

The guitar strings began to hum.

The guests turned as Bella appeared, small hands gripping her basket, curls bouncing as she took deliberate steps down the aisle.

She scattered dried rose petals—harvest gold and deep crimson and peach—onto the path as everyone smiled.

Patrick's breath hitched at the sight of her; she looked proud, confident, completely secure in her place in this moment.

Then the music shifted.

The world narrowed.

London appeared at the top of the aisle, framed by the trees and the slanting afternoon light. Her dress swept around her legs, the color of antique peach, and a crown of dried florals sat atop her head like something conjured from the woods.

Patrick felt the ground tilt beneath him.

It was the way she looked at him—steady and certain. A knowing kind of love lived in her eyes, layered with laughter, battles fought, and deep respect. His heart felt too big for his chest.

As she walked toward him, Patrick remembered every moment it took to get here: every doubt, every kiss, every argument and reconciliation, every whispered hope. London had become his peace, his fire, his every heartbeat.

The ceremony was simple. Honest.

They exchanged vows written in notebooks worn soft from days of being carried around and revised. Patrick spoke first, his voice cracking despite his best effort: "London, I used to think love was something you chased down. That it needed proving. But then I met you. And you showed me that real love…it's not about the chase. It's about being still. About standing firm, even when it's hard. You've been my anchor, my compass, and the light I didn't know I needed. I vow to keep showing up. Every day. No matter what."

London's voice was clear, but her hands trembled slightly as she read: "Patrick, I've always believed in hard work, in creating something from the ground up. And you've shown me that love grows the same way. You've softened the hard places of my heart with patience and kindness. You've planted joy and laughter and trust. And now, together, we harvest everything we've sown. I promise to keep tending this life with you, season after season."

They slipped rings onto fingers that had already held so much weight—and so much tenderness.

When the officiant finally said, "You may kiss the bride," Patrick didn't wait.

He gathered her close, lips meeting hers with fierce devotion.

There were cheers, applause, the sound of Bella squealing and clapping her hands. But Patrick only felt London. Only heard the quiet sob he swallowed when her fingers brushed his cheek.

As they walked back up the aisle, hand in hand, guests tossing more petals into the air, Patrick caught a glimpse of his mother dabbing her eyes. His grandfather had leaned over to whisper something into her ear. And though Myra didn't speak, she nodded, her fingers tightening around the small bouquet in her lap.

The reception unfolded beneath a canopy of twinkling string lights, draped from tree to tree like a blanket of stars. The soft, golden glow wrapped the clearing in warmth, casting a dreamy shimmer over everything it touched.

Tables dressed in simple linen overflowed with the bounty of the season—skillets of warm cornbread, pitchers of spiced apple cider, glazed sweet potatoes glistening with brown sugar, and platters of roasted vegetables that painted the table in autumn's richest colors. The scent of the slow-roasted meat lingered in the air, cozy and inviting.

Near the edge of the gathering, the dessert table offered a honey cake, each delicate layer nestled beneath swirls of buttercream, golden syrup cascading slowly down its sides like captured sunlight. Beside it, their wedding cake stood tall—elegant but unfussy, adorned with fresh flowers and a promise of sweet beginnings.

The whole scene sparkled—soft, intimate, and impossibly beautiful, like a love letter written in light.

As twilight settled and fireflies began to glow, Patrick stole a moment with London behind the farmhouse. The moon was rising over the marsh, painting everything in silver.

"You handled everything today with such grace," he murmured, wrapping his arms around her from behind.

"I didn't do it for show," she said softly, leaning into him. "I did it because I meant it. I meant it when I said I love you. I even love your mother… in my own way."

Patrick laughed, the sound cracking through the emotion in his chest. "You really do see people, London. Even when they try not to be seen."

"I think your mom just needed someone to look at her without judgment. Without expecting her to be perfect."

"And you gave her that."

They stood there for a long moment, the air sweet and sharp with the scent of pine and honey.

"I hope she can make peace with her father one day," Patrick said. "I want to know him, too. Not just because he's my grandfather, but because I want Bella to see what healing can look like across generations."

"She will," London said. "Because she's growing up with two parents who believe in love. Who fought for it. That's the best legacy we can give her."

He turned her in his arms then, holding her face between his palms. "You're everything to me."

"I know," she whispered. "You're everything to me, too."

Later, under the canopy of stars, they danced their first dance as husband and wife.

Bella stood on a hay bale nearby, clapping and singing.

The music was soft, acoustic, the lyrics about holding on and never letting go.

Patrick felt it in his bones. This was the life he'd wanted all along. Not the shiny one his parents had envisioned. But this—this life of grounded joy, of family built from truth and kindness.

As the fire pit crackled and their guests raised glasses to toast them one final time, Patrick's voice joined theirs. "To love. To choosing each other every day. To home."

London met his gaze, her eyes shining.

Home.
That was the word.
And here, on this island wrapped in fall's golden glow, they'd found it.

* * * * *

*Be sure to look for the next book in
Jacquelin Thomas's Polk Island series,
available soon wherever
Harlequin Heartwarming books are sold!*

Get up to 4 Free Books!

We'll send you 2 free books from each series you try
PLUS a free Mystery Gift.

Both the **Harlequin® Special Edition** and **Harlequin® Heartwarming™** series feature compelling novels filled with stories of love and strength where the bonds of friendship, family and community unite.

YES! Please send me 2 FREE novels from the Harlequin Special Edition or Harlequin Heartwarming series and my FREE Gift (gift is worth about $10 retail). I may cancel anytime by emailing ReaderServiceInfo@Harlequin.com or by calling 1-800-873-8635. If I don't cancel, I will receive 6 brand-new Harlequin Special Edition books every month and be billed just $6.39 each in the U.S. or $7.19 each in Canada, or 4 brand-new Harlequin Heartwarming Larger-Print books every month and be billed just $7.19 each in the U.S. or $7.99 each in Canada, a savings of 20% off the cover price. It's quite a bargain! Shipping and handling is just 75¢ per book in the U.S. and $1.75 per book in Canada.* I understand that accepting the free books and gift places me under no obligation to buy anything—they are mine to keep for free no matter what I decide.

Choose one:

☐ **Harlequin Special Edition**
(235/335 BPA G3CD)

☐ **Harlequin Heartwarming Larger-Print**
(161/361 BPA G3CD)

☐ **Or Try Both!**
(235/335 & 161/361 BPA G3CE)

Name (please print)

Address   Apt. #

City   State/Province   Zip/Postal Code

Email: Please check this box ☐ if you would like to receive newsletters and promotional emails from Harlequin Enterprises ULC and its affiliates. You can unsubscribe anytime.

Mail to the Harlequin Reader Service:
IN U.S.A.: P.O. Box 1341, Buffalo, NY 14240-8531
IN CANADA: P.O. Box 603, Fort Erie, Ontario L2A 5X3

Want to explore our other series or interested in ebooks? Visit www.ReaderService.com or call 1-800-873-8635.

HSEHW2603